Other books by Nanci LaGarenne

Cheap Fish

Refuge

the bitter end

SCAPE

GHOST

Scapeghost Copyright © 2023 by Nanci LaGarenne

ISBN 13-9798378983827

For Linda M, fly free, angel.

"When I discover who I am, I'll be free."

Ralph Ellison

Chapter One

The moon on the night of June 11, 1962, saved my life. On paper we didn't make it. No one had ever swam away from the Island and lived. The very reason it was built there in the first place. You can see the city from its shore, one and a half miles by water, as the crow flies. We heard all the stories of failed attempts to leave The Rock, the Island of Pelicans, better known as Alcatraz. We did not set out to fail, yet we had no idea the moon was on our side.

People talk a lot about the weather, mostly complaining about it. Rarely is anyone satisfied with the day they were given and happy they got another day at all. I will never be one of those people. I was, from that June night on, a big fan of the weather, particularly moonlit nights. Everything feels different when you are free. I am not a gambling man, but that night, we three took the chance of our lives and hit the jackpot. We made it. The moon and weather were a gift.

I had smarts, regardless of the fact I had not done much with the IQ I was born with, it came in handy. I cannot take credit for what happened, but the planning was exact and worked like a charm in the end. I had no specific knowledge of quarter moons and neap tides. I was aware the current in San Francisco Bay was extremely strong. You could get swept out into the Pacific easily. That night there was a beautiful first quarter moon, which created a neap tide, slowing down the current and taking the power out of it. Swimmers of channels anywhere try to do their crossings in neap tides. Less of a struggle. We were lucky. That particular June was exceptionally warm for San Francisco. A veritable heat wave. Not the usual "... coldest winter I ever spent was a summer in San Francisco," line of Twain's. The Pacific is cold. That June night, the air was downright balmy. The quarter moon, the neap tide and maybe the planets were aligned. I doubt Clarence or John were born under lucky stars. I sure as hell wasn't. Something extraordinary was in our favor that night. If I believed in God, I'd say science and divine intervention had a moment.

It is time. We are as quiet as mice. We hear every sound in the crawl space and our own heartbeats pounding in our ears. I feel my adrenaline rising. We have a rhythm; we keep going with sheer drive. We are stealth. Even our breaths are measured. Adrenaline guides our purpose. Escape. We inch closer and closer to freedom. Steady as we go. Forward. We are getting out. Fresh air. I feel it. We are almost there. I smell the sea. Deep breaths. "Keep going," I silently tell myself and my mates, as we get closer to the water.

It's dark but for that sliver of moon. Yes, there are lights on the roof, but not on us. We stay in the shadows. We are invisible. We know our way in the dark. We scale the fence. We are as agile as dancers, no wasted steps. Down on solid ground, we creep to the beach. Our rain slicker boats are waiting for us where we hid them. We move them to the shore. Quick. We get our life vests on and climb aboard our makeshift rafts. We push off; we paddle swiftly, quietly. Our very lives depend on it. Faster we go, faster, and faster still. We have to make time. The air is warm, the current calm and accommodating. Is the tide carrying us in the right direction? I see the other shore in the distance, it's far away, but it waits for us.

"Keep paddling," I tell myself. We don't talk, we paddle. "Forward," I mentally tell myself and the Anglins. No one is coming after us. Don't look back. Paddle. Breathe. "They could come after you..." I hear my subconscious volunteering. I ignore it. "Keep paddling, don't stop," only one mantra drumming in my head. We are doing this; we are setting ourselves free. Paddle, breathe, paddle, breathe. We are getting free. The moon is there, and I look up at it, wishing on it, not quite in desperation, but in solidarity. I am one with the moon. I will be free.

I concentrate in front of me, I cannot linger in any given moment. We must make time. Are there sharks? My research told me there had not been any shark sightings in the bay. But it's water, there must be sharks. I can't let my mind dwell on that. Keep paddling. Clarence mentions "gators." "No alligators here," I tell him. "What about...." he starts. "No sharks. Keep going," I say with confidence. He nods and keeps going. Keep paddling. Breathe. Paddle. Breathe. Is it time to swim? Not yet. Are they on to us? Have they alerted the boats? No. We've heard no alarms. Not a sound, but our breathing and the water swishing by. What they know is we are back there sleeping in our cells. Three heads under covers. Fake likenesses we made. No one will suspect a thing. Until morning. We will be ashore by then. Keep going. Paddle. Breathe. Paddle. Get free.

I am warmer than I imagined. There's a heat wave in San Francisco. Our luck in spades. The air is warm, the water is calm. No strong current pulling us out to sea. Steady on course we go. Paddle. Breathe. Keep moving. Don't think. Get free. The only sound is the rippling of water as we three paddle toward the light. To the shore. To the beach. To the wharf. To freedom. It's June, we won't freeze to death. People swim in this bay in February, and they don't freeze. It's June and the water is ten degrees warmer than usual with the lucky heat wave. Paddle. Breathe. We are going in the right direction, three rafts and three men heading to freedom. Paddle. Breathe. The rafts are holding us. Fifty raincoats sewn together. Brilliant. Don't gloat. Paddle, breathe, get it done, get free. Our brothers on the inside are with us in spirit, we know. "Get free," I hear them chant, "You damn lucky bastards," they'll say. But right now, no one knows we are gone. Paddle. Breathe. Swishing through the water. No waves. My arms don't ache, I'm surprised. I have superhuman strength. No one can stop me. I will be free.

Now we're in the water. Holy shit, it's cold. I don't care. I don't panic. I'm swimming. John and Clarence are swimming. They like water, they grew up on it. Southern water, but they don't complain. We are getting free. We dropped the bag we wanted the searchers to find, awhile back, near Angel Island. With luck and the current, maybe the bag winds up there. They'll think we drowned. Perfect. The rafts, we discarded too. They will find them, but not us. We are getting free. Swim. Breathe. Swim. Breathe. My arms ache. Keep swimming. My foot hits something. I feel my heartbeat. A shark? No sharks in the bay. Could be a sea lion. A porpoise. I have no time to care. We keep swimming. The shore is coming closer and closer.

The lights of the city shine like diamonds. Swim. Breathe. Get free. Swim. Breathe. Get free. I collapse onto the shore. I kiss the sand. The boys are with me. We untie our plastic clothes bags from our waists. We rest, briefly, take off our wet clothes. We throw them away in the nearest trash can. We don't talk, we change into our dry clothes we had in the plastic bags. We put on plain navy blue and khaki pants, white undershirts, button down chambray shirts. Casual officer's civilian clothes we borrowed. We washed all their clothes, part of our job inside; the very least they could do is donate some new duds to our cause. We're everyman and nobody. No one is down at the beach this early. The city is asleep. The ferry will soon be heading to shore. It's nearly dawn. We sit and wait under the cover of darkness and that delicious quarter moon.

"It's headed to Sausalito," I tell the boys, as it nears the shore. I read the letters on the boat. It might as well have said Heaven. I point. They nod. We walk separately onto the boat, mingle with the passengers, like we belong to this city, three nobodies, three workmen in watch caps and plain clothes, headed to a job early in the morning. Every day, the usual. To us, a day we have not had in a lifetime. I smell coffee as we board the ferry. We pay our fare with the money we nicked from the canteen before we escaped. There's enough left for coffee and donuts. John hands me a cup. I sip it slowly; I've never tasted anything so amazing in my life. It's manna. We are free. Be careful. Act natural. Be wise. We look at no one, no one looks at us. John holds a newspaper he found on the bench; he's sitting across the way. Is he reading it? Who cares? We are free. Clarence passes me a donut he takes out of a brown bag, on his way back from the canteen. Snack bar. Have to get used to civilian talk. He sits behind John, lights a cigarette. I watch him enjoying it. Smoking freedom. We're nobodies. We're everybody. I chew it slowly, savoring it. There's no rush. I look out the ferry window at the open water. I breathe in the salt air. It's beautiful. I am free. Is this what freedom tastes like? Hot coffee and a donut? A ferry ride? This morning is our first new day of life. I want to smile, I don't. Inside I'm leaping for joy. No more prison. I am free.

Every time I see one of those rain slickers, I have to chuckle. They were makeshift rafts, but they did the job. I'm no fan of open water and I know people dive into that cold bay year-round. I am not one of those people. We may have been crazy to take the chance, but folks diving into San Francisco Bay in February for exercise seems insane to me. I would have jumped off a cliff to be free. You do not know how it feels to be locked up unless you were.

We didn't stay in the city. We had more sense than to advertise ourselves. The manhunt was on, even though most people, including the authorities, figured we drowned. I planned on that line of thinking for the rest of my natural life. We knew we had to lay low and be smart. The Anglins thought about going home, they had family. That would have been suicide. Later, they would head north of the city, keep off the grid. Some beautiful places you can do that up north. We'd separate. That was the plan. I'm a loner, and it was smarter. They were searching for three escaped convicts; we weren't about to help them. Quiet and remote is what I would need. I would think it through and find the perfect hideaway. We had to be extra smart and sly as foxes.

I was born in a big city and spent my youth escaping from every place that tried to contain me. The inside of cold sterile institutions. They would never hold me. Every jail, every prison, I found a way to escape. Finally, the only one they said no one could ever succeed in escaping. No one escaped The Rock and lived to see the next day as a free man, unless he was a dead man. I wanted to be free in the very alive sense. You cannot keep someone yearning their whole life for freedom, in a cage. It was inevitable, freedom. I made it happen and I would make it last.

I had a yearning for fresh air and trees that I read about in books. I wanted to hear the rustle of branches in the wind and birdsong in the morning. I longed to gaze at the night sky, see constellations, and contemplate their brilliance. Most of all, I wanted to erase the sound of steel bars slamming shut, closing out hope and the future. I would see the moon from my own perch, staring at it for as long as I liked, no one stopping me.

I was born under a quarter moon, it turns out, September 1, 1926. A descending quarter moon. Some refer to this phase as the dark side of the moon. Perhaps prophetic, but in the end a stroke of good fortune. With that quarter moon on that famous June night, we achieved the impossible. You have to know that we were survivors. Alcatraz wasn't our first rodeo. The big one sure, but not impossible to leave, after all. We were not about to slip up and let them haul our asses back inside. We dropped that bag they found in the water on purpose, so they would assume we drowned. It worked, a natural conclusion. The end of those three inmates who dared to escape Alcatraz. And no one in charge had to look bad. According to them, we died trying. The current beat us. That was good news to us, let them believe we perished. It is often the little things that can save your life. And freedom is no small thing.

We found an open houseboat in Sausalito. The owners or tenants were obviously gone for some time or hadn't arrived for the summer. Clothes were gone from the dresser drawers and closets. Other clothes were stored in boxes under the bed. It would suit us for the time being. We were criminals, we knew how to be quiet. And how to listen real well for voices or footsteps in the night. No one came. They were too busy searching the bay for our bodies and the pier in the city, in case we made it there. There were surely cops galore on every highway north and south. We weren't in a car. We were sleeping on a houseboat in a quiet harbor in an artsy bohemian little gem of a city. One thing I've learned, if you lay low and stay out of the rat race, you don't become a target. Maybe it was chancy, looking back. But it worked. We had shelter, rest, and food. People never clean out their cabinets and the freezer had food. We were hidden and we had time to devise the next step, disappearing.

We took showers and John made pancakes and bacon. People tend to keep things like canned goods, coffee, and evaporated milk on hand. We relished our meal together, knowing we would part ways soon. We agreed that maybe one day, if we lived to a ripe old age, we'd meet up in Jack London Square and raise a pint to each other at The Last Chance Saloon. I was mostly a loner but by escaping together we had formed some kind of a bond. Surviving was the closest I had come to family. Pity we couldn't hang out and paint the town red. But we knew better than to celebrate while the biggest manhunt for our skins was happening. We had to let the trail go cold. The only way to do that was to stay out of sight. Thankfully this all went down at a time when the media was a newspaper and a local news channel. No cell phones, no internet, no video witness to everything a person does. Less technology worked in our favor. They would try like hell to find us. They were no match for our desire to stay gone. The worst mistake people make when they try to disappear is to draw attention to themselves in any way or have some hidden urge to be discovered. I had no one in the world missing me but the law. Clarence and John were resigned to freedom more than any sentimental feeling to look up their kin. Once you make that decision, you would be surprised how providence happens. We were presumed dead, swallowed up by the sea, our escape mission failed. Instead, we were alive and well and we aimed to stay that way, no matter what.

Chapter Two

The Anglin brothers left for someplace north and off the grid, a few weeks later. There was a caravan heading to a commune; it was perfect cover. They were disguised so well even their own mama wouldn't recognize them. Amazing what a little hair dye and hippie clothes could do to transform a man. They were survivors, they would do fine. Charmers when they needed to be. I had no worries about them. I wished them well, but we would not stay in touch. Common sense overruled sentimentality. I was ready to move on too. There were hippies and transients everywhere. I could blend in with a nice beard I'd grown and follow the pack. There was safety in numbers. My hair was longer and on the curly side now. When it was trimmed up short it looked mostly straight. This curlier version was "right on," as people said, ubiquitously. I was thirty-six years old, with a cool pair of John Lennon glasses, topping off my colorful shirt and a floppy suede hat, my own mother wouldn't know me from Adam. Not that she ever saw me again after handing me off to some foster home a minute after I was born. I can't blame her, she was only seventeen and probably scared out of her wits. My father? No clue. More than likely, she fell for the wrong dude. All I know is her name was Clara, and if she hadn't given me up, I more than likely wouldn't be here, but in an unmarked grave after being found in some trash can in a D.C. alley. Guess I was meant to live. The prophetic moon and all that.

You could get a decent secondhand wardrobe in thrift shops and Salvation Army stores, fill your belly on the kindness of stranger's leftovers and trip out too, if you so desired. I kept a level head. I was not in a movement, but rather on the move. It was intoxicating enough to be free. People on the outside had no idea. Maybe some did. I don't know what demons each person has driving them to escape their former life. I only know what drove me to risk my own. I could no longer be watched like someone's experiment, live according to someone else's rules, and be guarded like a caged animal. I made mistakes. I own that. I robbed banks, I didn't kill anyone. I would take nothing from anyone anymore. Only my freedom.

No one much cared where you were from, and everyone was friendly in California in the sixties. I could recite poetry or sing protest songs with the best of them. I'm smart, I know how to embody the moment. This one called for not standing out, but mingling, instead. Becoming part of the mixture, the happening. Revolution was in the air. Protests against the Vietnam War. Change. Music. Such good music. Without drawing attention to myself, I took it all in. Freedom tastes as wonderful as food when you're starving. I loved the philosophical buzzwords and hippie speak. I wasn't a radical, but "Life is radical, man," was as good a greeting as any. "Don't Bogart the joint," was a close second. I had some deep conversations with a few "Vets from Nam," as they called themselves. They fought for their country and were proud to have done so but not pleased with the devastation they saw and the killing fields. "For what?" they asked. If they truly belonged over there, why were they treated like garbage when they returned? So many had become addicts and were homeless due to what later was found to be PTSD. What was unspeakable became internalized. At the time, no one received proper treatment. These guys all self-medicated. Some checked out permanently. Vietnam went on too long. Nobody was arguing that point. No one got out of there unscathed, even if it wasn't obvious on the outside. I thanked them for going over to fight; I had respect for their courage and the belief that they were fighting for change. "We're speaking against the war now. If anyone can, it's us." I couldn't have agreed more. They said I had a good ear for people. "I like stories, man," I said. And they told me some more. One night we stayed up till the sun came up sitting around the campfire, sharing a joint or two. One of them, a cat named Rhodes, gave me his Army jacket. "You keep it. Take it where the road leads you," he laughed. "It's good luck, man." I thanked him and have to say, so far so good.

A professor on sabbatical from the East Coast was my cover. I had been an avid reader, inside, and my whole life, really. I could put my smarts to good use. No one was delving deep into my personal life. Everyone was searching, experimenting, living in the present, as the moment flowed. It was free love, peace and brotherhood and some very good dreams after the bowl got passed. I remained in control just the same. I hadn't risked my life and ventured this far physically and mentally to waste it being reckless. I never slept better in my life. It beat a prison cell. Now I was living. I would stay free. It was my one and only goal.

I found an interesting book on the houseboat, about a man called Joaquin Miller. He was a colorful poet in the 1800's and a frontiersman who settled in his later life in the Oakland Hills. His home, he called The Abbey and The Hights. Coincidentally, he also escaped from a jail in California, sawed the bars right off, they say. Horse thieving was the charge. The man was a non-conformist before it was popular. I liked that, and I liked his given name, Cincinnatus. I adopted it as my own. He didn't need it anymore and the name Frank Lee Morris never did me any good.

My hippie friends were taking a camping trip up to a place called Shepherd Canyon, near the old Montclair Railroad Trail. The trains had stopped running in 1941, so it was quiet, remote, and unpopulated. Perfect. I showed up with a bedroll and helped pack up a van and our happy group was on the road. I knew how to cook which came in handy. Communal living has its benefits when you want to remain in the background or just be part of a pack of wanderers. I followed the group; we hung out for a while at our campsite. When I had the chance, I took a lone hike and a good look around. I went hiking up in the hills. I read about abandoned logging cabins from the 1920's. The old logging road used to run down below in the 1800's, bringing redwood out of the Moraga Forest to Oakland. The first steam sawmill was at a place called Dimond Canyon. Deeply forested, not many people around; it was the exact place for me. I kept my discovery to myself and when the time was right, I wandered away on my own journey as so many were doing at the time. In reality I was searching for digs that were out of the weather and gave me the solitude I needed to disappear.

The cabins were deserted. After the loggers, they became getaways for city people from San Francisco when the railroad was running. Now they were abandoned. One in particular was in good shape so I let myself in. I knew how to pick a lock and the one on the cabin door was hardly a challenge. No one was around or had been for a while. There weren't mice or too many cobwebs and it looked like it was someone's sanctuary before I broke in. There were sheets over the furniture, an old blue plaid couch and matching easy chair by the window looking out to a porch. An old kilim rug lay in front of a small fireplace that had been used before, but not recently, from the ashes left behind. I checked the flue, it was closed. I'd remember to open it if I made a fire. I admired the built-in bookshelves on either side of the fireplace. Nice handiwork, whoever built them. There was a small television on a wooden stand in the corner. I doubted the reception was good up here. The selection of reading material that filled the solid wood shelves would keep me busy if I stayed any length of time. The floors were solid, these cabins were obviously built to last and withstand earthquakes. There were inside shutters on the windows. Good for privacy if anyone came nosing around or if the area ever got developed. Right now, the nearest cabin was down the bottom of the hill, and it was abandoned.

The natural light was good; light is important when you're in a remote dwelling. I'd had enough of dark tight places. Outside, the canopy of trees was magnificent. I climbed a wooden staircase of 100 steps to arrive here. The cabin looked out to beautiful, majestic redwoods, that went on forever, the sun coming through them in places like rays from heaven. On the south side of the hill it was sun dappled where the trees were smaller or had been cut, perhaps they were too near the house. The cabin was dwarfed by the enormous forest surrounding it. It was a treehouse for grown-ups. Not that I'd ever had one as a kid. It didn't matter, I was going forward. This moment felt right, in my gut. I was trusting my instincts.

I checked the kitchen for any leftover supplies. I noticed an old radio on the wooden counter. I turned it on, it worked. Good, I would have music and news. It was plugged in as was a toaster next to it. Someone obviously paid the electric bill so I would consider that while I camped here. There was a phone on the wall. I picked up the receiver and heard a dial tone and hung up. There was no one I planned to call, and I certainly wouldn't be answering it if it rang. There were a number of fat candles in dishes in all the rooms, and several boxes of matches on a shelf. I would go pioneer by candlelight and appreciate the respite from cold harsh institutional bulbs that hummed and invaded your dignity. I was aware of what I had been, and I paid for my crimes by being locked up like an animal. That was over. Every day was an opportunity to be a better man. Every bird, flower and insect, rainstorm or rainbow, a sign that life is ever changing, and I would notice or perish under my own ambiguity. I looked out of the kitchen window onto a world so wild and natural and so foreign from being behind cement walls for years. It awed me. I longed for a new life so badly, I would take whatever days I was given to be part of this landscape that made me feel alive. My senses were sharpened. I would never go back to prison. My heart and mind were open. It was a heady feeling. I had no idea nature could affect a person so much, the vastness of it, the majesty. Someone should paint these trees. They stood there like an invitation. Did I have any talent? I had all the time in the world to find out.

There was a new can of coffee and some canned evaporated milk in a cabinet over the sink. A few tins of peas, canned peaches, hearts of palm, a glass jar of sugar, a sack of flour and a box of steel cut oats. A feast. Every surface was clean. Dishes and cups were neatly stacked on open shelves. An old percolator was on the stove. The fridge was empty, unplugged, and spotless. If this cabin proved a safe place, I'd fill that fridge after I went in search of supplies, but that could wait. I had provisions in my backpack from the communal campsite that would last more than a few days, maybe a good week. Granola bars, a bag of homemade granola, and a bag of almonds and raisins, some beef jerky from the Vets and a bag of oatmeal cookies. I could stretch it if I had to before I ventured out and started poking around whatever nearby village there was. Someone in the hippie caravan had given me a map and it had advertisements on it for gas stations and shops. Not many. Good, less people, less questions.

The water was off, but I could easily turn it on when I wanted a shower and to wash dishes. At the back of the kitchen there was a washer and dryer. There were two bedrooms and a bathroom with a cast iron tub and shower. I couldn't remember the last time I soaked in a tub. What a luxury that would be. I went into what looked like the master bedroom. On the dresser was a framed photo of an older handsome man and a beautiful young woman. Her face was strangely familiar, but not from any recent hippie hook up. There were no women at Alcatraz. Except the one I saw. I remembered her. She came on island to tutor the officer's kids. I watched her from a distance when I delivered the officers clean laundry to a guard, their uniforms and civvies. That's how we were able to squander a few outfits for the escape. They never missed them, stuff got lost or damaged in the wash. The officers had bigger fish to fry, like very dangerous men. I was not among them. I didn't kill anyone. I was no Machine Gun Kelly or Al Capone. I was just a champion escapee. Maybe not so good at it since I always got caught. But that was before. The Rock was my ultimate punishment. No more. I was free. I would become a treehouse dweller with a new lease on life. Luck, like Rhodes the Vet said, was on my side.

I held the picture. She had mocha skin and big brown eyes. Her hair was shiny brown ringlets, loose and framing her perfectly shaped face, a kind beautiful smile. She looked happy. So did the older man. I ran my finger over the glass on her face like I was reading Braille. What could a photo tell me? That a father and daughter lived here? The man was white with very blue eyes. The young woman resembled him except for her exotic coloring and brown eyes. There was only the one photograph. I thought of the woman I saw at Alcatraz. This girl could be her daughter, they were so alike.

The prisoners did not mingle with the staff. The warden's wife and the officer's families lived on Alcatraz Island and took the boat back and forth to the city, but we did not get anywhere near them. All of them were white. Seeing this extraordinary woman across the yard that day by the laundry door, was a fluke. No one saw me looking at her. I have excellent vision, so I saw her clearly. Just once. I wondered where she was now.

I opened the top dresser drawer to see if there were any more photographs. I found none, but I did find an envelope with money. Not a lot, a couple of twenty-dollar bills. I went to the kitchen and found a notepad and a pen. I left an IOU in the envelope and borrowed a twenty. I would replace it. I was no longer a thief. With a little luck I could paint a few pictures and maybe sell something in town. Was that wishful thinking? As if in answer, when I opened the next drawer, it was affirmed. Two large sketch pads and a box of artists pencils just sitting there. Who was the artist? The man in the photo? The young woman? Maybe me.

Chapter Three

The village was a good hike from the cabin. After a fresh cup of coffee with sugar, I threw on jeans and a clean tee shirt, tied my hair back, laced up my boots and took an empty backpack for groceries. It was early morning and the birds serenaded me on my walk down the series of steps leading down to the village road. I didn't pass a solitary soul. There was a creek that ran through the forest thick with sassafras and eucalyptus. This was a land made for poets and writers. The solitude and beauty of nature were breathtaking. When the sun set in the hills and the moon came out with its millions of starry companions, a man knew he was alive in the most primitive way. Inside himself, where only the soul speaks. It doesn't reveal a person's secrets; it weaves them into a new story. One that doesn't chain you to the past but sets you free. The tree branches swayed with the wind, and I imagined the ancient people who listened to their message. Now I listened for the stillness inside me, bringing forth a communion with nature. I felt a kinship with this place of trees. I dared to consider the hope that I had finally found a home. I was tired of the past. I had run my whole life. Here in this moment, I was safe. Who could I become, I wondered? What might I contribute? I had no idea. Like the ancients, I would listen to the trees and let them tell me.

The first place I passed was a library. Established in 1930, this small brick building was in the Storybook design, truly something out of a fairytale village, its white trim like frosting. More importantly, at my fingertips all the books I wanted to read. Some were free on racks outside, so I didn't need a library card. I thumbed through a book of poems by Joaquin Miller, a legend in these parts, and put it in my backpack. I walked on and found a post office. I did not stop in to check the Wanted posters. I would pick up a newspaper in the grocery store I saw ahead, Godfrey's Food Store.

I knew by now I was old news; the escape had been two months ago. I wasn't expecting the headline I did see. "The Death of A Star. Marilyn's Tragedy." Marilyn Monroe was dead, at thirty-six years old. We were the same age. They claimed she took her own life with an overdose of pills. Was that the truth? If it wasn't, I can guarantee no one was talking. There is always more to the story and Marilyn Monroe did not have it easy just because she was a gorgeous star. Beautiful women are preyed upon and I'm sure she had her own demons too. It was a shame; she'd likely get more attention now than she did in life. People were vultures. I folded the newspaper under my arm and went in search of milk, eggs, butter, and bread. I added some cheese slices and two cans of tomato soup to my cart. I paid for my groceries and newspaper and walked outside into the bright day. I passed a small gift shop. Anne Hathaway Cobbledick, Proprietor, was painted on the window. "We sell local artwork and crafts." Bingo, I had a place to sell my paintings. When I got back to the cabin and made myself a grilled cheese sandwich and a cup of coffee with real milk, I aimed to get started on my art. I passed a cozy brick house that was a restaurant, Comb's Cottage. "Fine steaks, barbequed meats and custom-built hamburgers." My mouth was watering. One day I would sit down in a place like this and have a nice dinner like ordinary people. "One step at a time, Cincinnatus," I told myself. I inhaled the fragrant honeysuckle I passed in front of a small house built in the Storybook style and walked on. It was a sleepy village and people were going about their daily errands and work. No one took notice of me. I blended in with the everyday painting of life. The picture was freedom. I climbed the first series of steps to my new home.

Chapter Four

I filled up that cabin with tree paintings and moon carvings. The night sky was too good to waste and the whittling calmed me. I could easily pass for an artist. I was not a hippie, though I certainly looked the part. Like a skinny Grisly Adams. There was plenty of wood to carve. I turned on the water and drank my fill every day. It was the simple things I cherished most. I ate when I was hungry, not when someone told me. That was freedom. I froze extra loaves of bread to save. Bananas, apples, and artichokes were my favorite things to eat. California had some delicious fresh artichokes. Maybe one day I could plant a garden and grow them. I was starting to dream about the future. And the fact that I might have one. I found an easel and paint and brushes in a storage shed on the property. I got creative. It wasn't half bad, my tree and moon art. I would have to pay Miss Anne Hathaway Cobbledick a visit down at her gift shop in the village with a few choice pieces. Hopefully she could sell them, and I'd have an income of sorts. After I paid my debt of the twenty-dollar bill. I was on the straight and narrow and planned to stay there. When I heard footsteps on the wooden porch, I had a sinking feeling my luck had just run out.

The footsteps drew closer. A light step. A thunk on the table on the porch. A package set down. A jangling of keys. The screen door opened, and a key turned in the inside door. I moved behind the kitchen wall and waited. I watched the door swing open. There was no huffing and puffing, whomever came in had walked up that daunting staircase. Why hadn't I heard them? I chastised myself for not hearing anyone outside before someone opened the door. I froze where I was.

It was a woman. She had her back to me and was checking out my moon carvings on the table in the living room and commenting to herself. She stood in front of the easel staring at my tree painting. What was going through her mind? I waited, making sure she was alone. Maybe someone was parking the car. She took off her coat. She did not come towards the kitchen phone. She did not seem shaken, whatsoever. Who did she think painted the trees and carved the moon, ghosts? I waited. No one joined her, thankfully. I cleared my throat. She spun around.

It was her. The woman from Alcatraz. The one with the kids I noticed that day, out in the yard by the warden's house. She looked at me, staring blankly. Not an ounce of recognition on her beautiful face. There wouldn't be, we had not met before. Only I had seen her. Just the one time. She saw me now. She stared, saying nothing though her eyes spoke volumes. There was no screaming. She continued studying me. I let out my breath, calming myself. She was as cool as a cucumber. Why? I was a stranger in her cabin. I did my best not to look like a former inmate. I mean I didn't anymore, but I was guilty of escaping and of breaking and entering. She continued to stare. It was unnerving. She would not recognize my face from any photo she might have seen in a newspaper. Not under this beard with this head of long thick hair. And she had never seen me before. The staring contest continued. Who would break eye contact? I dared not move in case she felt threatened. I had no intention of harming her. I would just grab my backpack and leave.

I knew her face intimately. She was the girl I looked at every day in the photo since I'd been here. It was obviously an old picture, but it was her. I almost felt ashamed since I had touched the photo in the bedroom, as if I was touching her. The photo was a younger facsimile and the sadness I saw in the eyes staring at me now was absent in the photograph. This woman had been through something significant. She didn't wear it on her sleeve, but she couldn't hide it in her eyes. Not forgetting the situation, I was mesmerized for a moment. She was stunning, a touch exotic, and quite put together, in a city kind of way. But she was no stuck up prim and proper lady, I got a very natural feeling from her. There was an earthiness below the surface. She wore pressed black slacks, a button-down paisley blouse, black leather flats, and carefully applied makeup, not that she needed any. A hint of lipstick that she didn't need either, though it accentuated her full lips. Her skin was deep mocha colored magnificence. She was an ebony goddess. Large dark eyes rimmed in kohl, a mane of wild dark brown curls that she couldn't tame if she tried, her attempt to contain them in a velvet headband, failed. Long loose ringlets cascaded invitingly down her shoulders. She continued the staring contest, cool as ice.

"Who the hell are you and why are you in my cabin? Don't even think of taking one step towards me." For a second I was startled, to hear another voice in the cabin, beside the radio. I had been alone for a long time. She aimed her purse at me, her hand inside holding on to something. "I have a gun and I'll make you sorry, fast. I know how to shoot straight, Mister." Those dark eyes of hers didn't blink. Or lie. They commanded respect. I let her direct. She had the gun. I wasn't dying like this, that much I knew. I remained stock still. The woman was not kidding. She kept her distance and her arm up, keeping her purse aimed at me. I intended to be gracious. And smart. I spoke slowly and clearly. I was hoping she took it as humility.

"I found the door unlocked and needed a bed for a while. One day led to the next. I had no right. I hope you can forgive me. I mean you no harm. May I pay you with my moon carvings or a few paintings? Until I can sell something? I promise I'll be gone as soon as you can say, 'Cincinnatus."

"Just hold on minute. Are you homeless? Or did your wife throw you out? Probably for good reason. What's with the moon art? Seems a bit obsessive. The trees are beautiful. Did you say, Cincinnatus? As in Miller? What's that to you?"

"Not homeless per se. No wife, never married. Just between gigs, you might say. Looking for a quiet place to do my art. I'm Cincinnatus Jones." At that moment, I was officially reborn.

"Interesting," she replied. "So, you're a fledgling artist without a bed or a studio and you decided to squat here in these hills in this particular cabin and steal Joaquin Miller's real name. You do know who he is?"

"I'm not really an artist but thank you. It's more of a hobby. Or as you aptly put it, an *obsession.* I like the night sky, what can I say? As for my name? My mother was a fan of the Daniel Boone show," I lied. "Cincinnatus was the innkeeper. I am familiar with Joaquin Miller. I like his poems. If it's all right with you, I'll clear out my things and be on my way, Maam."

"Don't *maam* me, we're the same age. Sit down, you're making me nervous." *As a fox,* I thought. I sat in the nearest chair by the fireplace and kept my mouth shut. I know when a woman needs time to sort things out. I was out of practice but not dense.

"How long have you been here, Mr. Cincinnati Jones?"

Couple of weeks, give or take. I came out west some time ago, did some moving around with a bunch of friends. I'm a teacher back on the East Coast. Taking a sabbatical. I'll pay you for the coffee and oatmeal and use of the place. I was hoping to sell some of these carvings and paintings. I've been camping with some people I met in The Haight. I needed a bit of quiet time on my own. I don't like crowds. I found the cabin unlocked and deserted. I didn't mean to break in. I needed shelter and no one was around. It was presumptuous of me. I'm sorry."

"I don't need your money. The cabin was my father's. Originally, it belonged to my grandfather. Both are long gone. It was left to me, but I don't get much chance to come up. I used to teach in the city, the Alcatraz officer's kids that come over on the boat. I tutored the warden's kids too, on the island. You know three inmates escaped? Have you been reading the newspapers? You must have gone into the village? A person has to be careful, it's not healthy to hole up here too long. You could become a hermit very easily, trust me. Anyway, those inmates, no one knows if they survived the bay or drowned. They're assuming they drowned. What do you think?"

She was looking at me with such beautiful sincere eyes, staring into my soul. Make no mistake, this woman meant business. Perhaps she had known liars. I could hardly tell her the truth. I had to do more than my level best not to blink or look guilty. What were the odds, the one cabin I chose to "hole up in," belonged to an Alcatraz schoolteacher?

I cleared my throat. "I'd say they drowned. The water's cold, the current's strong, and they found their bag and a ripped makeshift raft. End of story. Would you like a coffee?"

"Right. I agree with you. Though I was secretly hoping one of them made it. What a feat that would be. And I can help myself, it's my cabin, thank you very much. The question is, what am I going to do about *you*?" She put her purse down. I guess I was not a threat anymore. I watched her pour a coffee, add milk, and sit down across from me. She had more to say I could tell, so I stayed quiet.

"Here goes. You didn't break anything. A kid could pick that lock or climb through what was probably an unlocked window. I mean, there's no crime up here. Looks like you've kept it clean and saved me from turning on the fridge, uncovering the furniture and gathering wood. No one uses it except me, and I don't use it much. Haven't in such a long time. It's too quiet. Especially at night. Anyway, I just come every now and then to see that wild animals haven't taken over. I never thought about squatters." She gave me the high eyebrows. I looked down, repentant. She went on.

"I like knowing it's here. I'm sentimental about the cabin. It's all I have left of…. Anyway, so if you keep it clean and fix anything that breaks, you can stay. Be the unofficial care-taker. No wild parties, though you don't look the type. You're not a drunk either, I know the signs. And I don't see any bottles around. You look clearheaded and you seem like a grown up. I know the opposite. Lost boys are a dime a dozen in San Francisco. Did you bake that bread? Full of talents, aren't you?"

She had a generous smile. Was she flirting with me? She was eyeing the new loaf of bread I'd taken out of the oven before she came. I was afraid I was dreaming. Was this a trap? My instincts told me it wasn't. There was something unusual about this woman. Maybe she was just eccentric or lonely. I didn't get a psycho vibe at all. Should I stay? Was it worth the risk? It wasn't like I was swimming in options.

"Please, have some bread. There's butter in the fridge." I started to move towards the kitchen and she held up her hand, then crossed her arms, looking me up and down, making me feel a bit naked.

"I'm not done, Cincinnatus. Let's not get too cozy just yet. I can read people fairly well and I get the very distinct feeling you're not dangerous. You might have a secret or two, who doesn't? That's none of my business. Unless you make it mine. Got it? I think you'll be my secret. Not in a weird way, don't worry, I'm as sane as they come. But I could do with some mystery in my life. Anyway, I'd like to take some of your tree and moon paintings to a friend's gallery in Sausalito, if you don't mind? You should stay Cincinnatus. You can work from here. You're quite talented. I paint a bit myself. By the way, I'm Patsy Vaughan." She reached out to shake my hand. It felt soft but her handshake was firm. This woman did not suffer fools. I took note of that, as I released her hand, reluctantly. What was I going to say to this Patsy Vaughan, woman of mystery? I decided to go for it.

"Okay, Pasty, thank you, I will stay. You paint watercolors, am I right?

"How did you know that?"

Scape Ghost

"A hunch."

She looked at me sideways. God, she was sexy, in a very serious kind of way. Why would she let me stay in her cabin? I was a stranger. What was her game? She looked too smart to be reckless. And I knew better than to gamble at this stage. Yet I cannot explain how I didn't feel threatened in the least. Maybe she liked secrets and secret men? Hardly a crime. Wasn't I a living breathing secret myself? Hey, if it got creepy, all I had to do was leave.

"Cincinnatus, I brought some groceries. Would you mind grabbing that bag outside the door?" I did as she asked. Patsy Vaughan was a small wobble in my plans. Everything would be fine if I stayed cool. And when and if it veered off course, I'd be gone before she ever returned.

"I was planning to cook," Pasty said. I liked her name. I liked the whole package and it had been a while since I'd had a real conversation, one on one. I was a convict, but I wasn't socially inept. I liked people, in small numbers, not constant companions. I could always get a dog, but that meant putting down roots. It was early days for that kind of thinking. Patsy didn't live here. She visited once in a while. This could work out perfectly. Especially the secret keeping part she mentioned. Patsy interrupted my reverie.

"There's plenty of food. I planned to stay for a few days. We can have a longer chat over dinner. About art, perhaps. By the way, I am a very good cook. You like it spicy?"

Was that a loaded question? I kept my cool so I could keep my head. I carried her grocery bag to the kitchen.

"I eat anything, but please let me cook for you."

"You cook, too? A chef and an artist. This may be my lucky day. You like seafood? I'll bring some fresh fish from the city next time. I am very glad I decided to come check my cabin today, Cincinnatus. Very glad indeed. Thank you for taking good care of it."

"The pleasure was all mine," I said, starting to feel we were trapped in an English novel.

She finished her coffee, and we sat outside on the porch and watched the sunset. It was very strange being there with someone. I didn't quite know what to do next. I mean, not in the way you think. But this was a good gig I had going here, I wasn't about to ruin it by seducing Patsy Vaughan. I was smarter than that. That doesn't mean she didn't sense what I was thinking.

"You're a good-looking man, Cincinnatus. Good time to be a man these days, huh? All that free love and flower people."

I was weighing my answer carefully. "Thank you. I like a fair amount of solitude. That doesn't suit many women. No disrespect. Women don't have it easy. It isn't fair. I'm aware of that. Things need to change."

"Who are you telling? You're either an enigma or a charmer. Maybe both. I'm going with my gut here. What do you say we rustle up some dinner and have a glass of wine? As I said, I was planning to spend a few days. Have you any problem with that?"

Was she kidding? I badly wanted Patsy Vaughan to stay. Besides, it was her cabin. Here's the thing though, where would that lead? I could not be found out. That was non-negotiable. Even if she was beautiful and smart, I could not fall for her and complicate my newfound freedom. And was she smart enough to know I was lying? I had a good poker face. I'd had to in my life. I could do this. Fact was, I needed a place to stay. Better than wandering around in plain sight, even under disguise. But people ask questions. I needed time to formulate a plan for the near and distant future. If I had landed in a field of four-leaf clover, why look for weeds?

"Wood is burning something awful in that head of yours," Patsy smiled at me. "Do tell."

"Sorry, I'm not used to company. I didn't mean to be rude. I could make us a fire."

"Right. We'll get to that in a minute. Out with it. Who am I going to tell? I'm a bit of a loner myself. I don't like complications. I don't think you're one, so we're cool, yes? I'm not looking for a boyfriend. I mean I like men, don't get me wrong. And you are certainly a man."

"I find you very attractive, Patsy. I hope that's not disrespectful. You're beautiful. And very nice. You didn't throw me out. Or shoot me. I will respect whatever you prefer."

She just smiled at me. I wondered what was going in *her* head. And if she even had a gun in her purse. I think she may have been bluffing, but I wouldn't push my luck. The thing is, I was only human.

"I'm flattered, Cincinnatus. No offense taken. We're grown-ups, remember? I can take care of myself. Have done for quite some time. A person I trust knows I'm up here. So, if I don't return, they will come looking for me. Not that I feel threatened, mind you. But a woman can't be too careful. Understand?"

"Understood. I'll get to that fire now." I busied myself with wood I had already cut on the porch and stacked. Patsy stood there watching me. I didn't mind. It was a different kind of watching than earlier. She busied herself in the kitchen while I built a fire in the hearth in the living room. I knew she was watching me. I lit the logs and stood up and leaned back, stretching a bit.

"Sore back, Cincinnatus?" Patsy was talking to me. I turned to look at her.

" A bit. I may have gotten carried away with the wood cutting yesterday."

"I have a good healing oil for that, in the bathroom. You can use it if you like. She handed me a glass of wine. "Hope you like Cabernet?"

I would like anything Patsy Vaughan was handing out. Vinegar in a jelly glass. Warm milk. I needed to get a grip on myself. "Thanks, it's perfect."

She smiled again. I liked her smile too. "Are you always this easy to please?"

She had no idea how much I'd like to please her right now. I took a swallow of wine. Easy does it, man. "Basically, yes, food, water, sleep, a daily..." I lost my train of thought; she was watching me again. It was unnerving.

"Yes? You were saying... a daily...."

"Walk. I like to walk." I recovered, tending to the crackling fire.

"Walking is nice. Good for the circulation and the mind. Like other things."

"Painting, for instance," I said. We were skirting around some very heady sexual chemistry, and I needed air before it might combust. "I'm going outside for more wood." Poor choice of words perhaps, but there it is.

"Right. Don't be long. I'll set the table. The loin is hot." Patsy went into the kitchen, and I took some deep breaths outside on the porch. The loin? Was she for real? What about my loins? Give a guy a break. No, I could do this. Remain platonic with this goddess and her loin or go with the flow and not get too involved. Both were a tall order. I carried a few logs inside.

"Ready to eat?" Patsy asked. I nodded and stacked the logs fireside and went to the sink to wash my hands. Patsy handed me a dish towel. She stood there as I dried my hands, her hand on the plates and silverware. We stood there looking at one another. "You have a piece of wood in your hair," she said. I reached up to brush it away.

"I'll get it for you," she said. "Cincinnatus..."

I didn't let her finish. I kissed her. She didn't recoil, she leaned into it, kissing me back.

"You feel better now that's out of the way?" she asked.

"Much better."

She laughed. "We'd better eat, then. The loin will get cold."

Ain't that the truth, I thought. But I would not rush things. Pasty Vaughan would have my full attention, when she was ready.

"Hope you like dirty rice," Patsy said, setting a bowl in front of me. "Something wrong, Cincinnatus?"

"No. Nothing at all. I've been alone too long. And you have a way with words."

"Thank you. That was a compliment, right?"

"Of course. Where did you learn to cook? This pork is very tasty and tender."

"My mama was Creole. We lived in New Orleans. What about the rice?"

"Filthy."

Patsy laughed. A delightful sound. "Dirty, you mean. Now if you don't behave, we won't get through dinner. So, where are you from?"

"New York, Pass the pork, please."

"You don't have an accent."

"My mother was an English teacher," I lied.

"And you? What do you teach?"

"English."

"Apple didn't fall far. And your dad?"

"My father died when I was a baby. I never knew him."

"Sorry. I lost my father too. Much later. "

"The man in the photo inside?"

"Yes. We were very close, especially after Mama died. He was a good man."

All this family talk was making me uneasy. "May I take your plate?" I asked.

"Thank you. Just leave the dishes for a minute," Patsy said.

"I'll take a shower then, if you don't mind?"

"Go right ahead, I'll put things away in the kitchen."

I was acutely aware Patsy Vaughan was in the kitchen and I was naked in her shower. I changed into fresh jeans and a tee shirt and joined her in the living room. She was seated by the fire. The lights were low and she looked positively ravishing by firelight. She'd lit a few candles.

"Expecting company?" I said.

She laughed. "Have you been sleeping in my bed, Goldilocks?"

"No, It was too big for one. I took the smaller room."

"Tonight, I'd like you to sleep in my bed."

"And you'll sleep in the smaller bed?"

She smiled. "No…"

"Patsy Vaughan, you are a naughty girl. We've just met. I'm not that kind of man."

"What kind of man are you, Cincinnatus? I think you better show me."

We didn't make it to that big bed. I lay Patsy Vaughan down on that kilim rug and made love to her like it was the last night of my life. Because maybe it was. You never know. I hoped like hell with my entire being that it wasn't. Patsy kissed me sweetly and I kissed her back a bit less sweetly.

"You're a bit dirty, yourself, Mr. Cincinnatus Jones."

"I see you like it that way, Miss Patsy Vaughan."

"Patsy *Billie* Vaughan, if you don't mind."

"As in Billie Holliday?"

"None other. What do you say we take a bath? I'm feeling a little filthy."

"Is that right? Then the bath can wait."

If I was to become Patsy Vaughan's sex fantasy, I was up for the job. The woman was obviously a romantic, not a psycho. It was going to be hard not to fall in love with her. I had to keep my wits about me. She kept this cabin hidden up in the hills for what reason, exactly? Sentimental, she'd said. Maybe she was a keeper of lost men. A do-gooder with a penchant for weekend trysts with strangers. My imagination was getting the better of me and yet the thought of being Patsy Vaughan's sex slave was not an uncomfortable feeling. I felt exhilarated. The sex was as intense as I imagined and better than anything I could have dreamt up. I think she was the enigma, not me. All librarian-like except that wild hair. She held nothing back. I had to hold my very former existence back. It didn't seem fair. But my freedom had to come first. We would keep it uncomplicated, or I would be gone. Patsy Vaughan was a woman who could unravel me and that wasn't an option. I was too smart to let that happen. Yet a strange new feeling was tugging at me. Energetically, like the pull of the moon. But I did not escape an inescapable prison, swim a bay to my freedom to lose it all by falling in love. That was not the plan. Freedom was a solitary affair. The minute I started thinking about another person I was in danger. Patsy would want more. I couldn't give more. I only wanted my freedom. A relationship was not on the table. I wasn't risking everything I survived so far for a woman.

Chapter Five

I came across a show years later on television, one of those cheesy solving a cold case type shows. It was about the Alcatraz escape of the Anglins and me. "They are alive!" the tv boomed with theatrics. There was no proof, just a lot of fanfare and someone trying to cash in on a story that never gets old. I had to laugh out loud watching it. They were saying among other things, that one day the escaped trio might return on the anniversary of their escape and blend in with the tourist crowd, but secretly knew they were returning to the inescapable island. A reunion. How corny can you get? I mean even if the Anglins and I had any inclination to meet up as old men, it would not be on the Rock, I can assure you. In truth, we would never, any of us, return. You cannot imagine being on that Island, trapped, as we once were. There was no morbid curiosity to see it again. We were not going to become nostalgic. We had cut our losses and had new identities and lives. We were no longer those men, those inmates of the Rock. It is enough for us to know we escaped and would remain free men. Though I speak only for myself, I knew the Anglins were no fools. We had all successfully disappeared and aimed with every breath in our bones to stay that way.

Patsy could never know. It would only compromise my life and put her in danger. She met a man called Cincinnatus Jones. A moon painter. A lover of trees. A free spirit. She liked her mysterious lover. There was no Frank Morris. He was a man in the archives of Alcatraz's history. He died in that famous escape. And that was the way it had to be. Maybe there was nothing to think about. Being alone can mess with your mind. I was wondering in all honesty if Patsy was someone I dreamed up that day.

She was not. Patsy came back for a second dinner, as promised, and she let me cook the fish she brought, red snapper, and some delicious crab bisque with a good bite, that she made to go with it. We had fresh sourdough bread from the famous Boudin bakery on the Wharf, the works. We ate like king and queen that night. And we made love. Less urgently, but no less passionately, in her bed. It was better than the dinner, which was pretty damn good.

I had been with women since the escape. It was free love days. Patsy was different. She was a lady. And a lion. She was smart and funny, and I liked her company. We could chat the night away on any subject. San Fran was her city, but she was willing to travel the world one day. She wanted to write about places she visited, keep a private travel journal. I don't know what kindness I might have extended to someone in another life to deserve Patsy showing up, but I was grateful. She never asked me to move into her place in the city, not that I would have. She liked that I was here for her alone, hidden in the hills, her secret lover.

I had to be careful. I was feeling something unfamiliar. Was I falling for Patsy Vaughn? I couldn't, even though she was intoxicating, life affirming. Dare I say, almost necessary? Like breathing. How long before she wanted to bring me into her other life? That would be out of the question. A deal breaker. People in love lose their minds. It is not a natural state. Euphoria is a drug like any other. Love is for ordinary people, not escaped prisoners. I was out of my depth. Patsy liked our arrangement, her secret life with me. Her words played over in my head, "People get possessive and want to know everything about you. I am not one of those people, Cincinnatus. Mystery is good. Anyway, I am too selfish to share you with the world."

I had been spared twice. How I deserved to meet someone like Patsy is the real mystery. She had no baggage, no ex-husband, no parents, no children. She was a free woman with a good job and a passion to paint. She no longer worked at Alcatraz. She taught art in the city to fledging artists. She was part of an artist's community. She had her own full life. I was a hobby. As long as I was a free man, I was satisfied.

I was the one with baggage, though buried, and it would stay that way. For Patsy's safety, as well as my own. I'm hardly innocent. I never killed anyone yet I stole what wasn't mine, so I don't get a pass. I paid my dues and I did hard time. I escaped to live the rest of my life free. I was never going to be released. I would have died in there. There was no need to purge myself and tell my story and beg forgiveness. Confession happens in the soul. Nobody needed to know what was none of anyone's business. More importantly, Patsy.

I worked on my moon carvings and treescapes and waited for Patsy to return. If you think I was lonely most of the time, you'd be wrong. I don't believe in loneliness. Now boredom, that's something else, that will break you wide open. You will be revealed to yourself. We're all broken on some level. Listen to me, talking like some damn guru. What did I know? I knew hopelessness, abandonment, the cold dark cage. The loss of not only freedom, but dignity. You look at those brick walls every day and hear the sea on the other side and know even if they let you outside to see it, you will never leave that island alive. That is a finality that kills you a little every day. That was a death sentence I could not accept.

I can see the birds now. The sunrise. I paint the moon. I am no old sage who gives advice, but if I were, I know what I would say to anyone suffering while trying to figure out this life. Live your life in a way that dares to reveal you to yourself and others. A way that sets your true self free. Don't hide from your loved ones, that's stingy. That is a kind of prison where you sentence yourself. Be generous in your spirit. Do what makes your heart beat faster, so you know you're really alive. Don't become one of those grey people, glazed over with disappointment, merely going through the motions. I was in prison; I know what a life sentence means. You know the job you hate, but endure for however many awful years you struggle to get a decent retirement? In the end, it will probably kill you before you get to enjoy the benefits. And it doesn't take digging through concrete walls and swimming across a bay to freedom to find that out. It takes leaving the window open just enough to feel the cold. It will be uncomfortable, downright chilly. Feel it. Shiver. The fear subsides. That's what I would say if someone asked me. So far no one has.

Chapter Six

I thought a lot about penance. It surprised me since I am not a religious man. But I had a need to give back. I may have been cut off from reality to a degree, considering my escape and history, yet I was aware. I still lived in the world. We were in a war in Southeast Asia. Had I not had such a colorful criminal history, I would have enlisted. Not that I necessarily agreed with our country's actions in Vietnam, but I value freedom for all people, so I would have done what was right in my own mind. It was on a quiet walk that I happened upon a fellow pilgrim. He was on his way to a meeting of war vets, he said, after a friendly greeting of, "Isn't this a day to behold?" I nodded in agreement. Maybe it was my look, the beard, and my "soulful" eyes, as Patsy called them, that caused him to engage me. Of course, it wasn't. It was the army jacket Rhodes gave me, back at the hippie camp. The guy assumed I had served in 'Nam. He invited me to come as a guest and listen to some vet's stories. Maybe I'd write them down, he suggested. I said I was more of a painter than a writer. "You don't know until you try," he said. I nodded again. "Look, the coffee is not half bad and there's free sandwiches." I told him I'd think about it. He gave me a highball and I saluted him back. Strange, I didn't deserve any salute. He wished me an open mind on my "journey." I thanked him. We parted ways at the bottom of the road. My *journey?*

I wandered in the woods for a bit, drinking in the primordial beauty, taking a picture in my mind to paint later. I headed back to the cabin for lunch. I thought about the friendly vet and his bi-weekly visits to the vet's hospital in the city. "I left the war, but the war didn't leave me," he said. There were not only visible scars, and legless survivors, but mental suffering and irreversible damage in so many of these human beings we called soldiers, but somehow forgot were people first. "The nightmares don't quit," the vet said. Turns out he was kicking a heroin addiction he picked up in Vietnam. He wasn't alone in that. Each soldier's story was different, but they all had a common thread. They had been fighting a war they didn't understand, and the political climate back home was volatile. No war was protested like Vietnam and the returning veterans had that to face on top of injuries and addictions. How were they meant to return to family and normalcy? No one bothered to ask. You were either for the war or against it. Yet it was in the grey area that the ugly reality lie. To this day, the feeling and stories aren't the same as other wars where the enemy was clear to our democracy and freedom. Vietnam was another animal altogether. The movies and books depicting it are darker and more reflective of the time.

World War II vets got a parade, clubs where they could find brotherhood and chew the fat for hours reminiscing about their time overseas. Talking about their ships, barracks, camaraderie, nicknames, and catching up years later for reunions, sharing war wounds and pictures. It was a different time in our history, a different climate where roles were accepted and unquestioned. The vet I met was adamant about one thing, all war is hell and evil must not get a leg up on humanity. There was shame in some of what he and his fellow vets witnessed. There was silence. While they weren't sorry they served, absent was the honor and tribute soldiers of other wars had bestowed upon them when they came home. It was a sore point, and the number of homeless vets only aggravated the wound.

What could I do to possibly alleviate their suffering? I was no journalist, no wealthy philanthropist. I was an escaped criminal leading a secret life. I could not share my prison life and escape with them. Maybe there was a way I could do something on a small scale to contribute to finding housing for those who wanted it. One day I might buy some clothes to donate to the vet shelters and hospitals with the money from my moon art. Books would be good, reading got me through many a prison stint. Reading takes you out of yourself and your life. Escaping in one's mind is the easiest way to transcend just about anything. At the very least, books are a temporary respite from a harsh reality.

I would go to the vet's hall, I decided. Helping someone else was one step closer to becoming a full human being. Those vets were heroes and they deserved not only a parade, but better treatment back home. While they were facing the worst torture and horrors their eyes could never erase from their minds, I was getting myself in more trouble with the law and living in a cell. The difference between them and me was that prison was my own doing. They were selfless heroes, and I was a common thief. I planned on giving back and earning my humanity. I felt guilty. Not so much for my crimes, but for the fact that I lied to that vet. I had a pre-existing medical condition preventing me from serving my country, I'd told him. What a crock. I had been serving time. The lowest of the low.

"Empathy is good for the soul," Patsy told me, when I told her about the vet on my walk.

"Did you hear that in a yoga class, or some woo woo guru's sermon?" I asked.

"No, actually the warden said it to me when I told him I felt sorry for the prisoners living at Alcatraz. Although they were paying for their crimes, to be locked away for the rest of their lives had to be the depths of hopelessness. No chance of rehabilitation."

The warden? Of the same Rock I was on?

"Really?"

"What's the matter? They were people before they became criminals," she insisted.

41

"I know. I'm just surprised a tough old warden would say such a thing."

"He had another side, apparently." The boys would bust a gut hearing that one. That bit I kept to myself. "I guess everyone does," I said, wanting to put the conversation to rest.

"The Shadow Self, you mean?" Patsy was studying me. I had a fleeting thought she knew I was an imposter. Then she smiled and the thought vanished like a cartoon bubble.

"Exactly. Anyway, it was good meeting the vet. He seemed like a solid guy."

"Good," Patsy said, "And so are you." Patsy, I believed, had only two good sides.

That night I looked up at the moon in awe. There is luck and there is grace. Only you can decide which one defines you. I was turning a corner and it scared the hell out of me. Prison is safer than freedom. You have to watch your back, but three squares, every day a guaranteed routine, no decisions to make, isn't all bad. There's no emotional growth either. The result is a dead soul. Oddly, I related to the vet. The un-hero to the hero. He saw terrible atrocities while the war I fought was in my head. We were strangers, worlds apart. One a giver, the other a taker. Were either of us really free?

Chapter Seven

I was having a quiet day imagining my next moon carving, thinking a full moon series might be in order since the night sky had been brilliant lately. I went outside for some fresh air and looked up at the trees on the upper road. I saw her. Hanging upside down, moaning. A broken wine bottle lay near her head on the step. I ran up the stairs, knowing I would be stepping into a rat's nest, yet how could I leave a woman hanging upside down?

I got her upright. She reeked of wine and cigarettes. Her eyes were bloodshot, and her hair needed a wash. Nothing was broken thankfully. But where did she come from? Other than Patsy, and the vet on my walk, I had not seen anyone up here. Why was she was hammered at two in the afternoon? How she didn't break her neck or fall down the entire 100 steps, is a miracle. Not that I believed in such things.

She thanked me, avoiding my eyes, obviously embarrassed by her mishap and drunken state. I told her it was no problem but that she might want to stay home and drink. She laughed. "Not an option," she slurred. I wasn't falling into that trap by asking why.

"Take care, then," I said.

"Right. You're my angel today," she smiled. She had nice teeth and I'd bet she was a lot younger than she looked. Angel? That was rich. She should only know.

"Glad you're okay. Watch those steps." I walked her down and waited until she was out of sight before heading back up to the cabin. I didn't want company, unless it was Patsy. I might have to be more careful in future. I did not want curious people lurking about and I didn't need a drinking partner. I knew enough drunks in my life not to become one myself. I am not bragging, just stating a fact. Liquor was not my vice. Drugs either. I got a rush from being a thief once, but those days were behind me. Fading into normalcy was my goal.

I read about Irish mist. Not the liquor, but the floating vapor that comes up suddenly and covers the mountains like an ephemeral vision. The hills in East Bay create that same feeling of magic and wonder. One minute you're staring at giant redwoods and the next they disappear from view and the moving curtain of mist mesmerizes you. I was awed by this natural moment every time. I knew what was under that mist as much as I knew who I had once been. The beauty of the mist was its sheer wonder, while my disappearance was staged, planned and executed. I was humbled, nonetheless. Like plants that reach their leaves toward the sun, I was reaching for a fuller existence. Every day the past got dimmer. A part of me would always remain hidden. Good and buried. The trade-off was incomparable. I was a free man. You protect your freedom at all costs. Human beings make mistakes.

It was a gorgeous day in the hills, so I took my moon carving outside. I heard someone on the stairs going to the upper road. Now what? When I didn't hear anything else I walked to the edge of the porch by the gate. She was holding her clogs in her hands and tiptoeing barefoot. "Sorry, I didn't mean to sneak up on you. I just wanted to say hello and thank you for the other day." The upside-down woman. Trouble.

"No need. Anyone would have done the same. You do know this is private property?"

"Not sure that's true. You know, there hasn't been anyone here for a while, so I didn't think..."

You do that a lot? Not think?"

44

"Oh man. Well, I guess I deserved that. Can we start over?"

"I wasn't aware we had started in the first place."

"Are you always this uptight?"

"Are you always this pushy?"

"Touché,' Mister…"

"Jones. Cincinnatus."

"For real? Cool. I'm Oakley. Just Oakley."

"Well just Oakley, I need to be getting on with my work."

"Right, sorry again. You're not looking for friends, I get it."

Or anything else, I thought. If Patsy gets wind of this chick, I will be out on my ass in no time. I watched her push a wisp of blonde hair out of her eyes. Do you know that feeling when you can smell danger? It grabs you in your gut. You either listen to it or you regret ignoring the warning.

"Well, I'll be on my way, Cincinnatus Jones." She smiled, revealing a slightly crooked tooth that could only look good on someone that looked like her. She had improved her appearance greatly since the other day. She breezed by me, leaving a wafting scent of patchouli behind.

"Look, Oakley, I don't mean to be rude. I didn't plan on company up here, that's all."

She smiled. "Really? Then you ought to tell that to the pretty lady who comes around on the weekends. Guess she's your type. Buttoned up tight city lady."

I realized later I should have left her hanging upside down.

"I don't have a type, for your information."

Easy, man, you don't need this. Do not further engage.

"Know what I know, Cincinnatus? I like you. And we could make beautiful music together, man. I expect nothing and I could make you happy for as long as you like. Or just for to-day."

"That's sweet. But I'm ok. Keeping things simple these days."

She nodded and started to walk away and dropped one of her clogs. I picked it up and handed it to her and she leaned in and kissed me. It was like lightning. I almost felt burns. I jumped back and she laughed. It was an endearing sound, and it was dangerous. That was any sane man's clue to walk away. I was not myself is my only defense.

I asked her if she wanted coffee. She probably would have preferred a drink or a joint, but she said yes just the same. We drank our coffee on the porch and then she asked if she could see the cabin. The answer should have been no. The self I wasn't, said yes.

She took a moon carving in her hands and traced it with her fingers. "This is amazing. Why do you make them?"

"It's a habit. An obsession. It eases my mind."

She looked at me and put down the carving. She was a little too close. She stepped closer.

"Like this?" She kissed me and held on to my belt. I was not able to move, as stupid as that sounds. She pressed into me, and I could feel her loose breasts under her cotton peasant blouse. There was no denying I was turned on and she knew it. I watched her remove her blouse and jeans. I led her to the bedroom after I locked the front door.

"You haven't had your mind eased recently, have you?" she smiled, afterwards, climbing on top of me, again.

"Not like that, no."

"You gotta relax more often. Let me show you something."

I was done. This was a moment I was not going to come back from without consequence. Yet at that particular time, that particular day, I didn't care. I might have begun a new addiction. Could I keep this secret from Patsy? Not in good conscience. I had to stop it before it turned into anything more than one reckless day. Oakley was a force of nature. A dream. The dream was over. I had to choose righteously or ruin everything.

Oakley left reluctantly but respectfully, after I told her while she was lovely, I had to do my carvings and art without distraction. I explained, though it wasn't any of her business, that Patsy owned the cabin and was kind enough to let a family friend use it. And I could not abuse that kindness by inviting anyone to stay with me. She seemed cool with that explanation and reminded me she invited herself, so there were no strings. I believed her. A man that's just had sex doesn't have the sharpest reading of things. This was not the last of Oakley, I had a strong feeling. Suffice it to say I was as stupid that day as I have ever been in my entire life.

I had a peaceful rest of the week and the moon carvings took up a whole wall now. I started to paint the moon on canvas. While I was painting, I didn't think about anything else. Like how my comfortable solitude could be taken away any minute. How stupid I was to let Oakley into Patsy's cabin. How I probably ruined everything because man is really a simple base creature.

I didn't see Oakley and she kept her promise to stay away. But I did find a note rolled up and stuck on the gate when I took a walk.

Dear Cincinnatus,

I won't bother you. But I was wondering how you heard me that day when I had removed my clogs. That's some sensitive hearing you have. You sure you're not hiding out and have a secret you want to keep? Or are you just a mysterious stranger? Maybe you're running from the law like a fugitive? That's really cool and sexy. Your secret is safe with me. If you get lonely, leave a cup by the gate and I'll know to stop in and say hello. Love, Oakley

There are two ways to react in most situations. In a normal calm manner, accessing before reacting at all. Or blowing up and losing all perspective and revealing oneself in a guilty or negative way. I had good sense, bear with me on that, though I recently proved quite the opposite. As I was saying, I had the sense that Oakley, while sweet and tempting and marvelous company, was not that smart. Certainly not clever enough to figure out I was an escaped inmate and one of the most wanted men in the United States very recently. She was a fantasy. The best way to handle it was not to overreact or react at all. Patsy was coming this weekend and I needed to have my game face on. Thankfully, I had a lot to show for my time with my recent moon sculpture prolific period. What were the chances Patsy and Oakley knew each other? Oakley had seen Patsy up here, she said. Did Patsy know this upside-down hippie chick that could very well be my undoing? I hoped not. Patsy was real. A drunk woman hanging upside down, was not.

Chapter Eight

Patsy was like clockwork. Friday at seven o'clock on the dot, she arrived at the cabin, groceries and wine in hand. I kissed her. We were that familiar with one another now. I don't know anything about normal relationships, not having had any in my life, but this felt normal.

"You've been busy, Cincinnatus. We've got to get these moon pieces down to the gallery this weekend. What do you say?"

"Not much else to do up here. Sure, I've got no objection to that."

"Something on your mind? You seem preoccupied."

Here's the part where I am at a loss. Not that I forgot how to lie, just that I did not want to lie to Patsy. And I wasn't stupid enough to think telling her the truth was a damn good idea either. Ah, the moral dilemma of man. Easy does it. Say nothing.

"How much time did you spend up in these hills?"

She smiled. It was a beautiful sight and I was humbled. I felt like punching myself in the face.

"Why, do you have cabin fever already? Or did you see a ghost?"

"A ghost? Very funny." Nobody was laughing.

"The cabins are haunted. I don't imagine that bothers you, or does it?"

There was no way in hell I was telling Patsy who showed up. Maybe I dreamt Oakley up. It was possible.

"It's just very quiet up here. I thought I saw someone walking down the steps. But there's no one living around here, right?"

"No, not anymore. Years ago, loggers. Later though, a young woman lost her life in a storm, as the story goes, a large tree branch cracked and fell on her, knocking her down the stairs. People claimed she came back. Her ghost? Is that who you saw?"

A ghost in hippie guise that haunts hilltop cabins? Is this what I was meant to believe? "I don't know exactly what or who I saw..."

But I clearly remember having sex with Oakley. A man doesn't forget sex, even ghost sex.

"These were logging cabins in the 1920's. They were deserted for years and that leaves prime real estate for ghosts. What?"

"So, I'm not crazy? That's a relief." In more ways than one. I dodged a bullet. No one but me knew about Oakley and her visit. I opened the bottle of Pinot Noir that Patsy brought with her.

"Maybe you saw Cincinnatus Miller. He lived in these parts once. The poet, Joaquin Miller."

I was well aware of Cincinnatus Miller, his real name, who escaped from jail in the 1800's. He had silver hair and was an old man. I did not have sex with an old dead poet of the male persuasion.

"Maybe. I could have sworn it was a ..." Shut your mouth, man. Don't borrow trouble. Women can smell a lie a mile away. I'd almost blown it.

"So tell me more about this poet, Cincinnatus Miller."

Patsy smiled. "I have a feeling you know more than I do about your namesake."

"I told you I was named for the innkeeper on the Daniel Boone show."

Scape Ghost

"And you're sticking to that story? Fine. So there's a story about the poet Joaquin "Cincinnatus" Miller, and how he escaped from jail. He stole a horse."

"Interesting. And he wore a chrysanthemum in his lapel every day."

"See? You do know about him. Maybe you will meet him."

"Patsy Vaughan, how do I know you're not a ghost?"

"I am very much alive, I assure you. Check me out, there's no obituary. And I told you, I worked at Alcatraz. A person doesn't make that up."

Hearing her say that name gave me pause. But not enough to let on. Wasn't I a ghost myself? Or at least Frank Morris was. He wasn't coming back to haunt anyone. I was out of my depth here. My head was spinning. I had to settle down. I couldn't tell Patsy about Oakley. And how she hinted that she knew I was hiding out. *Keep your secret,* she'd written in her note. *Are you a fugitive?* How could she know?

"Cincinnatus? Penny for your thoughts."

"Just thinking about ghosts."

"You know there are others." Patsy had a twinkle in her eye. She was clearly not the kind of woman who scared easy. Maybe she had a ghost fetish.

"Others?"

"There was this soldier. Maybe the Civil War."

She was playing with me now. I took the bait. "Were you alone with him?"

"I was. He was very persuasive. A gentleman, but he hadn't had a woman in quite a while."

I smiled and put down my wine glass. "Did he ravish you?"

"Come here to me, and I'll tell you all about it."

I exhaled. For now I was in the clear. If Patsy found out about Oakley or if she showed up again, I think I might see another side of Patsy Vaughan. One I wouldn't welcome. I better play my cards right and not show an ounce of guilt about Oakley. I thought about Cincinnatus Miller and tried not to think about Oakley. I had a sense of apprehension. Why? Was I waiting for a ghost?

Chapter Nine

I heard the music first. A lonesome harp wailing a soulful tune. The music got closer. I heard a fiddle. The two of them were like something from the movies. All raggedy pants and dirty chambray shirts. The one playing the harmonica wore a porkpie hat. The fiddle player's shirt was blowing in the breeze revealing a stained undershirt, a silver medallion hung to meet a tuft of blonde hair on his chest. I took a seat on the porch and watched as they continued their song. They seemed friendly enough and not about to do me any bodily harm. Just a pair of vagabonds with instruments, out of the blue. If I didn't know better, I'd say I was about to meet some real-life train hoppers. Tramps, they used to call them. Bojangles times two. This ghost stuff was getting interesting. I was convinced these guys were not of the earthly plane. I drank my coffee and waited for them to finish playing.

"You got any more of that?" The guy with the harp asked, looking at my coffee.

"Been traveling awhile, we could use a cup."

"Sure," I said, standing to get two more cups. "Where you fellas from? My name is Cincinnatus, by the way."

"Thank you, Cincinnatus, mighty kind of you. We don't make the best appearance, we realize. A bit rough from the road. I'm Cab. This here's Haggard. We ride the rails, wherever it takes us."

"As in Calloway? And Merle? Good stuff. I'm a fan of legends, myself. Take a load off, let me get that coffee." How cool was this? Bless Patsy Vaughan for letting me stay.

"I take mine with a measure of whiskey, if you can spare any," the fiddle player spoke in a dusty timbre. "Merle is one righteous fiddler no doubt but can't say I was named after him. Story goes my daddy asked my mama how she was feeling after the long-awaited birthing of me and she replied, "Haggard." My daddy, being a fiddling man himself, was all over that. Guess I can be grateful she didn't answer, "Like hell."

I laughed. "Good story. And I can accommodate you, Haggard." I looked over at Cab.

"Black's fine with me, hold the whiskey, it gives me nightmares," Cab smiled. For a train hopper, he had nice teeth.

I went inside to get their coffee, stopping at the window to see if they were still out there and not a hallucination. Cab was blowing softly on his harp and Haggard had his feet up on the porch rail. I wondered if they wanted to take showers and stay for supper. I almost laughed out loud. But then again, Oakley had certainly stayed the night. And whatever about her being a ghost, the sex was real enough, no doubt about it. Maybe she'd come back. She would love these guys.

"Here we are. One straight up. And one with a good measure." I handed the men coffees and sat down. "You fellas been up here before? I heard this place has a storied history."

Cab pushed his hat back. "Nope. Never visit the same place twice, if we can help it. Run with the trains. One place or 'nother. We do appreciate the welcome."

Haggard took a swig of his spiked coffee. "Now that will warm the very depths," he said, laughing, a cracked front tooth adding to the picture I had already started to paint in my mind.

"Nice place here. You alone? Not prying or nothing, just making conversation."

"No worries. Yep, here by myself. Doing some painting. Getting right with life, if you will."

"Sure, that's something nobody can fault you for, is it? How long were you inside?"

I wasn't sure I'd heard him right, but one thing I wasn't, was deaf. "Inside?" I was stalling. But how did he know?

"We know stuff. We ain't here anymore, in the traditional way, the living sense. So we know things." Haggard tapped his cup and smiled, revealing tobacco-stained teeth. I was surprised he had a full set.

"You're ghosts?"

"We ain't alive, Cincinnatus. Or whatever your real name is," Cab said. "Haggard ain't pulling your chain, brother. We been around, and then some. No worries, we ain't snitches. And dead men ain't no threat."

I scratched my head. "Right. I believe you. Yeah, I was inside. And now I'm here. Is that a problem?"

"No matter to us," Haggard said, finishing his whiskey coffee. "We're just passing through."

"I escaped. You wouldn't believe it if I told you the truth."

"We know. Cheers." Haggard held up his cup.

"You're safe. No worries, like we said, we ain't here no more. We'll be gone like the breeze again 'fore you know it."

"Fair enough. I'm a bit leery still, you understand? This is mind-blowing stuff."

"Indeed, we do understand. We don't know why or how, but I stopped asking questions about things I can't reckon, long ago. I can't rightly say I got quite right with life when I was alive. But I kept trying. You gotta do the same, brother. Keep going." Haggard put down his drained cup and took up his fiddle.

"We could use a shower if you might oblige us, Cincinnatus. We ain't got crumbs or nothing, just grimy from the road. A shower would set us right again. Your kindness is appreciated."

I hadn't heard someone call lice, crumbs since Alcatraz.

55

Help yourself, Cab. Bathroom is the second door on the right. Towels on the shelf."

Haggard whistled, "Indoor plumbing! Now that is a score if I ever heard one, ain't it, Cab?"

Cab nodded. "Don't mind us, we've been riding rough these days. We will be eternally grateful for the hospitality. We can play some more for you and Haggard can cook a mean stew if you got the fixins."

What was I to say to a pair of dead train hoppers with intuitive powers? What had I to lose?

"I never turn down a chance to hear good music. And the kitchen is all yours. I just have one request, if you don't mind?"

"No reefer?" Haggard asked, a gleam in his eye.

"Reefer is fine. I'd like to sketch you both, if you wouldn't mind. For painting, later."

The men looked at each other. "For posterity?"

"Yeah, something like that. Painting keeps me sane."

"We can dig that. Sketch us all you like. Capture our essence, ain't that what they say?" Cab said, freshly washed but with the same clothes he had on.

"I'll get my sketchpad," I said, walking inside. I wanted to make use of what was left of the afternoon light.

Cab sat for me first, while Haggard took a shower and started what he called "iron-dipped stew." He said years ago he remembered his granddaddy sticking a clean horseshoe in a pot of stew to add some iron. I didn't know if he was pulling my leg and I knew there weren't any horseshoes around, but it made for a funny story. The stew was delicious. I did see him tip the coffee pot into the stew and add a shot of whiskey. I'll have to remember that next time I cook stew.

Haggard was a good sport and sat for me, playing his fiddle the whole time. For men on the move, they were surprisingly relaxed and cooperative. I knew it wasn't easy to sit still, especially when someone was watching you. I knew that feeling all too well.

"You don't happen to know Cluck Old Hen, do you?" I asked my guests.

Haggard grinned, "Why I'd say you got a bit of the Appalachia in your soul, am I right?"

"Don't know about that, but I do love that tune."

"Cab, let's not keep our host waiting."

Now I have heard my share of good music, but these boys tore the roof off that song. I had to say if this was my last night on earth, I wouldn't die unhappy.

My musical guests hit the hay while I stayed up to do some painting. When I finally lay down myself, I half-expected to hear music from the other room. It was as silent as the gallows. Later, I heard a faint harmonica and a train whistle in the distance. Before I knew it, the sun was up and I crept down the hallway towards the kitchen to make coffee. I passed the guest room and looked in. The beds were made and not a trace of Cab or Haggard. In the living room, a half-painted portrait of Cab on my easel stared back at me. I went outside to the porch.

The train hoppers were gone. I looked around for any trace of them at all. There wasn't a note, but something gleamed in the sun on the porch railing. Cab's harp. I suppose he had more than one. I picked it up and blew a few notes. I was delighted I had this souvenir to show Patsy. Not that she wouldn't believe me, she was the one that told me about the ghosts in the first place. I put the harp in my shirt pocket for safekeeping and went inside to get coffee and look at my sketches of Cab and Haggard. On the hook where my coffee mug usually hung was something that looked familiar. Haggard's medallion. I looked at the design, it was Sanskrit and there was lettering on the back in script. "Tala." I had read a few books on Indian culture and specifically the Sufi poet, Rumi. I was drawn to the medallion. Tala meant music, the measures of it. Why did Haggard leave his medallion behind? I put it around my neck. Patsy was going to have a field day with this. I turned on the water to fill the coffee pot but noticed there was nearly a full pot already made. I smiled, filling a mug. I took it outside to savor the morning and relive yesterday in my mind.

Chapter Ten

I had a lot of time to think in prison. When I escaped, the fads were Transcendental Meditation and EST. People for some reason had a need to delve into their souls and psyches to find inner peace. Or maybe change their life for the better. I didn't knock it but joining groups and doing that touchy- feely 'how are you really feeling today?' stuff was not my deal at all. Neither was going to church or temple or any other worship of a supreme being. I believed I was responsible for my own life. My choices were mine to live with and accept. No god or the devil made me do it. Blaming a high or low power seemed like a copout in my opinion. Someone said, "Religion is for people who fear hell; spirituality is for people who have already been there." I like that. I would try my damndest to live an honest life from now on. Right now, that was a life of ghosts. Who else is a fugitive going to trust?

I started thinking about the loggers who built this cabin. Maybe I'd meet one of them. We could sit and talk for hours. I'd get the history from the horse's mouth. I could even tell him my own story. They were ghosts, they would not be calling the newspapers or the police. I knew deep down I wouldn't share my past. I was not paranoid, but I had that extra layer of self-protection people who keep secrets have. That mattered little because the ghosts already knew all about me.

Patsy said she had a surprise for me. I told her I didn't like surprises. She insisted I would love this one. It involved garlic, was all she would say. And a road trip. Six months had passed, so I felt safe enough to venture out. She understood my need for solitude and privacy. It would be just the two of us, and the garlic. Turns out we were headed north to Gilroy, the Garlic Capital of the World. We would smell, buy, and of course eat everything garlic. A lot of mushrooms too, un-psychedelic, which happen to be high on my list of delicious foods, if roasted just right. So, garlic and mushrooms, here we come.

Patsy was a good driver and a fun partner to travel with, in keeping with her pleasant and funny disposition I had grown to anticipate when she visited me at the cabin. She had arranged a diverse collection of music on tape for our journey. Everything from Mozart to The Stones with plenty of Miles Davis, Judy Collins, Sonny Boy Williamson, Howlin Wolf, Alberta Hunter and Nina Simone. Riding with Patsy and listening to such great music, I didn't care if she was taking me to the stink bug capital of the world. If ever there was a moment to freeze time, I was in it. I'm not a man prone to grand displays of emotion. If I was, I might have cried with joy. I was simply one lucky man. I would relish it while it lasted because the odds were it wouldn't. I swam off Alcatraz. No one found me. Or the Anglins. The likelihood of the three of us staying gone forever was slim. Then again, so is hanging out with ghosts. In the meantime, I was going to have all the fun one man could have until I couldn't anymore.

By the time we got back to the cabin the next day, we were garlic rich. Stinking of the damn stuff. Patsy started a garlic and oil linguini dish, while I chopped mushrooms to roast.

The train hoppers portraits were complete, and Patsy loved them. I didn't want to rush my time with Patsy, yet I was anxious to meet my next ghost. I felt like a little kid awaiting Christmas, not that I had any great memories of that holiday or any other stored up in my book of nostalgia.

I remembered the night before the escape. I could hardly sleep. We were dreaming in our waking state ever since we made that decision to go through with it. There wasn't doubt or even fear, really. Our need to be outside those suffocating walls of despair kept us focused and our adrenaline high. If it hadn't happened successfully, it would just be another anticlimactic tale. A yellowed newspaper headline in the wrappings of someone's garbage. Our capture would be compost with the coffee grounds or spoiled meat. Our demise, fish food in the ocean. Instead, I was a free man eating fresh farmed garlic that would make a vampire's eyes tear. Patsy and I, linguini aioli and bottle of Pinot Gris from the Napa Valley. My life could have ended after dinner, and I'd have died a very happy man. But that was not my destiny. My rebirth held much more in store.

Patsy left early Sunday night, heading back to her place in the Upper Haight. I was looking forward to my alone time and more ghost encounters, yet I wasn't really eager for Patsy to leave. She was fun, we had interesting conversations, and I liked being in the sack with her. The feeling was mutual. I thanked my lucky stars for Patsy and the ghosts.

I couldn't sleep, so I turned on the lamp and started reading one of the novels Patsy left behind. Political fiction would surely put me to sleep. I turned the pages of Allen Drury's "Advise and Consent," and found I was still wide awake. It was actually a good read. Patsy and I would have a good chat about it next time. I was contemplating what I'd just read, when I heard it, clear as day. A man's voice from the other room. He was reciting poetry. I threw back the covers and crept slowly into the living room. He sat by the window, the moon illuminating his face and gray beard. His feet in worn leather boots he rested on the coffee table in front of him. He had a crushed chrysanthemum in the breast pocket of his worn dark suit jacket. There was a candle lit in a hurricane glass holder I didn't see in the cabin before. He kept reading. I sat down on the couch, my eyes riveted to his face. His weathered hands held the notebook from which he read. I recognized the poem, "Kit Carson's Ride." This was too much. I was afraid to breathe. I relished every word he spoke.

*"Room! room to turn round in, to breathe and
be free.
To grow to be giant, to sail as at sea
With the speed of the wind on a steed with his
mane
To the wind, without pathway or route or a rein.
Room! room to be free where the white
border'd sea
Blows a kiss to a brother as boundless as he;
Where the buffalo come like a cloud on the
plain.
Pouring on like the tide of a storm-driven main,
And the lodge of the hunter to friend or to foe
Offers rest; and unquestion'd you come or you
go—
My plains of America! Seas of wild lands!
From a land in the seas in a raiment of foam.
That has reached to a stranger the welcome of
home,
I turn to you, lean to you, lift you my hands."*

I waited until he was finished. Should I speak? Offer him a drink? I was unable to make a simple decision. I didn't have to, he spoke first.

"I wouldn't refuse a cup of coffee, if you wouldn't mind. I've been working for a good spell, and it's worn me out. Not that I am complaining, mind you. When the words come, we have to pay attention, yes? You're a wordsmith, yourself?"

"Not exactly. More of a reader. I paint." I poured Joaquin Miller a cup of coffee. Can you grasp the magnitude of that sentence? I will never write anything that profound if I live to be one hundred. And let's face it, that's extremely unlikely.

"Art is many things. The medium is merely the way the soul expresses itself." He took his coffee and looked at my painting of Cab and Haggard. "Those men have a story on their faces. Came out through the music, I imagine. You captured something."

"Thank you. I recognize your poem. 'Songs of the Sierras,' right?"

"You are well read, I see." He had a twinkle in his eye.

"It has special meaning to me, that stanza you read."

"Indeed? Are you a seafaring man?" Again, the twinkle. "Or cowboy?"

"Neither. But freedom means a lot to me."

"Prison. That's it, yes?"

Joaquin Miller was long dead. He was a ghost. What was the harm?

"Yes. Most of my life. Not proud of it, but there it is."

"What's your name, son?"

"Cin.... Frank Morris, sir. I escaped from Alcatraz." I couldn't very well use his name as my own in front of him. I let out a breath I had been holding.

Joaquin Miller howled. He laughed so hard his whole face turned beet red. I don't know how ghost blood flow works, but the guy had color, I'm telling you.

"Brilliant. The military prison? The one surrounded by water. You some kind of fish?" He laughed again, then turned serious. "You are not a man of the water, you said. I may be inclined to believe this tale of yours, Frank. You may be a desperado."

I was uncomfortable with the sound of my given name. "I promise you, Mr. Miller, I am not lying. And it isn't a military prison anymore."

He studied me. "Just testing your mettle. And seeing if you had come clean, shall we say. I escaped from jail once, myself. Stole a horse. No swimming involved."

It was my turn to laugh. "You've had quite a life, if you don't mind me saying."

"No argument there. Done it all. The frontier, the law, the newspaper, the natural world, the eccentric edges, the precipices, the depths of men's souls. I have been to these places. I am everyman and no man. And right now, I am hungry."

I made Joaquin Miller a sandwich. I lied before. I just topped myself. This day was surreal. A cup of coffee and a turkey on sourdough with mustard, never tasted so good. We ate in silence, but I knew it wouldn't last long. The famous poet was a chatty guy.

"What did you miss most while in prison, son?"

"The trees, the sky at night. The breeze on my face while sleeping under a full moon."

"You are a man of nature, yourself. That will comfort you and elude you. I planted thousands of trees up here. People take that for granted. I can see you do not."

"Thank you, Mr. Miller. Every day I wake up and see this majesty, I am awed."

"Call me Cincinnatus. I prefer it. You should write poetry. Anyway, you won't go back. You will discover your own frontier and in doing so, discover yourself. You have dreams, don't you? They must not die. No one can call you a liar if you are sharing your dreams. There is such an expanse of imagination to be primed from the pump. Life is a deep well. Who cares what people say? They have limitations. We are who we are. Offer no apology. We ride hard and put pen and brush to good use. A wild horse knows no stable. You had to escape. You had to be free."

I was tongue-tied. I felt if I opened my mouth, gibberish would come out. I took the chance. "Your understanding and words are a true gift." That was lame, I thought. Well, he was the poet, not me.

Scape Ghost

"That all you got in your belly, cowboy? Polite words are fine, but how do you feel in your gut, desperado? Out with it, I can take it."

"I will never be caught, and I will never go back inside. This is a promise to myself. I made mistakes. I am grateful to be here. I won't waste a second of my life. May I be so bold as to quote you?"

Joaquin Miller nodded.

"*Ah! that night Of all dark nights! And then a speck -- A light! A light! A light! A light! It grew, a starlit flag unfurled! It grew to be Time's burst of dawn. He gained a world; he gave that world Its greatest lesson: On! sail on!*"

"Brilliantly recited. Now we must have a toast, as men of the page and canvas and open plains and hills have always done. What will your pour us, my friend?"

"Whiskey."

"Then we shall fall to our knees and rejoice."

I handed the poet a whiskey neat. I waited for him to make the toast.

"Let us drink to the moon."

"To the moon," I echoed. And we drank.

I painted Joaquin Miller the next morning when he was gone, exactly as I saw him that day in the cabin reading his poetry. I had sketched him after all. Though I believed I committed his appearance and expression to memory. I still wanted to pinch myself. The encounters were real. There was no doubt about it in my mind. I knew this much, there was a reason the ghosts kept coming. Maybe a few reasons. One, I was supposed to paint them. Two, I was learning something about myself with each visit. Or shall I say, visitation? If you're wondering if the real Cincinnatus, poet of the Hights left me a remembrance of himself, he did. I had his notebook. Inside were the writings of a man I had admired first in words and then had the privilege to know for a brief moment. Inside the worn vellum paper cover, was a crushed chrysanthemum. It would be a good while before I came down from this cloud. Patsy might find me hard to live with from now on.

I put my brushes in a coffee can to soak and took a walk. The trees I gazed up at had special meaning after meeting Joaquin Miller. I could not help feeling humbled by their giant lush presence. I walked on, enjoying the mostly quiet, except for birdsong. I decided to go a bit further before I turned back home. Home. I liked the sound of that. Home is not something I remember truly having any time in my life. Was prison where I belonged? All that had changed on that June night I dared to want something else. I would never regret my decision to escape. I was not a man of hubris, but I survived that water for a reason.

Chapter Eleven

1963

I walked into the village, picked up a newspaper, and treated myself to a jelly donut and a cup of coffee. I was still on a high from meeting Joaquin Miller. Could this day get better? I opened the paper. Alcatraz was closing. I read it again. Even if we had been caught, they could not have sent us back to that godforsaken place. I wanted to let out a cheer. I hoped somewhere John and Clarence were smiling. I finished my donut and accepted a refill on coffee.

"Big news, huh?" The guy behind the counter said to me. "Looked like a horrible place. Can't imagine being trapped there for the rest of my life. No wonder those guys tried to escape."

"They don't call it The Devil's Island for nothing," I said.

"It's like something out of The Dark Ages, if you ask me."

"I hear there was even a dungeon," I said, rather enjoying the conversation.

"Really? Like I said, I can't imagine what went on in there. Doesn't bear thinking about."

"I have to agree. Good riddance to that eyesore."

The guy laughed, "You said it. I'd buy you a drink but all we got is coffee. Take another jelly donut for the road. On the house, it's a day to celebrate."

I thanked him and left the newspaper on the table. I had pictures of that place etched on my mind. I had no intention of revisiting those memories. I walked back to the road towards the cabin, taking my time and breathing in freedom.

I felt a slight breeze go past me. I heard laughter. High pitched. Kids. It felt close, almost like someone had walked by me, though no one was on the path but me. I looked back. No one was there. I walked on a bit and turned around at the bottom of the path and headed uphill, back to the cabin.

I heard singing coming from inside and the lights were on. They shone on a small stained-glass window that was not part of the cabin before. Was I hallucinating? The singing continued. Some kind of a hymn. I opened the door and walked inside. Four young girls turned to look at me. They had beautiful shining brown faces and white dresses. They looked like angels. One was playing with a sash on her dress. The young one spoke first.

"Hello, sir, don't be afraid. We'll just sing you a few songs and be gone. We came a long way. To see the march." Her accent was thickly southern. Her smile was lovely. The march?

"You all seem kind of young to be traveling alone. Where is home?"

I wished Patsy were here. She was the schoolteacher. I had no experience with children.

"Birmingham, sir," the girl with the sash replied.

I felt my heart fall through the floor. "Alabama?"

"Yes, sir. Is there another?"

I spoke but my voice was far away. "You went into a church. There was another girl, one of your sisters." I'd read the newspapers. Reading about an unspeakable crime is one thing, having the victims stand before you is quite another. We looked at each other, these angels and me, letting the quiet surround us. I allowed the moment to sink into my consciousness and pierce my heart.

"Your sister?" I asked the girl who stepped forward.

"Yes, sir. Her name is Sarah. I'm Addie Mae."

I felt physically sick. I sat down and put my head in my hands, breathing deeply.

"You ok, sir?" the little one said. "You look mighty pale. We can get you some water."

I watched them all walk to the kitchen sink. One handed the other a glass and someone else filled it. The little one offered it to me. "Drink this, you'll surely feel much better."

I did as I was told and gathered myself. "Pardon me. This is a shock."

"Imagine how we feel," said the girl with the sash. "Why just 'bout a minute ago, Addie Mae was tying my dress sash; then we were gone."

I realized I was staring and crying. I never cry. Some would consider that a character flaw.

"Don't be sad, sir. We're here for the March, in your city tomorrow. Other places too. People are coming together. That's the whole point. You can come with us." Her innocence was humbling. I felt like two cents. No, make that zero.

"I'm sorry, I can't come with you. I have to stay here. There are people in the city looking for me."

"Like people that put bombs in a church?" The little one again, her eyes wide as saucers.

I cringed. "No, nothing like that. The men that killed you are purely evil. They hide behind masks. They are cowards."

"Will people always hate each other just because we look different?"

"I hope not. It makes no sense. Inside we are all the same."

"What is your name, sir?"

"Cincinnatus Jones."

"We mean your real name?"

"How do you know that isn't my real name?"

"We just do. It's okay. We know you can't hurt us. I mean you wouldn't hurt us. You're not a bad man. You were just very lost. Isn't that so?"

I was speechless. How did this little angel know all about me? She deserved an answer, that much was clear.

"My name was Frank Morris. I changed it after I was free. I escaped from prison. I am not really free though, as you probably know. I'll never be free. I'm one step ahead of the jailer as it were."

They all nodded like they understood. "I'm Denise," said the little one, "Denise McNair. I'm eleven. This here is Carole Robertson and Cynthia Wesley and ..."

"Addie Mae Collins, sir. We three are fourteen. My sister, Sarah, who isn't here, is twelve."

I was shaking and I realized I suddenly felt cold. It was as warm as a summer day outside.

"Would you girls like some lemonade and cookies? And please sing some more, if you would." I had a fleeting thought. I would go back to prison if these girls could be alive again. Of course, they couldn't, even if I gave myself up to the authorities. Were the murderers of these beautiful children in jail? Would they be executed for what they did to the innocent? I wanted justice for my new friends. I was offering them lemonade and cookies. Why didn't I do something useful like go find their killers and show them what it feels like to be locked away for the rest of their hateful lives? I would have to toughen up quickly. Crying like a girl wasn't going to help. What was happening to me?

"We would love a snack, thank you kindly, sir. Are you some kind of artist?" the little one spoke. I wanted to paint her, but my hands were shaking. I put four glasses on a tray and a plate of cookies, and I brought it over to the table.

"Yes, I like to paint. Pictures of the moon, giant redwoods, and people too."

"Would you like to paint us, sir?"

Would I? And then die, I thought. How in God's name did these angels come to me, a man with my past and lack of any belief in a higher power? Four angels, blown up in a church. Why?

"I would be honored, Addie Mae."

"Then I better tie Denise's sash right quick." She tied her friend's sash and then took my hands in hers. "You aren't like those men. And you aren't that man you used to be. You are peace and love and good things, Mr. Cincinnatus."

I wanted to fall on my knees and give glory. I don't even know what the heck that means.

"Sing with us, sir," said the little one, Denise.

"I don't know any hymns."

"You might know this one," said Addie Mae.

I had a front seat to a choir of angels who sang Amazing Grace like I have never heard it sung before and never will again as long as I live. I sang along softly, while I painted. The four girls kept singing until dark.

"We need to sleep," Addie Mae said. "The march is tomorrow. We won't disturb you in the morning."

"Please, take the other room. There are extra pillows and blankets. I would love to cook you breakfast before you leave. Pancakes and maple syrup and eggs."

I'll cook whatever you want as long as you stay alive and don't get blown up in a church.

"It's okay, Mr. Cincinnatus. We are at peace now. And you can be too. But there's a lot of work to do. It will take years, maybe forever." She thanked me. I was the one who should be grateful.

"Thank you, Addie Mae. The pleasure was all mine." I started to weep. My heart hurt. I wept because the pure beauty that was no longer alive because of hate, was standing right in front of me. Goodness destroyed by ugly racist fear. Mankind was an oxymoron, wasn't it? There were monsters living among us, masquerading as ordinary people. What hope was there for the world?

"Don't be sad, Mr. Cincinnatus," the little one, Denise, spoke again.

I looked at her. The world was a horrible place, I thought. Filled with hate and intolerance.

"And love, Mr. Cincinnatus. A love that forgives. Promise me you won't forget that?"

"I promise, Denise." I closed my eyes; I was suddenly tired.

When I woke, it was morning. I practically ran to the kitchen when I found the other room empty. No one was in the living room either. I looked at the window, it was an ordinary square again, the stained glass was gone. As were the four girls from Birmingham. I looked at my easel and there they were. Four beautiful angels in white dresses, one with a golden sash. There was something tucked under the canvas, I pulled it out. A page of sheet music, Amazing Grace. 16th Street Baptist Church was stamped on the bottom. I walked outside. The sun was brilliant. I looked up. "Why?" I yelled at the sky.

Chapter Twelve

Whatever about the moon art selling, I could not share the paintings of my ghosts, never go public with them, even under a fake name. Besides being too risky, no one would believe it. The Birmingham girls were my most treasured painting. I would show the painting to Patsy. I could not even imagine what her reaction would be if they brought me to my knees. Sharing their visitation with her was one thing. Telling her they knew who I was, was out of the question. The ghosts knowing my past was no threat to me. I aimed to keep it that way.

I could never for one minute forget I was hiding out. That did not have an end date. I would always be a fugitive. This Utopian existence I was experiencing could not last. People are not that lucky in real life. But while it lasted, I would savor every minute, each ghostly visit, each weekend with Patsy. Did I have stirrings, longing to do something more exciting or different? Why would I? I had been part of a historic escape from an inescapable prison. I was not a ghost. I was very much alive. What I did was not a feat to be celebrated, except in my own mind and of course the minds of the Anglin brothers. I wondered how they were faring. I hoped as well as myself. They were clever and resourceful, and they had each other. They were kin. We were never going to be interviewed on a talk show describing our escape. People would be fascinated though, that's for sure. And we'd be hauled back to prison before you could say Walter

Cronkite. We would instead become our own legends, the famous unsolved case of three inmates of Alcatraz who dared to dig through a wall and swim to freedom. All hinging on if we stayed gone and they never found us. We would never have a normal life, that was the price.

Patsy told me she wasn't in the mood to teach anymore; her mind was elsewhere. She wanted to have her own gallery and paint. She said driving to the cabin made her feel better, knowing someone she cared about was waiting to see her. I was crazy about her too. I wasn't worthy, but she had no idea about any of that. I'd venture to say even if she knew the truth, she wouldn't change her feelings toward me or about us. *Us.* I had never been part of an us. I was a loner. The escape was my only journey into teamwork. But that was a means to an end.

"Did you hear? Alcatraz closed. The end," she said. "Boy, I don't miss going there. The kids were great, but it was an eerie place. I suppose it's full of ghosts now. God only knows what went on inside that prison."

"I heard. The Devil's Island is no more."

"One day I'll tell you about my time with the kids. What a foreboding feeling I had every time the boat docked. And what relief I felt when it took me back to the city. You can't imagine how creepy it is on that island."

"No, I can't," I lied. "I don't even want to think about it," I said. That was the truth.

I wasn't about to give that thought any oxygen. Like Patsy said, "The end." The Birmingham girls had thrown me. They made me question humanity. I wanted to put it under a microscope and examine every cell gone haywire in man. Was hate and racism in the blood? If not, who was teaching kids to hate so much they took innocent lives? In a church, no less. They were not the God they believed in. What gave them the right? I was humbled to meet the Birmingham girls. I felt helpless, I could not bring them back. Now who thought he was God? I wanted justice. I felt vulnerable with something they stirred in me and that was not a feeling I was comfortable with at all. I would have been swallowed alive in prison. Vulnerability was useless to me before and could terrify any red-blooded alpha male. I was uncomfortable. Angry. I needed answers.

"So, no visitors this week, Cincinnatus?" Patsy was putting away groceries while I opened a bottle of wine. The painting of the Birmingham girls was in the back of the closet in the other bedroom. I didn't want Patsy to see it yet. The painting was not of a local free spirit who liked men and her drink, or a pair of vagabond train hoppers with musical talent, or even a famous poet and frontiersman. Nor was it of a war veteran, generous with his time and heart. I had painted four innocent girls, four murder victims of the most heinous crime known in the country. That deserved a conversation. They may have been ghosts, but to me they were angels.

How could the painting be explained if anyone saw it? Other than Patsy, no one would understand. I was a ghost of sorts myself and could not come out of the shadows. Why did they come to me? What possible good could I do with their visit? There was another girl, they said. A fifth one. She didn't die. Wouldn't she want to know her sister and friends were at peace? Was she not at least owed that, for the eye the killers took from her when they bombed the church? If she survived her injuries, she should know her sister was at peace. Maybe one day we could meet and I could give her the painting of the Birmingham Angels, as I would refer to it from now on, if only to myself. What was I talking about? When could I make such a visit and what would I say? Would the surviving girl understand? How would I convince her I was not some crazy person trying to profit from a tragedy so horrendous and unholy? Addie Mae would know the answer. But she was a ghost.

Patsy jarred me out of my reverie. "What's on your mind, Cincinnatus?"

I took a good swallow of Chardonnay. "Very oaky," I said. "With notes of vanilla and chalk."

Patsy laughed. "You love those wine snobs, don't you?"

"Do they really taste anything but the wine? Or are my taste buds not sophisticated enough?"

"A lot of it is embellishment and bull, if you ask me."

"Now that you mention it, I do taste bull and meadow, or is that cow?"

"Definitely bull." Pasty laughed. The sound anchored me. "We can play this game all night, or you can tell me what's going on."

"No bull?"

"You had another visit, didn't you? A female ghost? Is that why you're not telling me?"

I wished like hell it were that simple. "Take a breath, Patsy, you're not going to believe it."

I told Patsy about the Birmingham angels. She listened, not saying a word. I told her everything, right down to the stained-glass window. Her eyes kept getting wider with each word. Finally, I stopped talking. I went in the spare bedroom to get the painting. Patsy was still sitting by the fireplace where I'd left her. She looked up. I set the painting on the easel.

Patsy's hands went up to her face. "Oh, dear God." She burst into tears.

I held her and we stayed like that for a while, just the crackling fire making sounds. It was as quiet as a church. Patsy whispered something. Her voice muffled; her face half buried in my chest.

"Hmm?" I asked her, unsure who was holding who tighter at that moment.

"The window," she said, looking at me.

"I know. I thought I imagined it. It was real. Just like the girls. When they were gone, so was the stained-glass window."

"No, I don't mean that. One church window, a stained-glass window, survived the bombing. The one of Jesus with the children. I heard it on the news."

"Really? What do you think that means, that they didn't kill goodness and light?" I tried not to sound sarcastic.

"If only. It's deeper than that. Those girls were changing into their choir robes when the bomb went off. But they were not silenced. You saw them. They sang for you. This tragedy, these murders will always be an ugly reminder of how far apart people can be. Yet we cannot look away and live with ourselves, can we?" Patsy stood to get a better look at the painting. "They look alive." She started to cry again.

"They were alive, Patsy." I took her hand. "Right here in this cabin. Alive and beautiful and hopeful. Forgiving, if you can believe that. How can anyone forgive when this kind of hate exists?"

"They are in a better place. I know you don't believe it, but we don't know."

"I believe in those girls. In their innocent faith, in their love, even after they were killed by hate. How could I not believe it? They are, *were*, what is good in the world."

Patsy wiped her tears and smiled, "I love you."

I just stood there. Like an idiot, staring at her. What was I supposed to say? I realized I should say something. I wasn't daft, just conflicted. But how can you tell a woman you love her when you aren't who she thinks you are? Up until now we were having a good time. I was in love with Patsy but when people say they love you and mean it, isn't that the ultimate intimacy? What about honesty? I was sinking on my own boat of lies. Right to the fucking bottom.

"Nothing, Cincinnatus?" Patsy looked at me, her eyes wide, hopeful. That was the thing I lacked, hope.

I looked straight into her big brown beautiful honest eyes. "I am not the man you think I am. I have... well there are things. Things I haven't told you."

"You aren't a serial killer, are you?"

"No. What I am is a lost soul. I didn't know my mother or father. I have no family I know of, and I made a lot of bad mistakes. The only good thing I did was come here. I love you, I do. But I don't deserve you. You deserve much better."

"You think you cornered the market on sad stories? I'll have you know Oliver Twist is one of my favorite books. And please don't tell me what I need. I'm a big girl. I choose my own men, thanks. You came to this cabin for a reason. I know you have secrets. Things you may be ashamed of. Get in line."

"That's sweet. But I'm hardly some English orphan Dickens wrote about." Now Fagin, I could relate to. Or I could at one time. I guessed this conversation was bound to happen. I had just hoped to avoid it for as long as possible. Oh well. It had been fun. Nothing lasts forever.

"I did come to your cabin, not that I knew it as such. Because I needed to be up here, alone. Can we leave it at that? Or do you need to leave the whole thing alone now? Can't say I'd blame you."

"I have my own secrets, Cincinnatus. You're not the only one with a past. I don't scare easily, as you know, so tell me or don't tell me. I'm happy with the status quo. We don't need to get all dramatic and needy."

I had just been schooled by the schoolteacher. I decided not to be thick and go for it.

"Okay. Maybe we are ahead of the game." *Needy*? There's a first.

"How so?"

"We don't have to try hard to keep the mystery alive. We already have it. "

"See? You're a smart man. Let's go to bed."

"Yes, Teach."

Patsy laughed and threw her blouse at me. Honesty is overrated.

The painting of the Birmingham girls was still on the easel when we got up for breakfast. I knew there was a bigger conversation Patsy and I would have. I had the feeling she would agree with me, that we couldn't share the painting with the gallery in Sausalito, or with anybody else.

Patsy drank her coffee outside on the porch while I cleaned up the breakfast dishes. She came back inside.

"You know, even if you wanted to go public with the painting of the Birmingham girls, you can't. No one would believe it. Some might even say it was opportunistic and macabre. Besides that, I think they came to you because you needed them. Maybe we all did."

"We?"

"Collectively, humanity. Even if you never share that beautiful painting with another soul, you received a message. We are all a part of the same country, the same world, though we have unique experiences, cultures, and upbringing, or even the lack of an upbringing. You're already changed by this visitation. Something horrific you heard on the news was brought into your house, well, my house, but it happened to you. Right here, though it happened across the country. Hate is not one town. It's just more obvious there because of the segregation and history in the south. But we know the other kind that is just as volatile, the kind that hides in the shadows. Or people that talk in whispers in ordinary kitchens and at fancy cocktail parties in their walled-in yards about 'those people.' As amazing as your visitation was, those four girls remain dead. How are they going to be honored and remembered? That is the question. Did hate and racism end immediately after their deaths? No. Did the racist hypocrites who go to church on Sunday and hate and kill on Monday have an epiphany? Nope. There's a lot of work to do if we are to survive as a human race. It will take years, maybe forever. What? Why are you looking at me like that?"

"That was quite a sermon. Was your father a preacher? By the way, that is exactly what the girls, well, Addie Mae to be precise, said. 'There's a lot of work to do. It could take years, maybe forever.' It's eerie you both said the same thing."

"I'm honored. And it bears repeating. My father was a fireman, by the way. In San Francisco. He had the gift of gab though, no doubt about that. More on a barstool than behind a pulpit."

"Got it. So, what do you suggest we do? Go on as we were? You go teach and paint and I make moon carvings and wait for my next ghost?"

"We don't really have a choice, do we? Unless you want more attention than you can imagine, and a three-ring circus made of your Amazing Grace encounter."

"You're right. It stays our secret."

"Maybe one day we can take a trip down south and find Addie Mae's sister. If she survives her injuries, I can give her the painting. In the distant future, I mean."

"I like that. And the fact that you think we have a future, you and I."

Patsy kissed me and I knew for that moment in time, though the world was still a shit storm, we were okay. Our arrangement seemed to suit us both. With the world going to hell all around us, the constant of Patsy and I, was reassuring. I continued to paint the moon and had a spell where I painted the birds that came to sing in the trees by the cabin. I never took for granted that I got to see nature up close every single day. That would never change for me. All those years I spent locked up in a cage made freedom that much more cherished.

Chapter Thirteen

It was fitting that he appeared when I went into the woods for a walk. I had just sat down to sketch a forest scene when a man with a long beard and a walking stick appeared.

"Don't let me disturb you," he said, "I respect the solitude one finds here." He was about to walk on, but I was compelled to stop him.

"Please, you aren't bothering me. I've had enough solitude for two men, I assure you." I held out my hand to him. I knew he was a gentleman. He took it and a firm handshake was reciprocated.

"John Muir," he said. I stared at him. What could possibly be my reply to that? I may have been incarcerated for most of my life, but I assure you I knew who John Muir was. And here he was alive and standing before me in one of the very forests he helped preserve.

"Cincinnatus Jones," I said, hoping my grin was not too much. But what else could I do but grin? I was delighted, enamored, grateful, joyous and any other happy adjective that comes to mind.

"Cincinnatus is a good name. Like the very poet of this landscape himself, Joaquin Miller."

"Yes, I am a fan of his, and yours. Thank you for all you did for California. And the whole country, really. For saving the trees and forests and the way you revered nature. Such a legacy; nothing short of holy." I was rambling, but I was in awe, so I didn't care.

"Thank you, Cincinnatus. A man who admires nature's majesty is a wise man indeed. Shall we delve deeper on the dirt path?"

I nodded, putting away my notebook and walked alongside him. A small child with a chocolate bar couldn't have been happier. 'John of the Mountains,' and me.

John Muir looked up and pointed. "The Grandfather Tree. Five hundred years old. The only one left. Primeval groves once covered these hills. Ship captains would use these as their guidepost to navigate around underwater hazards, like Blossom Rock. They knew where the port was by looking at these giants. Navigation trees. Nature has always been there for us to choose to be in sync with, don't you agree?"

I did agree but I didn't want to speak. It was one of those moments dare I say, too good to spoil, but John Muir himself had asked me a question.

"Yes, one hundred percent, a testament to the amazing endurance of trees," I said.

Why stellar people of history were appearing, to lackluster me, remained a mystery. I had done no good to deserve such top people making appearances in the flesh. Why *me*? Maybe one day I'd know that answer.

The thing about these great men is they were passionate about their work and never short of words. John Muir chatted well into the late afternoon and when I asked him to come back to the cabin and stay for supper, he didn't refuse. I knew his writings and how he strongly defended nature as its own entity, not here for man's opportunity and amusement, but a stronger, more lasting alliance. He took the job he gave himself, defending nature's magnificence and fragility, so we would have mountains and valleys and streams to behold. People may fall in love with other people or things or manmade places. John Muir fell in love with everything nature provided and was a true steward of the land and water, for the whole of his life.

Scape Ghost

I asked him how he managed to have a wife and family too. I thought it a fair question. He said it was simple, "Louie, my wife, she understood. She knew the depth of my commitment to nature and how it affects our existence. So she let me go wandering, because I always came home. Louie came with me sometimes, but it wasn't really her thing. I respected that. Later I took the children, instead."

That was a good enough answer for me. John Muir had a vocation, and everyone close to him respected that in him. I was sure at times he was not easy to live with, being a man who was more comfortable out in nature, unencumbered, rather than the everyday trappings of an ordinary life. At least he was honest about it and there were no deceptions or delusions. Brilliant people are probably not the best spouses and parents when they are mostly gone on walkabouts or their heads in books and such; but look at the legacy he left for his family, alone. I mean the man saved California forests and helped create national parks. The Sierra Club, for Pete's sake. I was in awe.

"Are you a man of nature, Cincinnatus?"

"More recently, I am. I have grown to appreciate what I never imagined could be part of my life. I wasted time. Inside walls, if you know what I mean. Not in a monastic way. I have regrets."

"Regrets are quicksand. They trap and sink you. Let them go. You are a prisoner no more. You are here, and that is what matters. You can begin again every day you wake. Nature is in tune with that very way."

"Thank you, John. I am feeling blessed each day, for sure. And now after meeting you, I have a strong confirmation of purpose. I must contribute something. Mean something. This is such a beautiful place. The redwoods have humbled me."

"Well said, young man. I am pleased we met. You've no real family, is it? I don't suppose so with the life you've led before."

"No. Though I fell in love with the most amazing woman. Right here in this cabin. Though I fear she is wasted on me."

John Muir laughed. "Most good women, are, my boy. They have to be connected to the divine to put up with us."

"I never thought of it that way."

"Perspective is everything. Tell me about your paintings. A story behind each one, yes?"

I was hardly going to show off in the presence of genius. I hesitated and asked John Muir if he'd like a drink.

"You're stalling, Cincinnatus. I do admire humility, such a rare quality. But do show me. I am not here to judge or be judged. None of us are, in the end. We are merely here, like the trees, putting down roots, standing and growing old. Living and dying. Going back into the earth."

I showed John Muir my paintings. We drank a toast to nature and righteous men and divine women. It doesn't get better than that. Turns out he liked my paintings.

"Good to see you're not all hat and no cattle, Cincinnatus."

I was quite fond of the old fellah by this time. John Muir came to me. The enormity of that, if indeed it was real and not some fabulous dream, was staggering.

We got into some heavy stuff that day, John Muir and I. Inequality, violence, war, the future of the earth. We didn't solve any of it.

"We either pay attention now and make the changes necessary or we're going into the next generation leaving the mess for them to clean up. Vigilance is needed. We must be stewards." he said, surrounded by a redwood forest and such unspoiled beauty that could not possibly be taken for granted by anyone in his right mind.

Wisdom often comes when the barn door is already shut. People are people. We get busy and careless and want things to go our way, and if they don't, we are willing to stomp on whomever sees differently. There's disparity in money, equality, upbringing, the sins of the fathers and curses of the mothers, and a whole heap of nonsense we feed each other, in the name of whatever god or devil we worship. What is holy or sacred about hating your fellow man and killing for different beliefs or lording it over someone because you happen to think they are inferior? I am not preaching, just ranting, because in the end, what the hell do I know? I'm new to the self-realization game. Ghosts come to me, and I paint them. Maybe that's all there was to it. A haunted cabin and a fugitive soul. Was the cost of freedom this ghostly introspection? I should just enjoy the ghosts. I was not important in the scheme of things. I was just a man with the soul of a ghost.

John Muir was a revered man of nature who took the time to stare at trees and plant trees and let trees guide him. He truly felt he was no better than a simple oak or a majestic redwood. Forests are self-sufficient. They grow and live and shed leaves and when they fall sick and die, they are replenished with other trees. There is no judgement or hating of other trees that are smaller, larger, or different. Trees don't believe some handed down tree philosophy that makes no sense and never really served anyone but perhaps the believer. They cannot believe anything, for they are only trees. Yet time and again, man seeks out nature for answers. At the very least, we seek solace, an atmosphere in which to think, or to listen and be still in our minds for a moment. In essence, nature and trees can be a path towards the kind of wisdom we cannot get from one another. The kind we often long for our whole lives.

We might learn by witnessing and listening as our minds open and we connect with our hearts, coming into alignment with nature. Human nature wants to fix everyone and every situation, so we can feel better. We're unsettled with upheaval or sadness and differing opinions. Why then weren't we all born looking exactly alike, with the same brains and hearts and beliefs already programmed? Wouldn't that be easier? Who then would paint and write and sing and dare to step out of line, who would explore the universe and its infinite possibilities? We are better off as we are, as different to one another as we could be, and yet hopefully alike in the knowledge that change is inevitable and very good for us. United, we are capable of ending wars and all manner of violence. In stillness and quiet we find better ways to communicate. Hopefully, the trees and oceans will still be here as our witness one day. I shook my head. Who *was* I anymore? I must be forest drunk.

"John, what do you think?" I turned and asked my new friend.

I was looking at a massive trunk of a redwood. John Muir was gone. Our conversation, only a memory. I looked up at the canopy of branches and green swaying in the breeze. It was answer enough.

Chapter Fourteen

Patsy was busy in the city, so I had plenty of time to paint. Patsy believed I showed up at her grandfather's cabin not only to paint trees and ghosts, but for some deeper reason. What that was, I decided, was more important to Patsy than to me. I didn't profess to be anything more than a survivor with a lucky streak. I knew liars, thieves, murderers, and all manner of bad people. I had never waxed philosophical about life and spirituality before. I was a man only for himself. Until the ghosts changed that trajectory.

When the painting was finished, I left it to dry and took a shower. I would need more supplies this weekend. Patsy was always up for a car ride anywhere. Plus, she was a teacher, so she had a love of art supply shops. Wait until she saw the latest ghost painting. Against a redwood was a man leaning on the trunk looking straight out at me. I couldn't wait for Patsy to see John Muir. But it wasn't Patsy who showed up first.

"Hi, Cincinnatus." Oakley was reclined on Patsy's couch. "Should I still call you that, or do you want to use your real name?"

I started to sweat. My heart was racing. The jig was up. But she was a ghost.

"I prefer Cincinnatus. You know I have to kill you now?"

She laughed. "You don't do that. Kill people. You're a thief. Well, you were. And we're friends. Aren't we?"

"I was kidding."

"We're not friends?"

"I meant about the killing part."

"What happens now?"

"Nothing. Unless you plan on turning me in."

"I like you, Cincinnatus. Turn you in? I'm dead. Where's your girlfriend?"

"Not here."

She smiled a wicked smile. "Good answer. Paint me."

"Later. Do you have a secret you're keeping, Oakley?"

"Like what?" she said, moving to the chair in the corner by the window.

"Are you sure you want to sit there? What if someone comes by?"

"Who? No one can see me."

"Because you're a ghost? *I* see you."

"Would you like to see more of me?" She had her hand on the top button of her long gauzy dress. "Paint me in the nude and I'll tell you a story."

"Patsy won't appreciate that."

"It isn't up to her. You know I won't go away like the others. I'm the..." I cut her off.

"Resident ghost. So I heard."

"I saw you that night. I watched from the shore. You were amazing, the three of you. Fast swimmers. The moon was so beautiful. Quarter moon. Neap tide. I do my homework. A very warm night for a San Francisco summer, a perfect storm, so to speak."

"Were you swimming with us?"

"I'm a ghost, not a mermaid."

"So, you watched us. From what shore?"

"First on Angel Island. Then I realized you were headed to the city, so I moved there by the ferry landing."

"Did you watch us change our clothes?" This I asked of a naked ghost on a chair.

"You're a bit kinky, aren't you? I like that," she said.

88

"Maybe I should free fall off the porch and we can haunt people and places together. What do you say?"

Oakley laughed. "It doesn't work that way."

"Did you have some influence in keeping the authorities at bay?"

"I am not a magician. They are still looking for you, you know"

"I know. But they won't ever find me."

"How do you know that?"

"Because nothing bad can happen to me. Am I right?"

"So right. Now let's do something fun and not talk about this anymore."

She was a beautiful ghost with a short attention span. A man could do worse.

"What did you have in mind? Want to go haunt some wineries? You could procure some oaky chardonnay when the coast is clear. No one can see you, right? Except me."

"I have a better idea."

"Ghost sex?"

"I was going to say Jack London Square. The lopsided bar for a pint and lets go see that old deserted mental hospital, maybe some ghostly nuts will be wandering around."

"The logistics of you and I traveling together are a problem, so I think we'll stay here. Any more secrets you want to tell me?"

"You're not ready yet. Right now I think you're ready for me." She got up and walked her perfect naked body towards me.

I couldn't argue with that.

Chapter Fifteen

At the weekend, Patsy brought chocolate from Ghirardelli's and a picnic for us to take to Sausalito. I had moon paintings boxed up and ready. Patsy picked one up to rearrange them in the trunk. "What's this Cincinnatus, you got tired of the moon?" She'd found my rainbow painting.

"It was the most incredible thing, it hadn't rained. And you know how we get those crazy showers up here and then five minutes later the sun comes out? It wasn't that. No rain, not a drop. And suddenly, a rainbow. So vivid, like something out of The Wizard of Oz. I had to paint it."

"Beautiful. This is going to sell. I almost want it for myself. Did you have coffee yet? You look tired. Had a rough night?"

"Just not a lot of sleep. Too much coffee," I lied. I felt guilty about Oakley. And what was I going to do when Patsy found that nude painting of the 'resident ghost'?

"Cincinnatus? I brought a thermos of coffee. Why don't you have some?"

Patsy drove while I drank good strong coffee and popped a few chocolates in my mouth. Caffeine and sugar, not bad vices for an ex-con. "Thanks, I needed that."

Patsy smiled and patted my thigh. I passed her a handful of chocolate raisins.

"I can hardly wait for the gallery owner to see your rainbow painting. It's impressive."

Wait until you see what's back at the cabin, I thought to myself. I wanted to tell Patsy about Oakley but I wanted it to be

91

when we were back home. I didn't want her to be driving while I told her. There was so much to say. About secrets and ghosts. I needed a break. Not to forget, which I couldn't do if I tried, but to sit with it in my gut for a moment. *Face it, dead people dig you.* That's all well and good if it doesn't get you killed. I had a funny feeling about how Patsy would react to Oakley coming back and me painting her, especially naked. How could that turn out well? But how was I meant to control a ghost?

We were at the gallery. The gallery owner was saying how she loved the rainbow painting and wanted more. "You would be a great portrait painter. I can tell by your brush strokes. Have you ever considered adding people to your nature scenes?"

I cleared my throat. A stalling technique. "Um, no, I hadn't thought about that," I lied. "I'm not a people person."

She smiled. "You're an artist, I understand. The creative process is private."

I excused myself to look around while she and Patsy discussed business.

I walked into a side room. One wall was covered in surfing photographs.

I stepped closer to one. A woman stared back at me, holding a surfboard. Her eyes were the color of polished oak with a shading of green. Like the forest meeting the ocean. I was riveted to the photograph and didn't realize Patsy was standing in the doorway.

"That's True," Patsy said.

"What is?"

"Her name is True. She died in a surfing accident shortly after that was taken. She's beautiful, isn't she?"

"Her eyes are unusual," I said. But there was something else.

"True was an intuitive, she could tell things about people," Patsy explained.

Scape Ghost

"Everybody's got a story, right?" I said lightly, wanting to get the hell out of there. First a naked Oakley and now a dead woman who could predict the future. I didn't need to meet any more female ghosts. The one I met was keeping me on my toes.

"Ready?" I asked Patsy, starting toward the door.

When we were outside, Patsy kissed me. "Don't be spooked by True. She can't actually read your mind or know anything about your visitors. It was only a photograph. She's harmless."

"I doubt that. Anyway, I don't believe in that stuff. Though if you'd asked me a while ago if I believed people came back from the dead and had conversations with you or...."

"Sex?" Patsy laughed. She was having a go at me. I didn't mind. Hopefully she would keep her sense of humor back at the cabin.

"So, True? Not her real name, right? Short for Trudy?"

"Nope, her name is True. Actually, she and Oakley were friends. They surfed together."

My head was starting to ache. I laid my head back. "Can I grab a few winks, do you mind? I didn't sleep much last night."

"I knew it. You had another visit. They always take a lot out of you. Well, except for Oakley. That had the opposite effect. The ghost sex, of course," Patsy smiled. God help me.

I was already snoring while Nina Simone sang softly in the background of my dream.

When I woke, we were back at the cabin. Patsy headed for the bathroom, and I started unpacking our picnic bag and cooler. I was thinking about what we might throw together for dinner when I noticed one of my tree paintings was on the floor leaning against the wall. My eyes went above the mantle where now on full display was a naked Oakley. I guess ghosts could be troublemakers. Or maybe just one particular ghost. Patsy was in the bedroom changing so I made a quick swap, tucking Oakley's bare assets in the laundry room cabinet. I poured us both a glass of pinot noir and set out a plate of olives, smoked gouda and water crackers. Tomorrow I would dispose of the Oakley portrait for good.

Patsy flipped on the tv to catch the news and weather before we settled on a movie. All thoughts of Oakley naked or otherwise, vanished with the lead story. The President was dead. JFK was murdered in his motorcade in Texas, right beside his beautiful, devoted wife, Jackie. Gunned down like an animal, Jackie Kennedy's pink suit stained with her husband's blood. The country was in shock. We were riveted to the screen, as I'm sure was every household in America. Patsy was crying. "It can't be," she kept asking, "Why?" I didn't know what to say. Obviously, there was evil in the world, nothing new there. But the hope and class and civil rights that JFK brought to the country and the White House would be missed and mourned for years to come. In the meantime, Patsy and I sat holding each other, glued to the tv like the rest of the country on this sad day. There are rare times in life when everything stops and though the world keeps turning and the sun keeps shining, we don't notice, and we don't care.

Our somber mood had not lifted the next morning. Patsy slept in and we sat drinking coffee and eating toast on the porch looking at the trees. We'd had enough news with replays of the horror that had befallen the country. It was more than one man's assassination, though that was unconscionable. It was goodness being snuffed out by hate. I was convinced it was not an isolated crime of an insane person. Patsy didn't disagree.

"Remember when Medgar Evers was assassinated? So awful. Kennedy had given a speech about civil rights just two days before. These were men of substance, trying to build a country where everyone is equal and free. There are dark forces that keep trying to stop that effort. People who claim to be of the people but are driven by racism and twisted reasoning. It makes me angry and very sad. What do mothers tell their children after something like this? The world's gone crazy, little ones, I hope you can do better one day?"

"I don't have any answers, Patsy. I don't understand the ways of some men. We can only try and be better. Like that vet I met on my walk that day. He was just trying to make sense of an insane war and come back to some semblance of peace in his own tortured mind."

"Medgar Evers was a vet, you know. He fought in World War II. Only to be gunned down in his own driveway in a free country because of the color of his skin and daring to speak of injustice."

"I know. And the man who shot him is nothing but a coward. Like those men who hide in the shadows and pounce on the unsuspecting, driven by hate. We have a lot to fix in this country. Evil doesn't win, I know that much."

"You're an optimist, Cincinnatus. Why?"

"Because the opposite will destroy you, inside. Look at this beauty, it cannot exist if there is only bad in the world. Some just lost their way."

"You're a good person. How did you become so philosophical?"

"Time. Lots of time to think."

Chapter Sixteen

I slept like the dead. I heard a trumpet. Maybe I'd died in my sleep. This was no choir of angels, this was Jazz. An unmistakable riff. He played it again. I walked into the living room. Miles Davis looked back at me. I realized he wasn't looking at me, but beyond me. He was in the zone. They can come arrest me tomorrow, I thought, I have died and gone to heaven today.

I dared not interrupt. I took a seat on the couch. It was like my own private nightclub. Patsy was going to be so damn jealous. Miles kept playing. I didn't want him to stop. Could I request a song, I wondered? My Funny Valentine would be sweet. If I tell you Miles Davis played the first few notes of that tune right then, you wouldn't believe me. Anyway, I listened. Miles Davis stopped playing and rested his trumpet on the chair.

"Nice hideaway you got here, man," he said.

"Thanks. It's a friend's."

"Lady friend, am I right?"

"So right. You aren't dead."

"I'm feeling very alive. Why, have there been rumors?"

"No, no." I felt like an idiot. "Don't mind me, Mr. Davis. I've been having a strange time. Visits from, well, how can I put this?"

"Call me Miles. Dead cats? I get it. Listen, we all need inspiration. Who cares where it comes from, right?"

"I'm not going to disagree with that, Miles. But the thing is, you're not dead."

"I thought we established that. What's your name?"

"Cincinnatus Jones. Look I'm not crazy, I promise, or high or drunk. But everyone who came here was dead. I painted them all. I can show you. I don't only paint trees."

Miles Davis looked at my tree paintings and then at me. "There's a cat in that one, leaning against the redwood. He dead?"

"John Muir. He's dead, yes. Like I said...."

"Right, only dead cats. They come here and you paint them?"

"Yes. I know it sounds crazy, but I swear it's true."

"And you're sober when this shit goes down?"

"As a judge."

"Anyone else see these dead folks?"

"No."

"Word gets out, you're gonna have the coolest speakeasy on your hands."

I had to laugh. Miles Davis must have thought I was off my nut for sure. But he was being a good sport, or hoping to get out of here alive, in case I was dangerous, besides being delusional.

"I'll get my paintings for you. But how about a beer first? Or would you rather something stronger?"

"Beer's just fine, thank you. By the way, a band mate dropped me off here. Well, down below and I walked up. That's a lot of stairs, man. I don't know why I came inside and started playing. It was like it was out of my hands. Crazy, huh?"

"Who're you telling?"

We both laughed and took a pull of our beers. "Let me get those paintings, excuse me a minute. You'll wait?"

"Where am I going?"

"People have a habit of disappearing on me. Never mind." I went into the spare room. I chose The Trainhoppers and The Birmingham Angels. I heard the trumpet again. Miles

Davis was still in the living room. I resisted the urge to pinch myself.

Miles was quiet. I handed him the Amazing Grace sheet music from the 16th Street Baptist Church. "You paint before these apparitions?"

"No. I don't think I actually painted these."

"Now unless you're gonna share that stash of yours, we gotta be straight with one another."

"I don't take pills. I'm no lush either. It happened. Those girls were here. I don't know why."

Miles took a good swig of his beer. "I am familiar with sweet spots and losing oneself in music. Art is no different. But this isn't that, is it? You're talking a higher influence. You a believer?"

"I wasn't, before. I might be reconsidering. I have a checkered past, Miles. You have no idea."

I know bad cats, you're not one. You made mistakes. But you didn't hurt anyone but yourself. Am I right?"

"More or less, yeah. But still, why me? I'm nobody."

"We don't always get to have that answer, Cincinnatus. I'll keep your secret. I respect a man that changes his life for the better. You get chosen for something great like this, painting those angels, you just chalk it up to we don't know nothing about nothing in the end. Unless we surrender. Hell, what do I know, man? I'll tell you what, if I can impose myself a little longer, you can go ahead and paint me too. But I ain't posing or nothing, you understand."

"Thank you. I'm trying to be aware. I've led a jaded life. But I'd be honored to paint you. First, let me fix you some dinner if you have nowhere you need to be."

"New Orleans, next week. Let me play you something while you cook. A little inspiration."

Blue in Green never sounded better. It was the perfect song to mark this occasion and the conversation Miles Davis and I just shared. I made some hash browns while the steaks were broiling. Miles went into So What, another piece I loved. This had to be the coolest night of my life. Besides that infamous swim, of course. But come on, you don't get to hang with Miles Davis, especially if you're me.

"You know your way around a steak, I'll give you that. These hash browns and greens would make my own mama take notice."

"Thank you. You might say my taste buds have improved. For a time, I had little choice what I ate. Lucky you had a mama. Can't imagine what that's like. I mean there were some who tried. I didn't stay in one place very long. Maybe I should be playing the blues."

"You're not looking for pity, I don't imagine? We all make bad choices. I chase the dragon myself and I ain't proud of it. Cats get into all kinds of messes, don't we? And the blues has nothing to do with where you come from or your hardships necessarily. I play the blues, end of story." And play the blues he did, for the rest of the night.

When I woke, I was alone. I had had the most wonderful dream. And while it was fresh in my mind, I had to do a sketch before it disappeared from my photographic memory. After coffee I would paint Miles Davis as if he had been here. Of course, he could not have, because he was very much alive. Of that I was glad and the fact that I had a good night's sleep without a ghost coming to call.

Patsy was back the night after. She loved the Miles Davis painting, which I'd hung over the fireplace. Miles was blowing his trumpet with only the redwoods as his audience. The painting of Oakley I'd burned. I hoped that wasn't bad ghost luck. Common sense outweighed superstition.

"My brother Cole loved Miles Davis. He wore out Kind of Blue on our old record player."

Patsy never talked about family before. She wanted to seem "unfettered and alive," like Joni Mitchell sang in A Free Man In Paris. Patsy was more of an enigma than me.

"You never mentioned you had a brother. Where does he live?"

"He doesn't. He died in Vietnam. He enlisted early. He was too young, but he did it and now he's gone. You would have liked him. Everybody liked Cole."

"I'm sorry, Patsy. You haven't had it easy, have you? Your mom, your dad, and your brother. Is there anyone else?"

"No. You want to go to New Orleans?"

"Someday, yes. Why, have you been?"

"Not lately. My mama was from there. We can go together. When you're ready to leave here."

"Sounds like a plan. You hungry?"

"You made jambalaya? How did you know it's my favorite? If you make me beignets for breakfast, I'll marry you."

"Um...."

"Just kidding, don't look so terrified. I have no plans on marrying anyone. I like my freedom."

I breathed a sigh of relief. Marriage was not a subject for consideration. Who would marry us anyway? It would have to be a ghost.

"I was thinking you might like an appetizer, Cincinnatus." Patsy closed the shades and stripped in front of the fire. I was mesmerized, she was so natural and uninhibited. And more importantly, she was alive.

"Bourbon?" she asked, in a very sexy voice.

I nodded, riveted to her body in the firelight. "Sure."

"You'll have to come get it. This is a help yourself establishment. Patsy took the glass of bourbon she'd poured and dipped two fingers in the glass and rubbed the amber liquid on her breasts. "Cat got your tongue?" she moved closer.

I stepped in front of her. "My tongue is all yours."

I did what any person in their right mind would do at that moment. And then I lay Patsy down on the rug in front of the fire. If this was the last sex of my life, I could live off the fumes of memory for eternity.

"You outdid yourself last night, Cincinnatus."

"I could say the same to you, my lady. Though the bourbon was anything but ladylike."

"I meant the jambalaya. It was just like I remembered. How did you know I loved it?"

"I didn't. I never made it before. Something came over me after my Miles dream."

"Oh it's 'Miles' now, is it? I love how you befriend all your ghosts."

"Miles Davis is alive, remember? And I love how you have a way with bourbon."

Patsy laughed. It was beyond endearing. It got right under my skin in the most appealing way. The most comfortable pleasure I knew. I wanted to bottle her laugh in one of those mason jars on the shelf and open it whenever I wanted to hear it.

"I know Miles Davis is alive," Patsy said, biting into her second beignet. "You had one helluva dream, darlin. Do you think it was a coincidence that he was heading off to New Orleans and you suddenly made jambalaya? Perfectly by the way, to rival any true Louisianan's, I might add."

I sipped my coffee and bit into my first beignet. It was delicious. I might have been temporarily possessed by a Louisiana chef.

"I hadn't given that any thought. I dreamed of Miles Davis and I made jambalaya, no big deal."

"If you say so."

"I do. Let me paint you."

Patsy laughed again and I got a tingling sensation in my manly region. "You paint ghosts, remember? And dreams, apparently," she said, looking up at Miles Davis.

"You're a dream come to life. You just keep talking and I'll sketch you. You won't feel a thing."

"Shall I change?"

"No, I love that robe. It suits you. Very sexy and colorful."

"I bought it in the French Quarter. You'd love it there."

"I have no doubt. So, go on with your story."

"My mother cooked the best jambalaya in New Orleans."

"I thought you grew up in San Francisco?"

"That came later. Mama was Creole. We lived outside the French Quarter in a haint blue house. Mama practiced voodoo. Spiritually. She didn't stick pins in dolls if that's what you're thinking. But she did say she conjured Daddy. He was her dream gentleman lover. And he was crazy about Mama and later, me. She still practiced voodoo but in a more subtle way, shall we say. Daddy used to worry about all the candles Mama kept lit in the house. 'Well, that's why I have you, Cher. You're my fireman,' she'd say. Daddy worked for the New Orleans Fire Department. They were quite the couple. 'Fire and Smoke,' people in the parish called them."

I briefly went somewhere in my mind. I pictured Patsy growing up in her blue house in the Creole neighborhood in New Orleans. I pictured Patsy's mama with her voodoo and her fireman father. It sounded like a pretty good life. Until her brother died and later both her parents. People who she loved who loved her back. What must that feel like, to have a real family?

"Nothing is perfect, though. There were dark times. I choose to remember the good.

Like Mama coming here and cooking jambalaya and beignets."

"Your mama, here? *I* cooked last night. You smelled the jambalaya when you got here. And I got up before you this morning to make the beignets."

"I know it appears that way. But trust me, you were the instrument. Mama did the cooking."

"She wasn't here for the bourbon, was she?" I suddenly felt very uneasy. "Isn't there a ghost code of discretion?"

Patsy laughed. "No, she wasn't here, then. And if there is a code, it's unspoken. Mama wouldn't be shocked, anyway. I didn't lick my sensuality off the ground."

"Well, thank you, Mama." I leaned in to kiss Patsy. "You are so beautiful."

"You won't get your sketch done that way," she said, kissing me back in equal measure.

"But it will be fun. I must keep in mind you're the daughter of a voodoo priestess."

"Spiritualist."

"Right. Can you guess what I'm thinking right now?"

"You're insatiable, Cincinnatus."

"Is that a complaint, Miss Patsy Billie Vaughan?"

"Not exactly..." she teased, opening her robe. I put down my pencil and sketchpad.

Patsy laughed her delicious laugh, and I picked her up and carried her to the bedroom.

Chapter Seventeen

There was something eating at me. It could have been the undeniable fact that I was one lucky man to remain free all these years. Where was I in all of this, what was the point? A great escape and some amazing ghosts. There had to be more. Did it even bear thinking about? I should relax and enjoy it. Why wasn't surviving enough? I was comfortable, ate well, had regular good sex, and lived in a veritable tree house surrounded by redwoods. Sounds like bliss. It was in many ways. Yet the reality was I spent my days and nights with ghosts. Famous ghosts, unusual entertaining ghosts, ghosts that brought me to my knees and made me question everything, ghosts that made me consider a higher power, ghosts that taught me to stand up for others, erotic ghosts, and one beautiful non-ghost that loved me.

I had no right to complain. The alternative was being the old me and inevitably going back to prison. Not like I was missing anything. People were intrusive. There was no me I needed to reclaim, no role I needed to embody. I was no longer Frank Morris. He was a ghost. I answered to Cincinnatus Jones, because that is who I am. I believed that with a true conviction. Cincinnatus the painter, the nomad, the lover of nature, with an amazing girlfriend named Patsy Billie Vaughan. Still, there was that something I was feeling, and it was making me itch.

I liked Patsy's story about growing up in New Orleans. Was it just a story? She'd said in the beginning that people have secrets. What was hers? Was it harmless? Were Patsy and I kindred spirits, each with a past filled with secrets? Patsy was ruling my heart, that was for sure.

I don't remember sitting outside until it was pitch dark nor have I ever felt it this steamy up in these hills. Fog and mist, not oppressive humidity. It was as still as a graveyard. There was a distinct sound in the otherwise eerie quiet, a sound once described by the Anglin brothers to me, a northern boy. The unmistakable hiss and growl of alligators near water. I remember trying to imagine such a sound. You cannot. You must hear it for yourself. The hairs on my arms stood up. It wasn't alligators. Someone was here.

She came out to the porch where I sat. She was beautiful in her long blue dress and red turban, her cappuccino-colored skin glistening in the moonlight. She held a candle in a brass holder in one hand and sweet-smelling oil jar in the other. "Come inside, Cher, you'll be more comfortable. If it gets too hot, we can sit on the back veranda by the lake."

I wanted to ask her if she was Patsy's mother, but I knew she wasn't. She was famous this striking mysterious woman, I'd seen her photograph in books. She was the mother of New Orleans. She was the Spirit of Voodoo. Her essence was visceral, and she hadn't laid a hand on me. I got up and followed her into the cabin that was no longer the cabin. It was Maison Blanc, the infamous brothel and bar on Lake Pontchatrain. Candles were lit everywhere, and dark velvet parlor chairs and chaises beckoned. Blue goblets of drink awaited us on a low mahogany table by a couch near a window. Tall haint blue shutters were open to the back porch, where more candles were lit in hurricane globes. The alligator sounds grew nearer. The woman laughed, baring creamy white teeth. "They won't hurt you, Cher, don't mind them. Have a drink."

"Miss Laveau?" I asked, reaching for the blue goblet she handed me. "Is it really you?"

She smiled. "I am Marie Laveau. Welcome to New Orleans and Maison Blanc. Your first time?"

"To New Orleans, uh, yes," That didn't come out right.

"So, you've frequented brothels before? None like this, I guarantee you, Cher."

Whatever was in the goblet was making my tongue relax and stirring up other feelings in manly body parts. "Where is everyone?" Who was I asking about? I had no idea. I felt hypnotized and uncomfortable, out of my depth.

She laughed again. "Anxious, are we? Most would pay dearly for my company alone. But I'll happily introduce you to the women upstairs. Any preferences? Desires? You can bathe first, or have a swim in the lake, if you like."

I stared at her mesmerized and shivered suddenly. "No thanks to the lake, Miss Laveau, I'd like to keep all my body parts. A bath would be nice. It's so hot."

"Yes, you are too scrumptious for the gators, Cher. Follow me and someone will draw you a bath."

I followed Marie Laveau up a long wooden staircase surrounded by brick walls. Candle sconces lit our way flickering, casting shadows on the old brickwork. She turned at the landing and opened an arched Spanish style beautifully carved door. Water was running into a claw foot tub, candles flickered on a low table beside it, covered with glass jars of heady smelling oils. Frankincense, helichrysum, sandalwood, were written in fountain pen on their labels.

"You can leave your clothes on the chair." Marie Laveau pointed to a wooden chair with a cane seat by the wall. She took a seat in a red upholstered slipper chair across from the bathtub.

I stood motionless looking at her. "You want me to undress, with you *here?*"

"Are you shy, Cincinnatus? I've seen many men. Have you got something they haven't? You hardly had privacy where you were living before."

She wasn't talking about Patsy's cabin. She *knew.* I took off my clothes and put them on the chair. I stood in front of her and she took her time studying me. It was unnerving and titillating and suddenly I was the subject waiting to be painted, or in this case, something much more pleasurable. Someone had come into the room behind me, and I felt warm fingers caressing my back. Marie Laveau was enjoying my obvious reaction, though she remained in her chair, while I was gently being turned around sideways. It was Patsy's twin, except her eyes were deep blue in her flawless cocoa skin. I remained standing while the woman oiled every inch of me. She led me to the bath.

Afterward, someone led me to another room. What happened next, I could only begin to describe as sexual bliss. I would never do justice in the telling. Whether it was my own hunger unleashed in a New Orleans brothel or what Marie Laveau handed me to drink earlier on the porch, I don't know. Other forces were at work. There were cries of passion I'd only read about in books. And I had never been observed making love with anyone. I looked from the bed to the large standing mirror. We were not alone. Marie Laveau was sitting in a blue velvet chair in the corner by the open window, watching us the entire time. It was unnerving and exciting. We kept on and after we finished, the woman kissed me and left the room, closing the door behind her.

Marie Laveau held a fresh blue goblet. "Have some refreshment. You've earned it."

I walked over to her and took the goblet. It tasted sweet and potent.

"Gin and elderflowers. It heightens the libido, not that you need any help, Cincinnatus.

Are you spent? It doesn't seem so. Shall I touch you or are you too tired?"

"Please," I said, draining my glass. If this was to be my last ghost visit, I was intent on making the most of it. If this really was New Orleans, I would never leave. Patsy would find me.

Maybe it was she who sent me here. Marie Laveau was talking to me.

"Are you distracted?"

"Sorry. No," I said, meeting her eyes.

"Show me," she said, opening her robe.

I know you desire details. I cannot give them, because they were not mine to give. Perhaps she erased them. They belonged to that night and to that joining of body and soul and freedom and surrender. I gave myself to Marie Laveau in a way I have never given myself to anyone. I let her use me as an instrument of pleasure and I was humbled by her power. I'd never been comfortable releasing total control. I never had, completely, before that night. I was ashamed of that for Patsy because I loved her. But I had no choice, Marie Laveau opened me to my core and laid me bare before an altar I did not pray at or ask to be punished upon. I felt something not ever offered to me in such a way. Patsy was the exception. Yet did Patsy truly know me and I her?

I felt a strange connection to this dark bayou, with its impending danger and its sultry heat drawing me closer and closer to what? Myself? I felt intense passion like I have never known, but that is not what I remember most. Marie Laveau knew this. She made me feel much more than bodily pleasures and erotic ambiance and New Orleans in all its complicated charm. She made me feel vulnerable. She knew how to draw me in, I was willing and hungry, and she showed me how to accept it. I was starving for love and posing at it. She challenged everything I had known before. I lapped it up like a starving dog. I was ready to succumb fully.

We sat at a wooden table on the verandah overlooking Lake Pontchatrain. Marie Laveau fed me oysters, turtle soup, chicken with gravy, red beans, and dirty rice. For dessert there was bread pudding with bourbon sauce and chicory coffee.

"I have never had such a delicious meal. Thank you, Miss Laveau."

"You're welcome, Cher. Call me Marie. We have known each other intimately, don't be shy, suddenly. You're a passionate man."

"I only meant to be respectful, Marie." I accepted a glass of bourbon, the ice tinkling as I raised it to my lips.

"Come here," she said.

The alligators made their eerie bullfrog sounds. I stopped, distracted by their nearness. I feared we'd tumble over the balustrade and be at their mercy.

"Cincinnatus." I only heard her husky voice and saw her body in the candlelight.

I woke alone in the bed upstairs. I looked in the mirror across from the bed. I could see the verandah. Marie Laveau was sitting outside smoking, ice tinkling in her blue goblet. I walked outside without dressing. Marie Laveau handed me a fresh glass. I drank, quenching my thirst. It was only water. Out of the corner of my eye there was movement by the lake. An alligator was crawling through the balustrade. I lifted Marie Laveau to safety inside, put her down.

"You have been greedy, Cincinnatus." She closed the shutters as the alligator grew closer. I was alone outside. I screamed out for help, calling her name over and over. The alligator turned and crawled back down into the lake. I opened the shutters and walked into the arms of Marie Laveau.

"I have a jealous nature. Be careful to mind that, Cincinnatus." She stroked my back and led me a chair. "This, you will remember, Cher."

I woke, screaming for mercy. My body was soaking wet. I felt sharp twinges on my buttocks and back. I sat up and there was blood on the sheets. I got up to look in the mirror on the wall. There were lashes visible, but they were healed. I smelled aloe and lemongrass. I drank from the blue goblet, tasting the elixir of gin and elderflowers. I was tied to the bedposts. Marie Laveau was whipping me with a leather strap. I took my punishment until I could not any longer and begged for mercy. She applied ointments to my wounds and whispered in my ear. "Who is the Queen of New Orleans, Cher?" She was no longer Marie Laveau; she was Patsy.

I sipped clear water from a fresh blue goblet. "You are. You are my only Queen."

She laughed and kissed my lips, and I closed my eyes. I was alone in the room. I heard a laugh. Marie Laveau was sitting in the blue velvet chair. She brought me a cold blue goblet. I went to her. She led me to the bed, and I was absolved of any wrongdoing. I screamed out Patsy's name as the sun rose over the bayou.

Chapter Eighteen

The rain was coming down in sheets. The drains on the lower porch made a drumming noise that woke me. I reached for Patsy, but she wasn't there. I needed coffee. I threw on some jeans and a sweater; the cabin was freezing. I turned on the heat. While the coffee brewed, I started a fire. I poured some of Patsy's granola in a bowl and added blueberries and milk. I chewed and thought about what I might paint. I heard a noise coming from the spare bedroom. One of the canvases probably fell over. I was going to need to make more space for them somewhere. I put my empty bowl on the counter and took my coffee inside.

It was so warm in the spare room I had to take off my sweater. I could hear the fire crackling from the living room, and I heard something else. The croaking sound of alligators. I knew that sound. I smelled frankincense. My easel was facing the window. I turned it around. Marie Laveau stared back at me. The painting was haunting and beautiful. She was regal in her blue robe and red turban, oils in her hand and skulls at her feet. My back burned. I looked in the mirror. There were angry red lash marks across my back and buttocks when I lowered my jeans. I could hear laughing and ice tinkling in glasses. I remembered it all. The heat was unbearable. I took off my jeans. I had to get air. I opened the front door and stepped onto the porch. The rain felt amazing. I stood out there and let it wash over me. I set my cup on the gate ledge. I stood there until I felt I'd drown in the welcome deluge.

I toweled off and wrapped myself in a Navajo blanket and sat by the fire. I couldn't find my coffee. I got up and poured another cup. I was not going back in that bedroom with Marie Laveau's painting. I needed some time to process what happened in New Orleans or rather in my mind. Was it voodoo? Did Patsy have a twin, or had I only imagined her as the woman with the blue eyes? I touched my back. The lash marks were gone. I finished my coffee. I was still hungry. I put another log on the fire. It was just the right temperature in the cabin. I heard a bang. Even if all the paintings fell over, I wasn't going into that spare bedroom for love nor money. I heard knocking. Someone was at the door. Who would be out in this pouring rain?

I opened the front door. She was holding my coffee cup. "Oakley?"

She smiled and handed me the cup. "You took your time about it, didn't you?" she said, coming into the cabin. She took off her rain slicker and hung it on the kitchen chair. She was barefoot.

"What are you doing here?" I pulled the blanket closer around me.

She laughed. "I told you to leave a cup on the gate if you wanted me to drop by, remember? You look good, Cincinnatus. Satisfied. So beautiful standing naked in the rain. Someone should paint *you.*"

The patchouli was making me warm, not to mention the conversation. "Thank you, I didn't know I had an audience." I had to get her out of the cabin. If Marie Laveau got wind of her, I had no idea what voodoo she might conjure upon me. I realized she was dead but last night she was very real. Painfully real.

"You think too much." Oakley was watching me.

"Look, I had a rough night. A good night, but exhausting. It's complicated."

Oakley laughed. "Let's keep it simple then, shall we?" She whipped the blanket from me faster than a magician with a tablecloth.

"That's better," she said, taking in the view. "I'd say you've missed me."

I felt a strong sense of déjà vu. This was becoming a theme. I know, poor me.

There was no bloodshed or sacrifice and not one alligator reared its ugly head while Oakley was there. I didn't think about Marie Laveau, and it wasn't the Acapulco Gold we shared after we had ghost sex. I cooked fried chicken while Oakley played Joni Mitchell albums and stoked the fire, not to mention my loins. She didn't bring up Patsy and neither did I. I felt guilty. I was a traitor. But what was I supposed to do, send an ethereal vision away in a storm? What harm could it do? Oakley had not hurt me, and Patsy knew about our first meeting. The naked portrait was history. Still, I was a bit anxious this all might cave in on me later. I really wanted to sleep. Why did I agree to let her stay the night? She was afraid of thunder and lightning. It was raining the night she fell down the stairs.

"People believed I was drunk. Or heading down into the village for wine. I wasn't. I was home alone. My roommates were in the city for the night. I heard someone talking outside. First I thought it was someone on the stairs. I thought someone was calling my name. I opened the door and walked down to the entrance to the stairs. No one was around. I started back up. There was a loud crack and a bright flash. I could smell burning wood. I felt something push me back toward the stairs. I had nothing to grip, I was falling, and this huge branch was falling with me. Hikers found me at the bottom in the morning. It was a freak accident, Cincinnatus. I wasn't high and I wish people would stop perpetuating that myth of the drunken girl who leaves her little bottles behind. I had dreams. I wanted to do things."

"Become a magician?"

"No, a nurse. At the psychiatric hospital in Alameda. I wanted to work with the vets. There were so many around here that seemed so lost. My brother Cole was killed in Vietnam. I missed him."

"Wait, *your* brother Cole?

"Yes, why?"

"No reason," I lied. What a waste, I thought. This kind soul struck down in her prime, no one getting to know her generosity and depth. I myself had considered her just a hippie chick with a great body and a penchant to please. I was ashamed of myself.

"I'm sorry, Oakley. You would have made a great nurse. You have a wonderful bedside manner."

"I'm good in the sack, you mean?" She looked me in the eyes. I'd hurt her feelings. "Just because I don't look like your exotic city girlfriend, I'm not some airy-fairy hippie chick who couldn't have become something. What's Patsy's story? Do you know? Everyone has one. Why didn't she report you staying in her cabin? Don't you ever wonder? People are often not who they seem to be."

"What are you getting at?" Why was a ghost jealous of Pasty?

"Patsy's not who you think she is."

I was really tiring of this conversation, but I let her go on. Truth is, I wanted to know everything about Patsy. My mistake was letting Oakley be the one to tell me.

"Oakley, what does that mean? Do you have some grudge against Patsy?"

"Look, I helped her. She had no one else. She came to the hospital in bad shape. She had some kind of mental breakdown. I was doing my hours there while I went to school. I trained at the Alameda Psychiatric Hospital. Patsy was a patient. I was drawn to her right way. She was so delicate, but she was a fighter I could tell. She trusted me. I read to her. I spent extra time on my days off visiting her. I brought her art supplies. She liked to paint. She recovered and got herself an apartment in the city. You know she taught the warden and officer's kids at Alcatraz, right? Imagine, both of you on that island at the same time. It's kismet that you met. Anyway, she used to come up here to her grandfather's cabin. That's where we reconnected. She had gone back to the hospital and asked for me. She wondered why I wasn't working there by then; she knew I was close to graduating before she left. They told her what happened to me. She drove straight up here and stayed in the cabin. One night I heard her call my name. That's when I decided to pay her a visit. I couldn't bear for her to suffer another breakdown. She was so sad. You should have seen her face when I walked up on the porch. You know that smile of hers, it could warm you on the coldest night? She wasn't afraid. She'd missed me."

"What about *her* brother, Cole?"

"Cole is *my* brother. Patsy knew him. She doesn't have a brother. What does it matter? You have secrets, too. You didn't tell her you escaped from prison in one of the most famous cases ever. You've made up more than a few stories to survive. I get it, it's about trust. Patsy has trust issues too. Her father died coming home from work one night. He'd promised he'd be there for her, always. He stopped off at his local watering hole after a shift at the firehouse. He always called home, first. That night he didn't. Patsy loved him. Patsy's mother died when she was very young. She and her father were very close. He remarried. Patsy was fine with that, but later when her father died, she broke inside. Her stepmother was useless, checked out, in her own pain. Patsy's father held everyone together. Without him, the whole family was in bits." *The whole family?*

"You mean Patsy and her stepmother?"

"Yeah. Who else?"

"I don't know, that's why I'm asking. I feel awful that Pasty went through all that."

"Things happen, Cincinnatus. Patsy is stronger than she lets on."

"I think she's amazing. I love her. But what do I know about love?"

"Don't obsess, Cincinnatus. I'm telling you, you don't know her."

"How come you and Patsy never met before the hospital? You lived here, you said, on the upper road."

"Patsy and I traveled in different circles when I was alive. She wasn't the hippie type. And she wasn't up here much after her father died."

I had to end this Oakley thing. Patsy wouldn't be all right with Oakley dropping in whenever she felt like it. Ghost or not, it was bound to get complicated. I could keep her visits to myself, but I was tired of keeping secrets.

"Oakley, you seem to care about Patsy. Why keep coming here? There must be other places to haunt. Sorry, I don't mean to be facetious."

"I like you, Cincinnatus. We're having a good time. I'm the resident ghost, remember? Patsy could share, but she won't. She has to have everything for herself."

"Hey, where did that come from?"

"It's nothing, never mind. Whatever you want. Patsy, of course."

"Here's the thing, Oakley, I can't have these secret visits with you anymore. You have to stop coming here." She looked at me and didn't answer.

"You don't want to talk about it anymore? That's fine. As long as we're clear."

"I want to go to bed. If you're breaking up with me, Cincinnatus, I'm going to leave you with a very good memory. You can start your one-woman man loyalty project tomorrow. "

I just broke up with a ghost. I hoped the Anglins were having half as much fun as me.

So why did I feel like a heel? And why did I get the distinct feeling Oakley wasn't telling me the truth?

Chapter Nineteen

I needed to be outside. The weather had taken a turn for the better, so I headed for the woods. I needed some space. For a loner, I had more than my share of visitors and while I was honored and grateful, I was exhausted. I just wanted to walk by myself, inhale eucalyptus and not think about women or ghosts. There he was, standing at the edge of the cliff. His hands were in the pockets of a worn Army jacket. He didn't have the posture of someone who was going to jump. I walked up closer, keeping a healthy distance, respecting his solitude. Just two people, looking at the view of a postcard forest. He looked over at me. He was young, maybe eighteen, and the jacket was Army issue. A name stamped on the frayed pocket. Miller.

"Love these woods," he said. "I miss them."

"It's beautiful, all right. Don't get up here very often?"

"Not the same for me, anymore. I'm Cole, by the way." He took his hand out of his pocket to shake mine. He was ice cold but had a strong handshake.

"Cincinnatus," I said. "Cole? You don't happen to have a sister?"

"As a matter of fact, I do. Did. It's complicated."

"I know your sister, Oakley. In fact, she just left me this morning."

He laughed, "That's impossible. Oakley is dead."

"I know. She visits me. Met her a while ago, the resident ghost. We're friends now. She told me about you."

119

"Did she? So you're not spooked? What are you some sort of ghost whisperer?"

It was my turn to laugh. "Not exactly. Just one very fortunate guy."

"Cool. How'd you like to meet some less fortunate souls?"

"I've got no plans today."

"Wait till you die, you can't imagine all the free time you'll have."

I followed him down the path towards who knows where, but I was game.

Standing in a graveyard was not my idea of a good time, but who was I to question anything anymore? Cole pointed out his own headstone, which freaked me out. I mean what was I supposed to say? 'Sorry for your loss?'

"Surreal, huh?" he said, making me relax. "I was barely eighteen. I joined up because my best friend did. We had no other plans and dropping acid gets old, you know? Just kidding, we weren't stoners, just dreamers, but that didn't please the parents or pay the bills. We had this band, we weren't half bad, but so was everyone else we knew that started a band. We needed a solid gig. When that didn't happen, we ditched it for the military. My old man was proud. It killed my mother. Not literally, but she never recovered. My sister was wild, and Mom had a premonition Oakley would come to a bad end. No one believed her, but it turned out she was right. "I was the lucky one, Mom said. The golden boy with the dreams."

"Oakley had dreams," I said. "Did you know she was studying to be a nurse?"

"Yeah. Somewhere she got off track. Lost it, big time. And then...."

"She fell down the stairs. In the storm."

"Right. Horrible end. Life sucks sometimes. Both of us, dead. Well at least one of..."

"Yeah?" *At least one of us?*

"Nothing. Never mind. Just thinking out loud."

"I'm sorry, Cole. Life makes no sense. Why did I survive, for instance? I didn't deserve to; I did nothing to earn it."

"Don't go down that road, man. Survivor's guilt will rot you inside. A few of my buddies have it. Drugs, reckless behavior, depression. Hard to watch."

"You're right, sorry."

"Stop apologizing, man. It's fucking annoying. I met up with you for a reason. I know you paint some. Ever sell anything?"

"Mostly trees and moon paintings and a few carvings. A friend took me to a gallery over in Sausalito. They liked my stuff."

"You see True? Now she was fine. Oakley knew her. They used to surf together."

"I saw the photographs. Amazing eyes. Pity she died that way, doing what she loved."

"A rogue wave. She didn't have a chance. She was wild, man. Hot. I had the biggest crush on her. I was just a kid."

"Anyway, what was the reason we 'met up,' like you said?"

"Impatient, aren't you? It's not about me. I was gone before I knew what hit me. I want to help my brothers. The ones who are lying in hospitals, waiting to die. Others are homeless or lost in their lives. They got no reentry, man. One minute a guys on a killing field and the next he's dead, or he survives the nightmare, gets sent back home, but he's dead inside. It's no way to live. There's not enough money to care for the wounded soldiers with the numbers of them coming home every day. I know the war's over, but the damage isn't finished. Some are still missing. You can help."

"What can I do?"

"You can care, for one, Cincinnatus. And you can paint them. You've painted some interesting people. So you can't share them, I get that. But the soldiers will sell, I guarantee it.

You'll capture who they really were. You can open people's eyes. This is going to go on for years to come, these soldiers coming home broken. You can show them as ordinary people who served selflessly. Relate them to the rest of the country. Who they were before someone strapped a gun to their chest. They're forgotten, man. You could start a quiet movement. You hearing me?"

I didn't know about a movement, but he had this tiger by the tail, so I went along. He was as passionate and persistent as Patsy. You'd think they were related.

"I hear you, man. But I paint ghosts."

"The thing is you have no idea what you can do until you give it a chance."

"Any idea where I should start?"

Cole smiled. There was a warmth about him. He had the same blue eyes as the man in the photograph with Patsy, if my eyes weren't playing tricks on me. Actually, he was a younger version of Patsy's father, tall, built, and handsome. And that meant Oakley's story had a big hole in it.

Cole had more than ideas, plans drawn up, fund raisers in mind we could hold. He knew of abandoned buildings where new hospitals and therapy centers could be built. He knew guys that survived who he could put me in touch with easily. It sounded great. Except for one thing. Cole didn't know for one minute who I really was. I had come too far to get caught now. If that was selfish or un-American, so be it. No matter how long I live I'd always be a wanted man. Nothing could change that.

"There's one thing, Cole. I'm not exactly a free agent, if you get my drift."

"I know who you are, what you did. That's why I asked you. Nothing's going to happen to you. No one will ever know the truth. You can stay under the radar. I have specific ideas about how to do that. Oakley will help. You trust her, don't you? I mean I know she can be a real pain in the ass. She has a bad temper when she doesn't get her way. Be careful, man."

I didn't know how to answer him. Did I trust her? The jury was out on that. She was dead, what could she do to me? I was sorry about Cole and the vets, but I was one person. What difference could I possibly make?

"You can give back. It's karma. But it's your choice." He was reading my mind and I didn't like it.

"This is a big undertaking."

"I hear that. And escaping from Alcatraz was an ordinary occurrence, Frank?"

I cringed. I was uncomfortable hearing my former name. The reminder, always there.

"I don't go by that name anymore. That's the past, Cole. Why can't I just move on? Why do I owe anybody anything? I didn't ask for these spectral soul talks. I was doing just fine on my own, you know?"

He looked at me, the way one looks at someone with pity. Who was he to judge me? He was just a kid.

"Hey man, no pressure, do whatever you like. Ignore me, I'm just a bitter kid who made the wrong choice. I followed the crowd. I don't even know what the hell I was doing over in Vietnam. None of us did. So pay no attention to me. I told you I was a dreamer. Take it easy, man. Say hi to Oakley when you see her."

"Wait. Hang on a second, man. I'm not saying no." Jeez, the dead were impatient.

"I just need a minute to wrap my head around this whole idea. I know it seems I have what I wanted, my freedom, but it's not so cut and dried. I'm not against giving back, what I am strongly opposed to is going back inside. It sounds self-serving, I know, especially when you never had a chance to grow up and have a life. Everything's relative, though. No matter what I do, we can't trade places."

"I know you were in prison. *That* prison. The famous escape. I also know you went and talked with those vets in the village. Risky if you ask me. I know they moved you and you felt guilty for wasting your life, while they sacrificed theirs. I'm not judging you man, but you felt something. Where did you stuff that? It's numbing yourself from life. It's a fucking choice. Freedom, man, it ain't free."

Boy, the guy was intense. Like his sister. *Which one?* The ball was in my court, and I wasn't in the mood for playing. Everything that happened to me since the escape was beyond the normal comfort zone. Some ghostly advice didn't shake me. Just a little wiggle room would have been welcomed. I sighed loudly. I felt myself give in.

"Okay, you got me, Cole. I'm in, man. When do we start?"

"Outstanding. I was right about you. Thanks, Cincinnatus. I'll be in touch, man." He turned and walked away. I watched and suddenly he was gone. Just trees stared back at me. I looked down at his headstone. I noticed a bunch of purple pansies someone had recently left there.

"Nice meeting you, Cole." I touched his gravestone.

I was feeling manipulated. Oakley shows up with her big revelation about herself, and now Cole, the mysterious brother appears. I made an agreement with him, and I planned to honor it. Seriously though, who needed all this drama? Maybe I should have gone with the Anglins and kept it simple. Drift unencumbered. Instead, I was holed up in some haunted cabin in a redwood forest, spending my days and nights with ghosts. I thought of the murdered Birmingham Angels. Why did they come? I was undeserving. I did not believe that things happened for a reason, or destiny was responsible, or any other metaphysical musings that people bantered about. Maybe shit just happened, end of story.

Ghosts were not logical. Neither was swimming off Alcatraz and surviving. The ghost visits affected me, made me think too much. I wasn't converted to some divine plan. A ghost saw me escape? Far-fetched, I knew that in my sensible mind. The whole ghost appearance thing was fantastic, I had to admit. I had too much time to think. Imagined the whole thing. The solitude was seductive. I craved it. No one was watching me. No rules. No guards. It got lonely. Is that why the apparitions happened? Logical men don't lend themselves to supernatural fantasies. They were pretty damn good though if they were figments of my imagination. Maybe I'd lost my mind from the swim. Lack of oxygen, water on the brain. Maybe I drowned and this was me telling my story from the spirit world. Smart men don't believe in spirts. I had gone off the deep end. I was living a mad dream. "We are all sentenced to solitary confinement inside our own skins for life." Tennessee Williams said that. He was right.

I was not deluded. I accepted the ghosts. One thing remained; I was a loner. I might have been out of prison for a good while, I might have met Patsy, but people don't change because good things happen to them. They change because they have no choice. Because a gun is to their head, or they hit a wall. They're trapped or can't get over on people anymore. Maybe they're out of chances. Their usual way of doing things has expired. They become moldy like the bread gone past its use by date. You can still eat it and probably not die, but it won't taste as good as a fresh loaf you buy warm from the bakery. People eat cat food too. I won't describe the grub they fed us in prison. Yet was I changing? Would it matter in the end? The only thing I believed for sure is, I was never going back to prison. And that had nothing to do with anything supernatural or divine.

It's a good thing those thoughts stayed where they belonged, inside my head. If I shared them with anyone, I'd be committed, after I was arrested. Ghost man prisoner, that was me. Speaking of the dead, whom would I be meeting next? I wouldn't mind having tea with Sylvia Plath. I dug her poetry. It was edgy. Maybe that's what attracted me to Oakley, they were both tragic souls. There wasn't a particular phantom I longed to meet. Scratch that, on second thought, I'd like to meet Billie Holiday, Babe Ruth, and my mother.

Chapter Twenty

My mother came first. She was younger than I expected and prettier than I ever imagined. She knocked on the door a few minutes after I got back to the cabin. I knew who she was immediately. Looking into her eyes was like looking in the mirror of my past.

"I don't mean to bother you," she said, "I'm not sure why I'm here. I guess you have been wondering about me. Perhaps your whole life? Or maybe I don't bear thinking about. If you'd rather I leave, I'll understand."

"Come in. Do you mind if I call you Clara?"

"Of course not. That is my name. I never deserved any other title." She looked down at the floor.

"It's okay. You came. I don't expect anything. I'm a grown man, as you can see. I have no right to judge you. I take full responsibility for my life."

"I don't know what to say, Frank."

"Have a seat. I'll make us some coffee. I go by Cincinnatus, now. Frank is dead."

She sat in the chair by the window. Her lips quivered and it looked like she was about to cry.

"This is very awkward." She played with a loose string on her sweater.

"Look, we don't have to get all sentimental and apologetic, okay? I'm a big boy. You were obviously too young to raise a kid, so you did what thousands of other people did, you gave me up. I survived. There's no guilt trip to take. Relax."

She looked up at me with her soulful eyes and smiled. "You're very kind. Cincinnatus, is that like the innkeeper on Daniel Boone?"

"Not exactly. There's a poet from these parts I like to read."

"Joaquin Miller? I read him. I enjoy reading. I did, I mean. I probably should have spent more time at it, but life doesn't always work out the way you wish. I guess you know that."

"Ain't that the truth."

She laughed. It was a sweet sound. Can there be a primal connection with a certain sound one remembers, on a cellular level perhaps? In utero, maybe? I felt her laugh was stored somewhere deep inside me. Or maybe I wanted to feel it. I had no touchstone.

"How do you take your coffee, Clara?" I liked saying her name. It suited her.

"Milk and sugar, please. Oh, I almost forgot, I brought these for you." She handed me a bakery box. "I hope you like them."

I read the name on the box, Holmes Baked Goods. The aroma of sugared donuts filled my nostrils. I opened the box and took out a warm donut and bit into it. The sugared dough danced on my tongue. I remembered the taste like I'd had one yesterday.

"Sorry, don't mind me," I finished chewing. "These were always my favorite."

I set the box on the coffee table. "I haven't had one in years. Thank you."

"You're welcome," she said. "They're a D.C. staple. Or they used to be. I liked them best, too."

So, my mother and I shared the love of a good sugared donut and the poems of Joaquin Miller. If it all sounds flowery and tidy, it wasn't. It was real, though. The woman sitting before me was no more than a kid herself. How could I be angry with her, when she likely had no choice but to give me up? At least she had the nerve to show her face. My old man never did.

"I didn't know him long, your father. He wasn't ready for a child. Neither of us were properly prepared to be parents. And then he left town. It's not an original story. I didn't have a lot of choices back then, being on my own. I hope you can forgive me, someday. You seem to have turned out fine without me. Except the jail part. I'm sorry. You needed a mother."

"Prison," I correct her.

"Sorry. Yes, prison. How awful, I cannot imagine. But now you're free."

"Not exactly. I'll always be hiding from the truth."

That was her cue to run the hell out of there, vaporize or whatever a ghost does in such a situation. She remained where she was. My mother was brave.

"Freedom won't come easy, Cincinnatus. It never does. But you're smart, you'll figure it out. Are you the painter?" She was looking at the wall. "These paintings are very good. I like the trees, and what a beautiful woman."

"I paint, yes. Thank you. That's Patsy. This is her cabin. She's too good for me."

"Don't say that. I can tell by the look on her face, she loves you very much. You're lucky to have found her."

"She found *me*. Sorry, I don't mean to come off like a jerk. Seeing you brings it all back.

You know the first time I was only thirteen. Locked up in juvenile detention. Later, I got really good at it. My criminal career. I wasted a lot of years."

She seemed nonplussed. "People make mistakes, Cincinnatus. I came here to tell you that. I'm sorry you didn't have a proper upbringing and home. That was not your fault. I wish I had kept you. I know that doesn't do you any good to hear that now. Children need guidance and love. Did you learn anything? From your time in prison? Are you sorry for whomever you took things or money from, people you hurt? That's all that matters. You seem to be living a life that matters now. Love is what we all seek. And self-knowledge. If we are lucky, we realize it and hold on to it. I wasn't lucky. Not that I'm anyone to lecture you. I haven't earned the right."

"You're here. Thank you for saying you wished you'd kept me. I thought I was garbage, so I behaved like it. I'm not bragging or excusing myself. Just telling you how I felt. I'm not the same person I was in D.C. in all those foster homes and jails. Or who I was in prison. I thought I was a man without a soul. I've seen things and felt things I can't deny. I don't know why I got this chance. I don't want anything from you. You gave me life. You could have done otherwise, but you didn't. There's only one thing I need from you."

She met my eyes. "Anything. If I can give it to you, I gladly will."

"May I paint you?"

She smiled and then started to cry. "I wasn't expecting that."

"I wasn't expecting *you*. I was kind of hoping for Babe Ruth."

She laughed, "I like baseball too. May I give you a hug, Cincinnatus?" She waited, timidly.

I took her in my arms, and we cried.

I painted my mother. Then she made us popcorn and we drank Cokes and watched a ballgame on television. We stayed up talking into the wee hours. I shared my visit with the Birmingham Angels   and showed her the painting. She cried. "I'm very proud of you, son," she said. You can wait your whole life and never hear those words. Before she left the next morning, after insisting on cooking me a pancake breakfast, she handed me the small silver locket she was wearing.

I took my coffee outside and looked out at the trees. I fingered the locket in my shirt pocket. Taking it out, I gently opened it. There was a picture of a dark eyed baby on one side and a beautiful young woman with my eyes on the other side.

Chapter Twenty-One

Patsy phoned to say she had an art show in the city. She knew I wouldn't venture that close to my former home, and she wasn't calling to ask me to go with her. She was just checking in. She missed me, she said. I told her I was amusing myself, taking walks and painting when the spirit moved me. To that end, she asked if there had been any spirits who came to pay me a visit. I nonchalantly mentioned Oakley. I was not keeping that secret anymore.

"Really? She's back? I didn't think she would be." I sensed a bit of tension in her voice.

"Why not? You know how ghosts are unpredictable."

"Right. What did she have to say?"

"Nothing earth shattering," I lied. "You know Oakley, you can't pin her down."

Patsy laughed, but it was a nervous laugh. "I do know she likes to pin you down. But she better not mess with me."

Well, well. Patsy was challenging the resident ghost. "Them's fighting words," I said.

"Don't be silly, she's dead." The silence after that was deafening. I had to break it for her sake. From everything I heard from Oakley, Patsy had been through enough.

"You, on the other hand, are very much alive. Come back soon."

"Good, you miss me," she said, and I could hear the smile in her voice. "I have to go. I'll see you tonight. Try not to get into any trouble. By the way, if Oakley comes back, tell her I said to piss off."

"Roger that." I laughed, but when I hung up I couldn't help thinking there was more to the story Oakley told me. Perhaps she wasn't Patsy's savior at all. And if that was the case, then what was she?

I went down to the village for coffee and a new sketch pad. I wanted to be prepared when the next ghost showed up. The weather was crisp and pleasant for fall and though the leaves were not falling here in California, I could feel a shift inside myself. I felt an overwhelming loyalty and love for Patsy that pleased me. Perhaps there was hope for me yet. If push came to shove, Oakley was going to lose. I knew it in my gut. The resident ghost had to go.

The cabin looked different when I returned. It had an English flair. There were small diamond shaped panes in the windows. There was a brown-weathered low gate leading up to the porch, with a sign that read Devon Cottage. I smelled a fire. The ghost or ghosts were busy, I thought. There was a slender woman sitting by the fire writing in a small notebook and smoking. Patsy wouldn't like that. It smelled delicious in the cabin; something was cooking in the oven.

"It's Shepherd's Pie, Ted likes it. I hope you're hungry. Make us a drink, would you love, I just need to finish this poem," said the woman who wore a long tweed skirt and a blouse with a string of pearls. She reminded me of a bird with a broken wing. Her eyes were hazel saucers, trusting and tragic.

"You're Sylvia Plath."

"Yes," she said and continued her writing. She's not killing herself in this cabin, I thought.

"I'm already dead. I died in England," she said, nonplussed.

I made us both a gin and tonic. "I hope it's not too strong."

"After this poem, I certainly hope it is," said Sylvia Plath.

134

I laughed. "You do write some serious poetry. I mean, I love your writing."

"Thank you. I'm whiskey in a teacup. It's always a surprise and I don't know why. Maybe it's the pearls. Ted says I have no sense of humor. I am not frivolous and flowery, that's all. I am not apologizing for that." She sipped her drink. "It's lovely here. So refreshing after dreary England. Thanks for having me."

Did I have a choice? "You're welcome," I said, swallowing a good sip of gin.

"Are you a moody writer as well?" Sylvia Plath asked.

"More of a reader. I like to paint."

"Ah, a painter. How wonderful. Do you read Ted's poetry as well?"

"Personally, I always thought you were the better poet. I think he just has a lot of groupies. If he wasn't so good looking, I don't think he would have gone so far, professionally. In my humble opinion. Cincinnatus Jones, by the way." I extended my hand.

Sylvia shook it and laughed. "That's brilliant. I like you. I wish Ted could hear you. I'd buy tickets to that event. He thinks he can charm a spider. Jones? Is that English?"

"Irish. On my mother's side.

"Good. The English can be a cold lot. Ted is excellent at the silent treatment. It infuriates me. He runs hot and cold, like the tap. And they say I am the moody one. One wonders."

"Cincinnatus. What an interesting name. Like Cincinnatus Miller?"

"Yes. Do all you poets..." I started, leaving out the word *dead,* "know each other?"

"Not all of us," smiled Sylvia Plath.

"Ted is late," Sylvia said. "Probably stopped for a pint or a tryst." She sipped her gin and tonic, looking sadly out the window.

"Ted is alive, Miss Plath."

"Sylvia, please. Oh right. What a shame."

"Something funny, Cincinnatus?" Sylvia reached for a cigarette. I lit it for her.

"Just remembering a joke someone told me once," I improvised.

"Don't keep me in suspense," Sylvia said.

"Well, a guy goes to his shrink and says, 'my brother thinks he's a chicken. The shrink says, 'Just tell him he isn't, that's all.' 'I can't,' the man says, 'we need the eggs.''

Sylvia Plath cracked up. You don't picture that, I know. But she was having a joyful moment. She was a beautiful sight to behold. Yes, Sylvia Plath of The Bell Jar fame and her angry Daddy poems and her depression and eventual suicide. That Sylvia Plath. I wanted to hug her. I wanted her to be alive again. I wanted her to tell Ted Hughes he was a cheating asshole and that he and Assia and all his other paramours could go to hell, and she was just fine without him. Men would be lining up. Except she was dead.

"I know how that man feels," said Sylvia. "I often wonder if I need the eggs. Did you, Cincinnatus?"

I was about to answer when Sylvia Plath interrupted me. "Ted would waltz in and announce he was late. But never apologize. His hair would be disheveled, and his shirt buttons done wrong. I'd sigh and say, 'Drink, love? How was your tryst?' And he would get all broody and defensive but look as guilty as sin. Gorgeous and guilty. Good looking men get away with murder, you know. I imagine you've charmed a fair few women yourself, Cincinnatus?"

I was about to say, "Just one amazing woman and one relentless ghost," but I stopped myself. Sylvia went on.

"I'd kill for a drink,' is what Ted would answer after he got over his hissy fit. It would be all niceties for the remainder of the night. We'd make love. Ted is a voracious lover. Insatiable. He has rubbed off on me, I'm afraid. The way a wool sweater irritates your skin, but you can't bear to take it off, you fear the cold too much. Do you understand Cincinnatus or think it's rubbish? I'm a hopeless lovesick fool, am I not?"

"Personally, I would have burned such a sweater or donated it to the poor. I guess you can't do that with husbands."

Sylvia laughed so much she had to excuse herself to use the 'loo,' as she called it. "Make us another round, would you, love?" She said over her shoulder as she walked down the hallway to the bathroom.

"So, tell me, Cincinnatus. Such an interesting name you've chosen. Are you a fugitive outlaw and obsessed painter of the dead?"

"I used to rob banks. Now I listen to Jazz and meet voodoo priestess ghosts. And paint the dead."

"How exotic. Sylvia said, passing me the dish of olives.

I won't deny I was a little turned on. Is that weird? Not at all, I told myself. Remembering the Oakley ghost sex and Marie Laveau.

"You paint nudes, too."

I can't say I didn't see that one coming. "One, yes, but I burned it. The night is young, I could do another..." It's not often you get to toss sexual innuendos around with Sylvia Plath.

"Aren't you cheeky? Ted always said I have an amazing back. I wouldn't mind posing for you later. Though the woman over your mantel is much lovelier. Might she mind? She is no ghost I take it?"

"Patsy is my girlfriend. This is her cabin. She'll be sorry she missed meeting you."

"She's a good one. Don't screw it up. And you can tell her about tonight. Right now, I'm all yours," Sylvia said, smiling at me. It was unnerving to say the least. I left Sylvia by the fire, while I checked on the dinner.

"Can I ask you a question?" I asked Sylvia Plath, over a delicious shepherd's pie.

"Of course." She looked at me. Her eyes were so sincere. It seems honest women always wind up with cads.

137

"Why did you put up with Ted?"

"You have seen him, Cincinnatus? Even in photos, he is virility on two feet. He knows it too. So dangerous. To answer your question though, Ted is in my blood. He would have to be surgically removed, all my blood drained and fresh blood injected. Good thing I can write. Otherwise, I might stick my head in the oven."

"Please, don't do that," I suddenly begged, feeling ridiculous because that is exactly what she had done. Neither writing, nor her children or family and friends were enough to keep her from her fatal ending.

"I promise," she said, meeting my eyes. For a split second, I believed her.

I'll say one thing, Sylvia Plath cooked a mean Shepherd's Pie. She let me paint her, fully clothed, and we shared a brandy in front of the fire.

"You only get one, and on the odd chance, two, to truly love someone with your entire being. That is what I had with Ted. He was just too selfish to appreciate that kind of love. If he didn't write, he'd probably just have been any old tosser who looks for the next thrill around the corner. Fame is heady stuff, Cincinnatus. One is truly better off without it."

"Shall I read you some poetry?" I boldly asked.

"I would love that. Have anyone in mind?"

I picked up a book by the fireplace and started to read Mad Woman's Love Song.

**"I shut my eyes and all the world drops dead.
I lift my lids, and all is born again.
(I think I made you up inside my head)**

**The stars go waltzing out in red and blue:
And arbitrary blackness gallops in:
I shut my eyes and all the world drops dead.**

Scape Ghost

I dreamed that you bewitched be into bed.
And sung me moon-struck, kissed me quite insane.
(I think I made you up inside my head)

God topples from the sky, hell's fires fade:
Exit seraphim and Satan's men:
I shut my eyes and all the world drops dead.

I fancied you'd return the way you said.
But I grow old and I forget your name.
(I think I made you up inside my head)

I should have loved a thunderbird instead:
At least when spring comes they roar back again.
I shut my eyes and all the world drops dead. I think I
made you up in my head."

"Well done Cincinnatus. Thank you for a most enjoyable evening. Be sure to read this poem to Patsy."
Sylvia leaned over and kissed me on the lips. She was as warm as the apple tart we shared for dessert.

"The pleasure was all mine," I said, standing.

"Stay honest. Good night, love." She walked down to Patsy's room and closed the door.

I sat back down in front of the fire. I had the feeling if I went into Pasty's bedroom, Sylvia Plath would not be there waiting for me. She had lived and died for one man. I cleaned up the kitchen and shut the lights. The fire was embers. I slept in the guest room and dreamed of Patsy.

In the morning, the door to Patsy's room was open. I walked inside. No one was there. On the bed was a single sheet of vellum paper with a handwritten poem, Mad Woman's Love Song. It was signed, For Cincinnatus, Love, Sylvia Plath.

Chapter Twenty-Two

I heard laughing outside. I could smell grilling meat.

"Women troubles?" the guy at the barbecue grill asked, turning around.

I was speechless. Too bad my mother hadn't hung around.

"You're Babe Ruth," I said lamely.

He laughed, his eyes squinting, "Last time I looked, yeah. Nice place you got here. Hope you don't mind, I'm starving." He bit into a hot dog. "Want one?"

"Sure. How about a beer to wash it down?" I didn't wait for an answer, I went inside to grab two beers and pinch myself. The Babe was here.

"Thanks." He took a good swig. "So, this your place? Don't see any little woman around." Whoa, Patsy would hate that. Not to mention Oakley. The Babe better steer clear of loose branches.

"My girlfriend's cabin. She's in the city."

"What about the other one?"

"She's a ghost."

He roared. "Then you're golden. How do you take your dog?" He took a good swallow of beer.

"Well done, please. You know I'm a huge fan of yours. The whole team. This is unbelievable."

"I go where I'm welcome. You and I got things in common."

"You escaped from prison?" I chewed my hot dog.

He laughed again, "Good one. No, I had some trouble as a kid. Parents sent me to a home for wayward boys. It had a good ending. Yours did too, it appears."

"It kind of did. I'm here, the escape was a success. Not the same as hitting it out of the park, but close."

"If I had to swim to survive, that would have been the end of the story. I like to drink too much, and I eat like I have two assholes. I'm lucky no woman bashed my head in, either. I pressed my luck there more than once. I have a greedy appetite for women, too. Maybe you can relate?"

It was my turn to laugh. "If I had to hit one out of Yankee Stadium, that would be the end of my career. You're a god. As far as women, one at a time suits me better."

"What about the ghost?"

"Bases loaded."

Babe Ruth almost split a gut laughing. "I like you…"

"Cincinnatus."

"That's not your real name."

"No, I borrowed it. It feels like mine. I've worn it awhile."

"I understand. How much says I can hit that tree way down there?" Babe Ruth picked up a bat.

"I don't bet."

"You any good at pitching?"

"I told you, I was a jailbird. And one night, a long-distance swimmer."

"Yeah, I heard you, but can you throw a decent ball?"

"I have a feeling we're about to find out. What if you hit the tree and it boomerangs instead?"

"You forget who I am?"

"Not for a minute. Ready when you are." I pitched a few balls to The Babe, and he hit the last one out of the park.

"That calls for another beer," he said. "When are your girlfriends coming around?"

"Not anytime soon, sorry. Though I think you and Oakley would get along pretty good."

"Annie Oakley?"

"Not quite, but she would appreciate the reference. For a ghost, the woman is a pistol, man."

"You got a good gig going here, Cincinnatus. Don't mess it up."

"I don't plan on it. Hey, what do you say we go find ourselves a ballgame? I know some vets who like to play. They'd be thrilled to meet you."

"Won't that cause a ruckus? Me being dead and all?"

"Nope. They're dead too."

"Excellent. Lead the way. Bring the beer."

Babe Ruth didn't meet Oakley there, but he did meet her brother, Cole, and a whole bunch of vets from another war, years before Vietnam. The DD's they called themselves. Real characters, the lot of them. There was Bose, Booker, Vodka Harry, Yeah 'Youse, Mick, Tony, Freddie, and Dee. You couldn't get a straight answer from any of them, but they were dead serious about their nicknames. Dee loved baseball. He wanted to be a pro. "It didn't happen," he said, "the war did." They all loved The Babe and had a day they'd never forget. Cole and I were old buddies by now. He hadn't expected me to come through so quickly, he told me. "Thank The Babe," I said.

"I will," he said. "Something's different about you since we last met. You meet someone before Babe Ruth showed up?"

"My mother. I was an orphan."

"You know The Babe has a soft spot for orphans. Someone helped him at the right time and it changed his life. He likes to give back."

"You trying to tell me something?"

"No man, just talking. Let's play ball."

If you never played sandlot baseball, I cannot properly describe what a thrill it is, especially with a bunch of dead vets who were pitching and catching with The Babe. Cole hit a home run and I got a few walks, but that's beside the point. On that lot in Oakland, we became kids, enjoying the swing of a bat and the chance to belong somewhere. The Babe wanted in on our vets' project after Cole pitched him the idea. We cracked open the cooler of beer and sat shooting the breeze on the sandlot for a good hour after the game. The Babe was hungry again, so we headed back to the cabin with the vets. I took a bunch of steaks out of the freezer, and we had ourselves a cookout that would have made the Anglins proud. I wished my old friends could have been there, but you can't have everything. If we ever met up one day, I'd tell them all about it. If they were experiencing half of what I was, we'd have a lot to talk about.

Oakley showed up after all, wearing a Yankees cap and jersey with The Babe's number three on the back. The Babe loved her. She was her usual charming self and didn't mind him calling her Annie Oakley. Cole was happy to see his sister, so everyone had a good time. With timing on my side, the party would be history before Patsy returned from the city.

The guys didn't want to leave. The Babe wanted a poker game. You don't argue with Babe Ruth. I got out the cards and poker chips. Patsy's grandfather was a fan of the game and kept a good supply of both in a drawer in the kitchen. The Babe wanted cigars. I had to draw the line. Patsy would hate the smell of cigars in her cabin, and I can't say I blamed her. We moved the game outside to the porch. I saved face and The Babe got his cigars.

Bose dealt the cards. Booker placed the first bet, half his chips. Dee laughed and said, "You ain't got a snowballs chance in hell to beat this hand." Freddy was all in before he even got started. Tony raised Bose. Mick had all aces, and The Babe was not happy. "New dealer," he bellowed. Yeah 'Youse took over and The Babe was king's high. These guys were all WWII vets on the same Navy ship. The Babe and Vodka Harry went head-to-head on the next deal. Vodka Harry folded. The Babe had a full house.

I don't know what time the cards got put away and the guys all left. I did capture The Babe on canvas and some of Cole's friends from Vietnam and the DD's. Oakley helped me clean up and by the time Patsy returned from the city, there were no traces of poker, beers, cigars, or Babe Ruth. Well, besides his portrait. Oakley made herself scarce too. But not before she planted a good kiss on my lips. "I could stay," she said. I took a deep breath. "Or you could go," I said. She didn't push her luck. That should have been a clue, but I was too high on baseball and The Babe to pay attention.

Chapter Twenty-Three

I slept like the dead. Considering what recently transpired in this cabin, it was ironic. If that was what the afterlife was like, I had better catch up on all my sleep now. I wasn't famous like my ghost visitors. Infamous maybe. I doubt anyone was putting me on a list of dead people they wanted to meet, come the day I was six feet under. Then again, you never know, there's no accounting for taste. I smelled coffee. I truly hoped it wasn't of the ghost kind. I was not in the mood for another haunting just yet. I wanted to savor The Babe and the vets. And keep the living away from the dead, mainly Patsy and Oakley. Maybe The Babe was right, I needed a score card.

Patsy was standing in the doorway to the bedroom, a cup of coffee in her hand. "That for me?" I smiled at her and patted the bed next to me. She handed me the coffee and sat down.

"Good morning, sleepyhead. I didn't have the heart to wake you. Ghost dreams?"

"Funny you should say that." I swallowed a good gulp of coffee.

"You had company last night? I hope it wasn't Oakley?" Patsy smiled when she said it, so I knew she wasn't mad at me, just curious. Maybe more than curious, come to think of it.

"Actually, she was here, but only for a short time. She met Babe Ruth." I took another good sip of coffee and watched her face. She could have played poker with us.

"That so? You're a big fan of The Babe, are you?"

"Huge fan. We played a sandlot game down in Oakland. These dead WWII vets joined us. It was a blast. How was the art show?"

"It was good. Sounds like you had more fun."

"I also met Cole Miller. He's Oakley's brother. Funny, you both have brothers with the same first name." I realized after I opened my big mouth that antagonizing someone with possible lingering mental issues was not a smart thing. But I didn't feel unsafe with Patsy. I loved her. And love does strange things to your sensibilities. And if Oakley was lying, what did I have to lose?

"Waffles or eggs? Or both? Or I can get in bed with you and breakfast can wait. Unless The Babe wore you out or Oak...."

I didn't let her finish that thought. I covered her mouth in a deep kiss. Luckily, she responded and thankfully I had rinsed my mouth with mouthwash earlier. I gathered Patsy in my arms, helping her get undressed. I had a plan. Sex and sustenance, then a much-needed heart to heart. I know when to push an issue and when to let it be. No confrontations before waffles or sex. I'm not Freud, but I'm no idiot.

Patsy made killer waffles. The Babe would have loved them. And he'd probably skip the chat and let sleeping dogs lie. He certainly would have kept Oakley on deck. But I wasn't Babe Ruth. I worshipped the man's baseball record. He was a legend. But he and I had different styles.

"Good waffles," I said.

"Oakley coming here triggered me. I didn't feel it happening at first. Her presence rattles me. She needs to move on. It's awful what happened to her. But we can't bring her back."

"I'm sorry about your brother. And your parents."

"Thank you."

"Don't worry, Oakley is history."

"If only."

"She has nothing to do with us."

"She's not finished."

"What does that mean?"

"My father's name was Colton. He knew Oakley's mother. They met one night in the city at the bar my father frequented. They had an affair and fell in love. Cole is my brother, too."

"Holy shit."

"Ah, she didn't tell you that part? She wouldn't, of course. It's a possessive thing. You see there was no love lost between Oakley and her mother. Her mother always favored Cole. My mother was already dead, so the affair didn't affect me the way it affected her. All I saw was that my father was happy again. I had no siblings before, and my mother was gone. My father never stopped loving me and I had siblings to play with. But her parents broke up over it, and there was a new daddy around. My father loved Oakley. But she was unreachable."

"What are you saying?"

"Cole wasn't supposed to die. When he did, something happened to my father and Oakley's mother. To all of us, we loved him so much. He was easy to love. We all came apart. Her mom started taking pills, she was out of it most of the time. Oakley needed her. My father tried, but his drinking got worse. Then he was killed that night he was drunk, the car accident. I had just graduated from college. I was ready to teach. Oakley was close to graduation from nursing school. She'd started her training at the psychiatric hospital in Alameda. Cole enlisted. I met someone but he was bad for me. I finally left him. Cole was killed in Vietnam. I had some kind of break down. Oakley took care of me in the hospital, but she wasn't right with Cole's death either. She just hid it better than me. She was self-medicating. Easy access to meds in the hospital. She was always in a dreamy fog, clouding all her pain. Anyway, I recovered and when I got out and went to see her, she was gone. Her mother told me she was dead. I was in shock. Her mother was numb. Any warmth she had was gone with my father and Cole. I went up to the cabin that weekend. I was as sad as a person could be. That's when Oakley came."

"This is incredible. No wonder she came back. It's because of you. She wants to be near you. It's really touching, Patsy."

"Yes, it would seem so. But it's not as genuine as it comes across, trust me. She needs to move on and let us have our time together. I love her, I always will. We are sisters, if not by blood. Cole's our kid brother. But I'm not sharing you with a ghost. What's so funny?"

"She said you don't like to share."

"I shared my dad, didn't I? And Cole. She is rewriting history. Oakley has a bit of arrested development. Don't forget she died young. She needs to leave us alone. It's not up for discussion. Maybe she can find a ghost to love."

"The Babe liked her."

"Why wouldn't he? So what do you think?"

"She liked him too."

"I meant about us."

"You and me, kid. Three's a crowd. Any more waffles?"

Patsy laughed and all was right with the world, for the moment. "You're insatiable."

"So was Ted Hughes."

"What?"

"I had another visitor. Sylvia Plath. I'll get her portrait for you."

"After we go walk off these waffles. I need a ghost break."

"You? How do you think I feel?"

Patsy and I did our usual loop in the hills and I told her about my mother visiting me, without certain details. "You're so lucky, Cincinnatus. I'd give anything to see my dad again. And Cole."

"Be careful what you wish for."

"I meant I'd be alive, like you."

"You never know. We share Oakley, right?"

"Don't start that again." Patsy gave me a playful punch in the arm.

I laughed. "Just teasing you. That ship sailed. Or sunk."

"Good, so don't go diving on any wrecks. I'm telling you, regarding Oakley, you're out of your depth. She has a mean streak. Be careful."

"That's what Cole said."

"Then pay attention."

"Yes, Teach. You're all right. I like a woman who knows what she wants and what she doesn't."

"Then we're golden. What's so funny?"

"That's what The Babe said."

"Then you should listen to him."

"Hang on, that's not all he said."

"I can imagine. Sort through and take away what matters."

"You just make that up?"

"Yep."

"I like it. I wonder who is going to visit next?"

"Who's on your list?"

"Billie Holiday."

"Cool. You know Nina Simone is playing in New York this weekend? But she's alive."

"Of course she's alive. Since getting on a plane is out of the question, I have to hope she decides to play San Francisco sometime. Miles Davis came. One never knows."

"That was a dream. I have no doubt you'll meet Nina Simone in your dreams, too."

We headed back to the cabin. A nice cold drink was in order. Patsy was going to make her homemade lemonade. We both had new novels we wanted to crack open and relax on the porch deck in the sunshine. I was digging the simplicity of the moment and Patsy. I put on Nina Simone's Pastel Blues and opened the door to the deck. The strains of "Nobody Knows You

When You're Down and Out," carried soulfully through the cabin and out to the trees. I fell asleep, my book in my lap, page lost, dreams in charge.

When I woke I had an urge for an espresso. Patsy had turned me on to it, so I decided to brew a pot for us. What would the guys on the old cellblock think? I laughed to myself. Just as quick as that thought popped into my head it exited like a cloud disappearing.

Patsy preferred her espresso with a lemon peel and sometimes a splash of Sambuca. I stuck with a lemon peel, and I took two small cups outside, listening to Miles wailing on trumpet and watching the trees dance in the light breeze.

I had been ghost visited by amazing people, including the ones on my list and a reappearing of Oakley and Cole. It was thrilling every time. Was it over? Patsy said the cabins were haunted. The idea of an unlimited number of ghosts appealed to me. Each ghost that came made a lasting impression on me. Cole had something important to tell me, regarding the loss of souls in war, the vets who returned and what they needed and how I might help them. My mother and that unbelievable day was my own history unearthed in a way I would never have known otherwise. The ghosts of Oakley and Cole were part of Patsy's history so therefore interesting to me. No need to try and figure it out. The ghosts seemed to be my purpose for now, or maybe for longer than I knew.

The hills around Patsy's cabin remained mostly unin-habited so there was no imminent danger of discovery. When I started to sense such, it would be time to leave. I had not lost my ability to sense trouble, though I'd been free for five years. A prisoner has that sixth sense ingrained in him. Etched in his cells. I resembled nothing of my former self. For some reason I was spared. What was it other than my disguise that kept me free? I can't say, I am no sage. I only know where I came from and what I did, until the escape. I still have the soul of Frank Morris, though I have embraced the heart of Cincinnatus Jones.

Scape Ghost

Like a tree top philosopher of sorts, I was good at ruminating and hosting ghosts and doing some painting and
cooking. Would I go so far as to say if it all ended tomorrow and
I was found out, I would calmly accept my punishment? No. I
was never going back to prison, no matter what happened. I
would never trade my freedom for love or honor or forgiveness.
If that is a character flaw, then go ahead and label me. I would
not become a criminal again, that part of me died and good riddance. Yet, given the choice between the ledge and the prison
cell, I will go for the ledge. A free man does not go backwards.

Chapter Twenty-Four

"I think we need a road trip," Patsy announced. "Let's go to Pacific Grove. I hear Joan Baez is playing at a small venue there. The monarch butterflies are there, that alone is reason to go. Then, of course there's whales and dolphins. I know a place where we can stay that you will just love. We can relax and take beach walks and you can take a break from the ghosts. The scenery and vibe there is almost unreal, it's so beautiful and soul-affirming. Sound good?"

"Yep, exactly what I need. *We* need." She sensed I was also going somewhere in my head that wasn't good. My own weighted down feeling about the future. I was happy she had a suggestion that had nothing to do with ghosts. I would bring my sketchpad, but only for the butterflies. I couldn't wait to get out of this cabin and on the road.

"By the way," Patsy said, "We can stop in Gilroy and buy more garlic." She was elated.

"Not many women, people really, get that excited about garlic."

"If you don't already know it, Cincinnatus, here's a news flash, I am not many women."

"You certainly aren't, and for that I am beyond grateful. Garlic and butterflies, here we come."

"Don't forget Joan Baez."

"Who could?" I noticed a small dark cloud pass in front of Patsy's face.

"What is it?" I was almost afraid to find out.

"Just thinking about Oakley and if she is really gone. Are you missing her?"

"Oakley who?"

"Very funny."

"By the way, where did this shell come from? It's beautiful." Patsy was holding a conch near her ear. "You can hear the ocean, smell it too."

"No idea. You can have it. Or better yet, let's take it to Pacific Grove and throw it back into the ocean."

"Yes, let's do that. Perfect." Patsy seemed overjoyed by the idea. "You know, it smells like True."

"You miss her, Patsy?"

"She was a good friend. She had the most amazing eyes, like the sea wrapped in moss. True was an intuitive, you know."

"So you said that day at the gallery. Did she read palms? Do tarot cards?"

"Don't poke fun at the dead."

"Sorry."

"I'm just messing with you. But True had a sense of things. Doesn't mean she could prevent them from happening. She was a beautiful person. Maybe she can distract Oakley."

"Why would she do that?"

"Because she loved Oakley."

"You mean more than a friend?"

"Much more. Where did this shell come from anyway?" Patsy was still holding the conch.

"I don't know. I just noticed it when you picked it up."

"It's True. She's around."

"Will she be visiting, do you think?"

"I wouldn't be surprised. Anyway, I have an idea. We could bring a few paintings to Pacific Grove. I know someone who runs a gallery. They get some good walking traffic there."

"Fine. I don't mind. It's getting crowded in the spare room."

Scape Ghost

"It's settled, then." She kissed me. Patsy was the kind of woman who knew how to wrap up a conversation. She wrapped herself around me. One day I would tell her the truth. Why didn't I trust her enough already? Would I ever be really free with this secret between us? If I told her who I was, would she still want to be with me? More importantly, would she turn me in? I felt awful thinking that way, but old fears die hard. I wanted to be Cincinnatus Jones and never have heard of Frank Morris. For the moment I would leave it alone. Maybe another ghost would present a solution. My mind was open.

I wasn't into formal meditation. The kind that was all the rage at Esalen. I had all the solitude a guy could want at Patsy's cabin. But I wouldn't turn down a chance to see Joan Baez and Dylan live if I could help it. The folk concert at Esalen was Patsy's surprise. In true Patsy fashion she arranged a perfect place where we could hear the music without being in the middle of the crowd. Her friends in Pacific Grove had a house practically in the backyard of Esalen. They were quiet laid-back types who didn't ask a lot of questions. And they respected Patsy's policy of utmost privacy. Patsy told me they were her dear friends for the duration. I envied her. They liked my moon paintings. My Tree Period, as Patsy called them, the gallery owner in Pacific Grove had bought. Patsy had delivered them while I waited in a cafe next door. The fewer strangers I met, living ones anyway, the better I'd remain unfound. It was enough that all the ghosts knew me. I still had a bit of fugitive residue.

Patsy told me on the ride down, that while her friends were mainstream professionals, they had once belonged to a confidential group that helped abused women in the country escape and travel safely west to restart their lives. "They know how to keep secrets," she said, looking at me in a way that suddenly gave me pause. Did Patsy *know?* Had she been keeping not only me a secret, but my biggest secret as well? If so, she was a better actor than me. I didn't know if I should be happy about that or worried.

I parted with the Trainhoppers, one of my favorite paintings and encounters. Only after the husband told me about his affinity for old trains, train stories, and Bluegrass. I had Cab and Haggard etched in my memory, so it felt okay to let them go. I would never forget them. They were in good hands. Patsy's friend insisted on paying the gallery price, even though I wanted him to have it as a gift, for their hospitality. I could see he was not a man to argue with on certain points.

"I pay for good art," he said. "And I am sure you will put the money to good use. Patsy told us about the vets you met. I don't like war and I don't like ignorance either. Those guys got a lousy homecoming and no reentry plan. That fact cannot be swept under the rug. By the way, your choice to remain anonymous on your paintings is sacrosanct to us. Patsy is a dear friend. And therefore, you are now, as well." *What did he mean by that?*

The husband was a tall man who carried his height like he'd earned it. He had a long white beard in sharp contrast to his dark brown skin. He happened to play the harp, I would find out after dinner, he loved Neil Young and favored worn chambray shirts, similar to Cab's, only clean. I could easily imagine him as the third Trainhopper. His name was Sinclair, like the writer Sinclair Lewis; his mother had been a fan. Everyone called him Sink. He held a doctorate in linguistics and taught at Stanford. His wife, a nurse turned midwife, was called Circe, like the goddess and enchantress in The Odyssey. She was a dead ringer for Judy Collins, turquoise eyes and all. They made a formidable couple. Hobby farmers who grew their own vegetables and kept chickens for eggs and liked entertaining guests in their modest house with an incredible view of the Pacific. The meals they served were delicious and impressive. Heaping platters of homegrown Swiss chard and fresh pasta with pure imported Greek olive oil Circe's family sent her, baked eggplant with melted goat cheese, grilled carrots with spices and a local honey glaze, and a crusty loaf of aromatic homemade rosemary bread. And mushrooms. With that garlic Patsy loved. We lingered at their outside table, talking for hours. Patsy seemed so at home. I had no choice but to feel welcome. Even relaxed. I envied her, these good friends she trusted with her life. Other than the Anglins and that famous night, I didn't have those kind of people in my life. Until Patsy. *Could I trust her with the truth?*

Sink and Circe weren't vegetarians, so they let me cook Cab's iron-dipped stew one night, and Patsy made homemade buttermilk biscuits and we drank a few bottles of Pinot Noir that Patsy and I had picked up on the way. We had their farm fresh tomatoes with fresh roasted garlic and grilled artichokes we bought in Gilroy. I shared my Trainhoppers story with them, without saying they were ghosts, but transients instead, that I met one night at a bar by the old Oakland Mole Railyard. Sink loved it. Meanwhile, the music drifted right onto their patio, and we were in heaven. It doesn't get better than Baez and Dylan and Joni and Judy, good food, new friends, the Pacific breeze and Patsy. Sink and Circe turned in after we were all well sated with wine and a joint after Dylan sang Knocking on Heavens Door. Patsy and I made love under an Indian blanket on an old brass bed on wheels that I helped Sink roll out of their barn earlier.

"Highly recommended for star gazing," Sink said, with a wink before he and Circe went inside to their bedroom. "There's plenty of blankets in the house if you want to sleep out here, too," Circe added. "It gets a bit chilly, but I imagine you'll keep each other cozy. Keep the fire pit stoked. You'll be warm as toast."

"I think I could live here," I said to Patsy, as she drew close under the blankets.

"It's beautiful, isn't it? You're free, aren't you? You can live anywhere."

"We're all free." *Did she know?*

"Yes, but you've been on a… I don't know what to call it, a soul quest. You've changed, haven't you?"

"From what?" I had to poke the bear a little or I'd lose my mind thinking about it.

"I don't know. Only you can know. I'm just a witness."

I allowed that thought to penetrate my mind. *A witness to what?* Five years can be a long time in normal living years, but when you're a fugitive from the law, it seems like yesterday. Even one presumed dead. I would remain aware of my surroundings and my anonymity probably for the rest of my life. If it was a free life, what did it matter if I came clean with Patsy? I looked at her and touched her beautiful face and body, lit by the moon, a brown goddess with skin like silk, and sighed. "I want to sketch you again. Like this, without a stitch on, on this brass bed. What do you think of that?"

"Kinky. Meet me here at sunrise." Patsy laughed. That sound of her laughter. I was undone. I pulled her to me, and we loved each other until the sun came up.

A farm breakfast, enjoyed on Sink and Circe's patio was beyond delightful. Sink played albums we all liked. Patsy was a huge Joan Baez fan and Dylan was a troubadour of the time you could hardly ignore. The vets I'd spoken to dug his music. You might think they were conflicted with Dylan's message or Joan's, but they weren't. They served in a most confusing war that was Vietnam. As Sink said, "You can disagree and still want freedom for everyone, and defeat oppression without becoming the oppressor. Besides, music transcends politics. Or at least it should."

We all agreed, clinking coffee mugs on it. I really liked Patsy's friends. Sink was a fabulous storyteller. His deep captivating voice held my attention. He spoke of growing up in the South and moving out to California when the country was still in its infancy in many ways equality-wise, but there was undeniable freedom he resonated with, out here.

"I was just a man getting on with life, getting my education, making an honest living and giving back so others might follow. In my soul I am neither black nor white. I am an ordinary man living an extraordinary life. That I get to share it with this amazing woman is such a thrill, even after all these years. Circe gives me the benefit of the doubt even when I am dead wrong. Not without the clock ticking for me to wake the hell up, mind you." He smiled and Circe did too. "Circe is fair and always honest. Often brutally, which I need. Men can be thick. Her delivery is gentle, so you wouldn't even know you'd been schooled. You know what I mean, Cincinnatus?"

"I do."

Patsy smiled, "Circe can tell you what their secret is, can't you, Circe?"

Circe put her coffee cup down. Sink kissed her softly.

"Sink always puts me first. Not his family who were very uneasy at first about us taking on a biracial relationship, not our kids who may have balked at times when they were self-centered adolescents, but have turned into quite lovely functioning adults, and not his work. That is the glue, knowing I matter to him, above all. And I reciprocate, of course. Why wouldn't I? He's made it easy. We made that decision a long time ago and it's served us well. You know how they say, 'it's not what you said but how it made me feel'? Well, I have always felt loved and supported emotionally and we've always been a team. Even when we disagree. The world is hard enough to navigate. Why be with someone if you don't feel valued? That isn't love."

"No, it sure isn't. It's called something else," Sink said, looking out at the ocean.

"Control?" Patsy asked him.

"That's a mild word for it."

"Slavery," I said. Patsy looked at me.

"Exactly, Cincinnatus. Spot on," Sink said. "We don't own people. People are free to feel how they do. If you don't like

161

it, then the other person you profess to love would do better to cut ties and move on. Marriage may be an institution, but it is not meant to be a prison."

I inwardly winced at the word prison.

"Easier said than done," Patsy said.

"Never easy. I'm a nurse and a midwife, so I have seen a lot. But the freedom on the other side is always worth it.

"I agree about freedom," I said, I thought rather nonchalantly. Did I imagine Patsy looking at me sideways?

"Cincinnatus is changing his life," Patsy said, touching my arm. "An extended sabbatical from teaching back east. Painting is something he discovered out here, well, at my cabin. I think he may have found his calling."

"Good for you, man," Sink said. "We are honored to have the chance to get to know you. I can tell from your paintings what a passionate person you are. An old soul. That doesn't come from living an easy life. There is often a deep well of angst to draw from."

"I can't disagree with you," I said.

"Well, you could, but this is my house," Sink said.

"*Our* house, you mean, darling," Circe said.

"I stand corrected," Sink said, "Our house. A very, very, very fine house."

We all laughed. Joni was singing A Free Man In Paris and we were inside the most interesting and enjoyable day with the promise of more to come.

We were quiet on the ride back to Oakland. Patsy had, as usual, organized good road trip music for us. Chet Baker was playing after Aretha serenaded us down Highway One. I liked Patsy's friends, Sink and Circe. I envied their easy way with one another and their life with the Pacific as a backdrop. Their little garden. Even the chickens. Would Patsy and I ever have that? Perhaps a modified version, off the grid. But Patsy had her gallery, and it wouldn't be fair to ask her to change her life for me. She had worked hard to be where she was, why would she want to complicate things? We had good times together and I loved her, yet never having had that feeling about anyone before, I had doubts. Was I good enough for Patsy who loved with her entire being? I didn't know if I was capable of such generosity and honesty. It was terrifying. Are people better off on their own not having to think about another person's happiness? Maybe my existence from here on in, was painting ghosts and loving Patsy and thinking any further was useless because it was already fated to be what it would be. I could screw it up if I wasn't careful.

I dug what I saw in Sink and Circe's relationship, their consideration for each other. Maybe I just liked the way it looked but had no damn clue how to emulate such a thing even if I tried. At the bottom of it I knew, was fear. I didn't want to fail and disappoint Patsy. I didn't want her to see through me and find the real man underneath. The loser I was before she met me. He was not the guy Patsy loved. She loved an artist named Cincinnatus Jones. A guy she discovered squatting in her cabin in the trees. It was a romantic cliche and those don't stand the test of time. It wasn't real life. It was a fantasy. What if I were caught and hauled back to prison? Patsy would suffer. I couldn't let that happen. I closed my eyes. I was getting a headache. What if it had nothing to do with me and my ego? Patsy could kick me to the curb at any time and call this a fabulous fling and say, "Have a nice day, Cincinnatus, or whoever you really are under all that hair."

Patsy was slowing down and pulled into a gas station with a small cafe next to it.

"I need some coffee," she said, "and a little snack. How about you?"

"Yeah, sure. Sounds good. The music is putting me to sleep," I lied.

"Really? Because I noticed your jaw clenching and you seemed lost in thought to me."

"I can't fool you, can I? I really had a great weekend. I liked your friends. I wouldn't mind that kind of life."

"Modify. You're creative. I'm not going anywhere, if that's your concern. Unless you want me to. Before we continue this conversation, which I'd love, I seriously need caffeine."

Patsy kissed me. I filled the car up with gas and watched Patsy walk over to the cafe.

She returned with two cups of coffee and two cinnamon buns. We got back in the car and munched and sipped while Miles played us home. "You know, Miles chases the dragon."

Patsy was nonplussed. "Everybody chases something. Comes a point it outruns you and you die. You have to decide how you want to live. He makes fabulous music, that's for sure."

"Are you saying he couldn't if he didn't self- medicate?"

"No. But maybe he thinks so. Isn't that the dilemma? There's all that pop psychology about what doesn't kill you makes you stronger. Sometimes we only think we need a crutch. Life is a scary ride."

"How did you get so smart?"

"I made mistakes. Had my dark nights of the soul. I'm still learning. What are you smiling about?"

"Just wondering if your bed would fit through the door of the cabin."

"You liked that alfresco sleeping, hmm?"

"Yeah, the stars are calling."

"Let's talk about it after you make me a drink. I'm just going to change."

"Deal. But first I need to ask you a question. It's been on my mind for a while."

"You're not going to propose, Cincinnatus, are you?"

"No. Did you want me to?"

"God, no. I'm quite happy with the status quo."

"Patsy, why were you so trusting of me when we first met? Did you think I was a ghost?"

"You mean when I pretended to pull a gun on you? Hardly trusting. Honestly?"

"Of course."

"Well yes, at first, I entertained the idea. I didn't mind you as a ghost. I told you the cabins are haunted. But then I knew you were no ghost. You were mysterious enough to keep me interested. And I never felt I was in danger for one second. Does that answer your question?"

Yep. Sort of. When did you know I was real?"

"When you stayed. Can I change now?"

"I like you the way you are."

"Then I have the brass ring, don't I?"

"I'd say I grabbed that first when I found your cabin."

"It's a big ring, we can share it. G & T, please, lots of ice and lime. Be right back."

I went into the kitchen to make our drinks. How was Patsy so sure I wasn't leaving and reappearing each time she arrived? What made her a ghost expert?

"Umm, delicious." Patsy took a healthy sip of her G&T. "You can make a drink."

"Maybe I was a bartender in a past life. Maybe your friend True would know?"

Patsy looked at me. "Maybe she would."

Chapter Twenty-Five

I stared at the portraits lined up against the porch railing. I wanted to see their faces in the natural light. The sun cooperated, shining on each in one moment, then it shifted, shade falling on them, creating a much different look. The trees swayed in the light breeze. I put Cole in the middle and his two sisters on either side. Patsy, so beautiful in her New Orleans robe, smiling her radiant smile. Oakley, serious, in the nurse's uniform I'd embellished for her. And Cole, beaming and handsome in his Army jacket. Suddenly it hit me. Popped right out like a spark. The name on Cole's jacket pocket. Miller. Oakley's name, not Patsy's. Wasn't Cole, Patsy's father's son, the love child?

"I did it for Oakley," a deep voice came from inside the living room. A man walked out to the porch and stood looking at the portraits. I waited. I was used to ghost decorum by now. He was an older version of Cole. That fact was certainly not lost on Oakley.

"You must be Cincinnatus. I'm Colton Vaughan. Nice to meet you," he shook my hand.

"Same here. But I'm confused. I thought Cole was your..."

"Love child? Don't worry, I'm not touchy on the subject. He was and I was crazy about his mother. She wanted Cole to be named after me, and to pacify Oakley, we gave him their family name. It was her concession to her daughter for ending the marriage. But you'll never hear Oakley tell it that way. Honestly, it wasn't an easy time for the kids, and I don't blame her for being angry. Cole loved Oakley from day one and vice versa. Patsy too. But Patsy wasn't needy. Cole understood that, even as a kid. Patsy was fine with all of it. She was willing to share me and Cole with Oakley. That's Patsy. Oakley was cut from a different cloth. She was possessive. When Cole was killed in Vietnam, we all became unhinged. I'm not proud of my drinking, and I never should have driven that night. I deserted my family. I am ashamed of that fact. Oakley is still holding on to old grudges and pain, from the grave. It's sad. She never could let a thing go. That's Oakley. How's my daughter?"

"Patsy? She's wonderful but you already know that."

"I do, but I wanted to hear it from you. You love her?"

"Very much. She's special. But I don't deserve her."

"None of us did. It's too late for that kind of talk. Patsy has decided you're the one. If she's good with you, and you're a good man, there's no problem."

"Yes, but there is, Colton."

"That's in the past. You've redeemed yourself. I know you like your life now. You've done good things. And you make Patsy happy. What she doesn't need, is a man who can't forgive himself. You have to come to terms with what led you here. That's a solitary job."

"Thank you. Listen, can I get you something? Coffee? Are you sober in the afterlife? Sorry, no offense."

"Coffee would be great. Don't apologize. You do that a lot, don't you? And yes, I'm sober for all eternity. What a concept, huh?"

"I am a little offended," he said, when I handed him his coffee.

"Oh?" I was taken unawares. "Patsy told you I bake? I think she left some donuts."

"I'd love a donut." I saw Patsy in his smile and Cole written all over him.

"But I was referring to your other paintings. Can I see them?" He had Patsy's subtle charm. I'm sure when Oakley's mother met him, she was swept away. He was very likable.

"Of course. Right this way. I'd be honored if you let me sketch you, if that's not too weird."

"Get me that donut, and I'm all yours. So, your girl-friend's dead father, not weird at all, is it?" He laughed. I joined him. It let out a little steam from the heady situation.

I went inside to collect my sketch pad and pencils, and a couple of donuts for Colton and myself. Patsy's dad was a very nice man. There was no way of knowing how a day would turn out.

"Anywhere special you want me to sit?" Colton asked when he finished his coffee.

"No, just be natural."

"Natural? Ah, good choice of a word. Then I suppose I'd better come clean and tell you what I really think." Here it comes, I thought, he hates the fact that I am an ex-con. Not the kind of man he hoped his daughter would meet.

"Don't look so uneasy. I was just going to say that while you and Patsy were both on Alcatraz Island, you had no idea what was in store. Perhaps Patsy was your good luck charm. This was meant to be. What do you think?"

I let out a breath. "You know, Colton, this cabin and the ghosts I've met, not to mention your lovely very alive daughter, have affected me. I am not the same man. So you're saying it was Patsy from the beginning? Not Oakley who watched us swim to shore?"

"Now you're catching on. Patsy's the one. She is her mama's daughter, a genuine, tried, and true person. She might not have witnessed your escape, but she is part of your free-dom, yes? Oakley, on the other hand, likes to make up stories. Sometimes they're harmless and sometimes people get hurt."

I started to sketch him as he talked. "Oakley was jeal-ous of Cole, because he was part of her mother and me. She

169

seemed fine with Patsy, though I had my doubts. But with Cole, Oakley could feel her mother abandoning her, replacing her. She wasn't, but Oakley sees things the way she wants to, not the way they actually are. She showed a coldness towards her mother. Oh it wasn't obvious, unless you were there living with it. Patsy accepted her stepmother. And she went out of her way to embrace Oakley. On the surface, it all looked fine. We went along that way, as families do. Until Cole enlisted. Then all hell broke loose.

I wasn't thrilled about him enlisting. Of course I wasn't. I loved my son. But he wanted to go. I couldn't deny him his sense of duty and honor. His mother was suffocating him. She loved me, but she couldn't see straight where our son was concerned. She seemed to forget she had a daughter. Oakley felt that abandonment. Patsy was ignored too, but Pasty didn't need her. She'd had a good mother. And she had me. Oakley felt I took her mother from her and made her father leave. That was not the truth. I loved her. We all did. You've met her, so you know she's charming. But she resisted me. I wasn't her father, she said. She pushed us all away.

Oakley was reckless. Her mother would say she wouldn't make it to twenty-five at the rate she was going. It was a prediction that later came back to haunt us all. Cole dying in Vietnam finished her mother. After that, she was emotionally absent to any of us. You know my story, the alcoholic's lament, hiding in the bottle. I knew better, I saved people. It was my job rescuing people from burning buildings. I was a good guy. But I couldn't bear it. I was a coward. It's a real shame. After Cole, I got lost too. You know, Cincinnatus, you can't make people love you." I nodded and kept sketching, thinking, do the dead go to therapy? This was very interesting.

"You know a different Oakley, I understand that. She's not without her calculating ways, trust me. There's a lot of pain hidden under that easy breezy manner. Cole refused to jump when she said so. Neither would I. There were rules in our house. Someone had to keep it together. If I hadn't turned to the sauce, we might have all had a fighting chance. Even after Cole was killed. We all make choices, Cincinnatus. We can't undo them; we can only learn from them. We may forgive ourselves, but we must make amends. I thought it was too late for me."

"No Twelve Steps in the afterlife?" I wasn't trying to be funny, but what a waste. Three people dead in a family. For what? At least I only hurt myself.

"In a way, these are my steps. Oakley is going to hear me. That I love her and that she didn't cause her father to go away. Her mother had a right to be happy. She wasn't before. Oakley needs to know that. I just stepped in where there was an opening. I tried my best to love them. I failed, apparently. Patsy didn't send Cole to Vietnam. She talked to him on her own for hours to keep him from going. Oakley blamed her for no reason. She could hurt her the most because Patsy loved her unconditionally. She trusted her. And it almost killed her. You sure got more than you bargained for today. Here's your chance to run, Cincinnatus. A sane man would. A lesser man might."

I put down my pencil. The sketch was complete. "All I know is I am luckier than most. So I'm staying put. When I do go, Patsy will come with me. When it's safe for both of us."

"That's all I needed to hear. And I wanted to meet you. Don't worry about Oakley. Like I said, we have a long talk ahead of us, she and I."

"Thank you, Colton. It was a pleasure. Don't be too hard on Oakley. She was just looking for someone to love her the most. You can't blame her."

"You're right. I don't begrudge her that longing. But she has an agenda, and that won't do. That isn't love. Patsy doesn't deserve that. Neither do you."

"I don't disagree. You know Babe Ruth liked her. Oakley, I mean."

He laughed. "That right? Cole said you were funny. Be good to my daughter, Cincinnatus."

I had half an inclination to say, 'Which one?' But I thought better of it.

"Life is for the living." He shook my hand and walked down the stairs to the woods. He looked back up. I waved to him. Life may be for the living, but if not for the dead, where would I be?

Chapter Twenty-Six

I was putting the finishing touches on Colton Vaughan's painting. The more I thought about what he said and how his face appeared in the portrait, so like Cole's, I felt a calm assurance that things were going to work out. Oakley would listen to Colton and realize he loved her like his own daughter. She would let go and find peace. That isn't how life goes though, is it? We don't have neatly tied up solutions. People don't cooperate because we want them to do so. We come into the world wailing our heads off and we go out the same way, holding on and moaning for dear life. Probably doomed to come back and try it all again. It was a cynical view of things, but I never claimed to be saved. I left the painting on the easel drying and went inside to get a cup of coffee. When I came back out, it was gone. The scent of patchouli was heavy in the air.

"Handsome, isn't he? So like Cole. My mother didn't stand a chance." Oakley held the painting in her hands.

"Hey, Oakley. He's a very nice man. We talked. I didn't expect you back." I took the painting and set it on the easel.

"I'll bet. I don't take orders from Colton Vaughan. He doesn't know me. Neither does Patsy. Only you understand me. That's why we're meant to be together."

"Look, I only know what you let me see. Obviously, there's a lot more underneath."

Oakley grinned and played with her shirt. "You know what's underneath, Cincinnatus."

"I'm talking about what's in your heart. You have to resolve your issues with your family."

"Thanks for the advice. But I'm good. All I need is you. Let's keep it simple. Or this could get ugly."

"Is that a threat? Is that how you want this to go? More people get hurt? Are you good with that? Because I'm not. And guess what? I don't take orders from you."

Oakley laughed. It wasn't that sweet laugh I knew and enjoyed.

"I'll turn you in. You won't have Patsy either." She took a stance. Crossed her arms.

"You're a ghost. How exactly will that work? I'm curious"

"You don't need to know. And there's Patsy...."

"Oakley, listen hard. Touch one hair on Patsy's head and you will be very sorry."

"I'm a ghost. What are you going to do, kill me?"

She had a point. What was I going to do about her? This was beyond me. I looked at her and she stared me down. Even The Babe wouldn't have liked her right now. I drank my coffee and sighed. The gate slammed shut. We had company. The Calvary was here, Colton Vaughan and Cole. And bringing up the rear, True, the dead surfer.

"We meet again, Cincinnatus." Colton looked at me and then at his portrait. "Nice work. You flatter me."

"He does that." Oakley looked from me to Colton. "What is this, *Daddy,* an intervention?

Isn't someone missing?"

"Patsy can't be here, you know that. And yes, I think you need intervening, Oakley. You wouldn't listen to me."

"Save it, Colton."

"Easy, Oak, we're only here because we love you." Cole moved closer to his sister.

"Don't 'Oak' me. You left me, with *her.*"

"Mom loved you. Colton loved you. Like you were his own."

"No. He left too. Everyone leaves me."

"I think you're remembering it wrong," True said. "May I interject? We all got along once. We surfed and hung out. Talked about the future."

"Yeah, we surfed and smoked pot and fucked surfers. It wasn't exactly a sisterhood. And the future got screwed too, didn't it? Look at us now."

"Wow. Sorry you saw it that way. Our deaths were accidents."

"Were they? Fuck you, True. You have no idea."

"Watch your mouth, Oakley. She's your friend."

"You're not my father, Colton."

"But I am the one who stuck around for you. Until I...." Colton looked down. This wasn't going well.

"Right, until you didn't. You drowned your problems and killed yourself. Was your drinking above my drug habit? We both escaped."

"I made big mistakes. One was not reeling you in sooner. We all gave you too much power. Poor you, right? We did you no favors. You turned our love against us. I'm sorry you didn't feel I loved you. I did. We all did. You're hurting people, Oakley. It has to stop. I won't allow it."

"You mean St. Patsy, of course."

"Knock it off, Oak."

"Hit a nerve, did I, bro? You always did have a thing for Patsy."

"Now that's enough. Cole doesn't deserve that. And it unconscionable to imply such a thing." Colton's vein in his neck was throbbing.

"Is it? Stranger things have happened. Ask my mother." She looked at Colton. He was obviously at a loss. Oakley continued. "She didn't tell you? Of course she didn't. Why would she? It wouldn't paint her in a good light. Not protecting her own daughter from that monster she married." She shot me a look. "Don't look so surprised, Cincinnatus. Why do you think I'm so good in bed? He broke me in good and early, my father. But she didn't throw him out, did she? Not until Colton came along. Her hero, Mister All About Her. She acted like a lovesick puppy. Pathetic." She wiped her tears and looked at Patsy's father. "It was the happiest day of my life when Mom found you. And then you had Cole. I just wanted you to myself, for a little while. A normal father. Couldn't she give me that, at least? Patsy was lucky, she had you. I wanted that too. To be loved like I was special. Then Cole died, and you were killed in the accident. Why did you leave us? I was stuck with her, a living corpse. You both deserted me. There was no reason to go on after that." Oakley started to cry.

Colton put his arm around her and sat her down on the couch. "I'm so sorry. I had no idea. Your mother was wrong not to tell me and completely wrong not to protect you. You poor sweet girl, having to endure that alone. Can you ever forgive me for deserting you?"

Oakley blew her nose. "I do forgive you." She looked at Cole, "I'm sorry I said that before. It was mean."

"Forget it. But you have to move on. Our parents are dead. Your father suffered his own hell for a long time. He had a long slow death. As did our mother. Colton didn't mean to leave you. I didn't either, Oak."

Oakley started a new round of tears. I wanted to take her in my arms, but that wasn't what was needed now. That's what she'd always used to push the pain away, her body. The next guy. I went in the kitchen to make more coffee. In a way I had been better off without a family. The world was a terrible place sometimes. I could hear Colton's voice outside. He was tender with Oakley, but he had to be what she needed, a father. The one she didn't have in her early years.

"Oakley, you have every right to your feelings about your parents. I won't deny you that. This is about you, after all.

I just want you to know that we all love you. We don't want anything from you in exchange for your love. We never did. That was someone else. That was his crime. And your mother's too, for not stopping him sooner. Do you hear me? Can you forgive us for not knowing? And Cole and I and your mom, for dying, and leaving you alone?"

Oakley blew her nose again. I could see her through the kitchen window. She was a different woman than the one who came to see me that first day. And yet I saw the same vulnerability on her face now that struck me the first time. If I weren't such a tough guy, I'd nearly break down and cry myself. Instead, I poured coffee and kept my mouth shut and stayed witness to a family trying to heal. Oakley caught my eye through the window. I suddenly got a chill. She was lying. She had issues with her father, no doubt. He left. But sexual interference was a big stretch of a lie. What was she doing? And then it occurred to me. This was Oakley's pity party, and she was the star.

"I forgive you," Oakley said to Colton. "And Cole." She stood up. "I need to use the bathroom. Be right back."

"Something on your mind, Cincinnatus?" Oakley took a mug of coffee and sipped. Butter wouldn't melt, I thought. She was quite the actress.

"Why not tell him the actual truth? Not sad enough?"

"What? That both my parents deserted me and started new families? The hell with me, right? How boring. No, this got his attention. Anyway, who am I hurting? They're all dead. Are you judging me?"

"Hey, it's your party. I just want..." She didn't let me finish.

"Yeah? You just want what, exactly?"

"I want you to be yourself. Happy and free."

She laughed. "Too late. I'm dead, remember? Know what I want, Cincinnatus? You. But you don't want me. You want Patsy. The end."

"I'm sorry, Oakley."

"That's not good enough."

"I know, but that's all I got." I kissed her cheek and went outside with coffee.

Oakley walked over to True. They hugged. I watched them. What was this about?

"I'm sorry you went through that," True said. "I wish I could make it all go away."

"You can." Oakley took True by the hand. "Take me surfing."

"That I can do," True said, surprised, but smiling. "Is it okay with everyone if we leave?"

Oakley came over to me. There was a sea change in her eyes. Victory. She gave me a hard kiss on the lips. "It's been fun, Cincinnatus. But I have to go now. The waves are calling. Tell Patsy goodbye for me. No hard feelings. Be happy together. Keep painting. You're beautiful, man. I'll miss you." The old Oakley was back, minus the pain. She hugged Colton and Cole. And then she and True walked down the stairs to True's red Jeep. Two surfboards stuck out the back. I leaned over the railing to watch them drive away, The Grateful Dead's "Cassidy," blaring from the Jeep's speakers.

As relieved as I was to see the back of Oakley, my concern was for Patsy. Was she safe? Was Oakley really going surfing with True, the last wave of the ghosts? How could I trust Oakley after her performance? Patsy would surely have answers, but Patsy wasn't here, and she had not called to check in. I must have been pacing and hadn't realized it.

"Sit down, Cincinnatus. You're making me nervous," Colton said.

"I can't relax. I'm worried about Patsy."

"She's fine. On her way here, actually. It's been quite a day. Oakley is done wrecking lives. Time for her to be finally free."

"So you weren't surprised? You knew about her father?" I was testing him.

178

"I know he left and found someone to love and had other kids and wanted nothing to do with Oakley. That horrible tale she made up was just that. A terrible lie."

"Why did you play along?"

"She's been through enough. We all have. No one suffered from her lie, but her. It was in her mind. It was a small gift to give her in the end. Oakley never learned how to be straightforward in relationships. Oh sure, she's aggressively charming with men, but that's different. She won't go where it hurts the most. Inside her heart. She feels abandoned. Her father leaving, me dying, Cole, her mom. Only Patsy remained and she didn't hang around herself to appreciate Patsy. Today she got what she needed from me and Cole. She was starving for attention for years. You got a perfect glimpse today. Sad."

"Will she stay away?"

"Yes. You have to trust me on that."

"I will, Colton. I'll take care of Patsy."

"I know that. Well, I'm going to clear out now and give you and Patsy some privacy."

"Thank you. And thank Cole for me, too. He sure left in a hurry."

"You're welcome. Cole wanted to make sure Oakley and True caught a good wave."

I nodded. These ghosts were a trip. I told Colton I'd be right back, I wanted to grab a jacket inside. When I came back out, he was gone. There was a black fireman's hat on the table. I picked it up. Captain SFFD Engine 41 was printed on the front. Inside was a note.

Cincinnatus,

Thanks for the hospitality. Thought you'd be interested to know that my firehouse was on Leavenworth Street.

All the best, Colton Vaughan

I had a good laugh and waited for Patsy.

Chapter Twenty-Seven

I didn't dream about prison anymore. It was only a matter of time before something went wrong. A slip of the tongue on Patsy's part. Maybe somebody follows her one night, leading them right here to the cabin. I couldn't risk it. I had to face this head on when Patsy returned tonight. Maybe it was time to go, alone. Even if traveling as a couple would draw less attention, we couldn't romanticize this whole thing. This was my life. If it put me in danger of landing back where I vowed never to go back again, what was the point? I could give up Patsy, even though I loved her. What I would never give up for anyone, was my freedom. I know Cole and Colton were on our side, but they were ghosts. And ghosts can't protect you from reality. Even if they said they could, I wasn't betting my life on it. I was getting into a funk thinking about Patsy and the future. I had to shake off the mood. It was unproductive. Maybe I could paint. I went outside for inspiration and fresh air to clear my head.

I started to line up brushes and mix paints. I had a canvas on the easel and a family of deer in the woods below posing in front of a redwood. Back to nature was in order. People were giving me a headache. That's when I noticed the magazine. Gallery Happenings from Sausalito. Someone left it on the outside table. The deer weren't going anywhere; they were happily munching on leaves and berries. I sat down and opened the magazine and glanced at the index. Patsy's name jumped out at me. "Former Alcatraz schoolteacher heads show at True Duncan Gallery." I turned to page 36 and there was Patsy's beautiful face staring back at me. She was posing in front of one of her watercolors. I read on: "Patsy Vaughan picked up right where True Duncan, surfer cum artist, left off, Duncan having lost her life doing what she loved best, surfing Cronkite's waves. 'True left her definitive stamp on this gallery,' Vaughan said, 'her peaceful and creative vibe is felt here by every artist that walks through the door. Some say True herself, visits from time to time. I certainly have felt her presence. Whether that's wishful thinking or strange to some, it's nice to think she never really left us. She was a good friend. I met her at a time of transition in my own life. I've always been interested in painting and after teaching the children of the warden and officers at Alcatraz, I was ready for something totally different, something I could be equally passionate about."

Patsy was as free as me. Neither one of us had anything further to do with Alcatraz. She ran a gallery, and I painted ghosts. I left the magazine open, so Patsy and I could talk about it when she came. Right now there were deer waiting for me to paint them. I picked up my paintbrush and dipped it into the brown paint. I suddenly smelled the ocean. I felt a slight tingle go through me. I turned around. There was True.

"Hey there, Cincinnatus. Nice day, isn't it? The waves at Cronkite were amazing."

"I thought you and Oakley caught your last wave, the other day?"

"Oakley did. She's gone. Nothing to worry about. With Patsy, too. I see you read the article. I just wanted to tell you in person. I knew you were worried. Oakley put you through the ringer. She could have easily set your mind at ease, but that wasn't Oakley."

"So, you'll still be floating around, so to speak?"

She laughed. "Yep. I can't explain the rush, surfing Cronkite again, knowing I have nothing to lose if I wipe out. It's beyond thrilling."

"I'll take your word for it. My one big thrill, my close call of a lifetime is good enough for me."

"Right. The escape. Had to be an incredible high, making it to the other shore. Not being found."

"A definite kiss the ground moment. But I can't take it for granted. I don't sleep with one eye open anymore, but I stay aware, let's just say."

"Makes sense. I'd love an Anchor, if you have one."

"Nice cold ones on the door of the fridge. Help yourself."

"Thanks. Want one?"

"Sure, I'd love a beer. That article made my day."

"Not me?" Was she flirting with me? I thought Oakley was her person.

"Icing on the cake, True." I concentrated on the deer while she grabbed us a few beers.

True sat on the couch on the porch and put her long tanned legs up on the wooden coffee table. "This really is a beautiful place, isn't it? Pity we all didn't meet up years ago. We could have had one helluva time." Her eyes were like seaweed tangled in wood.

"Cincinnatus? You okay?" She touched my foot with her toe and I felt electricity run straight to my man parts.

"Look, I'm glad you stopped by and all, but...."

"I'm making you feel things you don't want to feel?"

"You could say that. I'm only mortal you know. You're beautiful and tempting. And you're a flirt. But I love Patsy. And then there's the fact that..."

"That I'm into women?"

"Well, yes."

"Yeah, Oakley, she's hard to resist, isn't she?"

"I'm finished with all that."

"Good. Don't run out on Patsy. She'll stand by you, understand? Don't ruin it. You'll be fine. Well, gotta go, the waves are calling." With that she headed down the stairs and was gone. I wasn't sure why she showed up in the first place. To tell me to hang in there? What did she really know? More likely she was making sure Oakley didn't put in an appearance. These ghosts were fascinating to say the least, but I was looking for less complicated visitors in the future.

Besides painting and entertaining ghosts, my favorite time was when Patsy was here. Mornings when I woke, and she lay sleeping beside me were both puzzling and affirming. How did this good thing happen to me and how wonderful that it did. Each time I would quell the doubt by telling myself not to keep wondering why and simply go make a pot of coffee and let the day have its way. The concept of uncertainty was still an enigma to me. Despite the fact that I had hosted more of the dead than the living, none of it was by choice.

"Ah the smell of coffee and you. What else do I need?" Patsy came up behind me and wrapped her arms around me.

"Bottoms?" I felt her bare backside under the shirt she was wearing which was mine. She wriggled closer.

"Your coffee is poured, Patsy Vaughan."

"Thank you. How formal. And it's Patsy Billie Vaughan, if you don't mind."

"Could you possibly get any more fetching?"

"What an old-fashioned word. I like it. This coffee is heaven."

"Shall I fetch you some more? And an egg? Toast and jam, Miss Pasty Billie Vaughan?"

"You do, and I am all yours."

"Very fetching. You're on. This may be the best moment. This morning and coffee with you. Paradise."

"That's perfect, Cincinnatus."

"It's not original. Johnny Cash said it first. 'This morning, coffee with her.' His definition of paradise."

"You can't argue with The Man in Black. It makes me like him even more. You know my favorite song of his?"

"I Walk the Line?"

"Folsom Prison Blues."

I swallowed my coffee. Was Patsy messing with me?

"I would have thought Ring of Fire."

"Not as fetching," she smiled.

"Eat your eggs Miss Patsy Billie Vaughan, before I fetch you right here on this table."

"How frisky, Mr. Full of Surprises."

"Cute. Full of something, that's for sure."

Patsy went outside after breakfast and did a few yoga stretches facing the trees. Every time she reached skyward, I had a delicious view. I went out and wrapped my arms around her.

"No surprise there, Cincinnatus," she laughed, feeling my enthusiasm against her. She turned around and unbuttoned her shirt. She started to walk inside. I took her hand and pulled her back.

"Out here. You're beautiful in the sunlight."

"You're quite the nature boy, aren't you?"

If that bed on wheels under the moon and stars in Pacific Grove could be topped, this morning did the job. Sunlight breaking through a canopy of trees, birdsong, and an amazing woman called Patsy Billie Vaughan. If a bubble burst at this very moment and I was back in my cell on that inescapable island, I would have had the best damn dream of my life. But what if it was neither dream nor reality? What if Patsy and I were both ghosts after all? Perhaps my body was never found in the days or months or years following the escape. I couldn't exactly go ask anyone if they had seen me around. Even without the beard and long hair, I had become someone else. There would be no residue of Frank Morris anymore. No remnant of him anywhere on me. Too early for DNA, that was in the future back then. How do I know I didn't die that night? We were presumed dead, the Anglins and me. But here I am. Or here I think I am. This was not psychedelic drugs talking, nor booze. I was struck by love, not lightning. But suppose I was dead? Patsy too. Maybe Sink and Circe were ghosts too. Everyone else I'd met, who knew

Patsy, was dead; it wasn't an illogical conclusion. I didn't go to hell. I went to a cabin in the Oakland Hills. Patsy herself was the resident ghost. It was fitting, she'd worked at Alcatraz. She conjured me. Tried to save me. But I was beyond saving. I could never be free. So I became a ghost. It was a good story, but it wasn't the truth.

Chapter Twenty-Eight

1968

I took a walk down to the village to pick up a newspaper and some new brushes. The headline assaulted me. **Dr. King Murdered**. Martin Luther King Jr., a pacifist, and speaker of freedom and equality for all, was assassinated. The country was shocked and in mourning, as they had been for JFK. It seems those who strive to do good in this world are silenced by hate. A lone person may have pulled the trigger, but hate is a fever that spreads like wildfire. There was blood on more than one person's hands, no doubt about it. The killer was an escaped convict, who avoided the law for years. I felt no kinship with this person. I caused no one any bodily harm in my crimes. To take a life, unless in self-defense, requires a psychotic mind or a hateful depravity for humankind. I was sorry I had picked up a paper at all. But one cannot hide from the ugliness of life while enjoying its beauty. I was disgusted and put the paper down and went to get my art supplies and couldn't wait to get back to the cabin and be alone. The world had gone insane.

They were deep in conversation, heads bent over coffee cups; one of them smoking a cigarette. From a distance, I didn't know them. On closer look, I knew him. I read his poetry. He wrote of freedom, albeit for the African American people, but freedom is a subject that resonates with anyone denied it, for whatever reason. His poems spoke to me in prison. They spoke to me about dreams denied and how we must hold on no matter; "Hold fast to dreams..." he wrote. Or die yearning for the very freedom those dreams promised us, if only in our minds. Langston Hughes spoke to the people, for the people, and I was an admirer of him for that reason, as well as for his beautiful poetry. I was speechless but they took no notice of me. I watched them.

Did I know her? Her hands were animated and strong. She created art, she was a sculptor. Her art spoke to the people. It was life-size and powerful. People were her subject. Her name was Augusta Savage. Patsy was a huge fan. She was going to be so jealous to hear that Augusta Savage came to visit. And *him*. What a score.

They saw me. He stood up. "Please, stay where you are," I said. "Don't mind me. I'm honored you're here. I'll grab a coffee and join you, if you don't mind?"

"It's why we're here. I'm Langston Hughes, by the way," he reached out his hand to me.

"I know who you are," I met his eyes, and then hers. "You're Augusta Savage. As beautiful as your sculptures." I gushed, reaching out my hand.

"You know me then?" she replied, shaking my hand. I felt her strength.

"Of course. You're famous. Your sculptures are amazing."

She laughed and clapped her hands. "Well, isn't that something. Did you study me in school?"

"Not exactly. More self-taught. My girlfriend, Patsy, loves your work. Both of you. Boy, will she be sorry she wasn't here today."

"You do realize we're dead?" Langston deadpanned.

188

"Ghosts are my best visitors."

Langston shook his head "Are you serious? What kind of place are you running here?"

"Oh I'm very serious, Sir. And that's a very good question."

"Are you the painter?" Augusta Savage asked. "I mean now, of course."

Of course, she knew about me. They all did. And it was still unnerving.

"I am. But hardly one, compared to you, Maam."

"There are no comparisons. We are all variations. Whatever form our art takes. Please call me Augusta. Excuse me, what is your name?"

"Sorry. I'm Cincinnatus Jones."

"Well, Cincinnatus, you are a talented portrait artist. Quite a collection you have. I would love, I mean *we* would love, to hear all about your many visitors. Wouldn't we, Langston?"

Langston Hughes nodded and blew out a stream of smoke. "Undoubtedly," he said.

I poured more coffee for my distinguished guests and proceeded to tell them about my most incredible visitors, starting at the deep end with the Birmingham Angels. As I described in detail that unforgettable day and the voices of angels singing Amazing Grace in this very cabin, Langston Hughes and Augusta Savage were visibly in awe. I know they were wondering why these angels chose me. I still wondered about that myself. I may not have vocalized that wonder, but I felt it. And now as I felt it even stronger, an unworthiness came over me.

"Don't do that," Langston said.

"Sorry? Do what?"

"Try to figure out why a thing happened. It happened. You went to jail. You escaped. You moved on. Those murdered girls came here for a reason. You must realize that. Augusta can explain it better, I'm sure."

"Children are very in tune with the soul, Cincinnatus. And they are trustworthy with their hearts to people who listen. Perhaps there was a need in you as well. The small child you once were that still resides within you. Does that make sense or scare the living daylights out of you?" She smiled. "We all retain an innocence, if we dare look."

"I'm hardly innocent. I was just honored they came."

"That isn't what I meant."

Women were always calling me on my shit, I thought. "I know. And yes, there was that lost little boy I used to be, unloved and abandoned, get in line, yeah?"

"Do tell," Langston said, leaning forward.

"You're making me self-conscious."

"Give it up, man."

"Okay, okay. I didn't feel any of that innocence in myself when those sweet girls came here. I felt undeserving. Like when my mother came. I hadn't thought of her in years. It was a closed chapter. Suddenly, she was here."

"Mother issues. We all have them," Langston said.

"So I painted her. It was surreal. Like this whole ghost thing, don't you agree?"

"I find it so interesting and wonderful," Augusta said. "I must hear more."

And so we spent the rest of the afternoon and early evening, chatting away like old friends. The unlikely trio of us, trying to figure out the problems of the world and when there would there be equality of skin color and sex and humanity. We wouldn't figure out anything earth shattering because as Addie Mae herself said, "It could take a long time, maybe forever."

We talked about humble beginnings and all the reasons we don't become who we were ultimately meant to be, yet in spite of the variables, people can still succeed and even make a difference. Langston Hughes was a firm believer that adversity makes you fight harder and be more compassionate to others who are judged on the basis of their skin or sexual preferences.

Augusta Savage spoke about being doomed to hell by an unforgiving God for daring to depict people as she saw them, in all their hurt and passion and reality. Thankfully, she didn't accept that sentence and continued to create art that meant something to so many people.

"We're not here to be comfortable, Cincinnatus. We're here to make others uncomfortable and feel something. That is where the heart and soul connection happens. Art has always made us look when we'd rather close our eyes or turn a deaf ear."

I listened. One, because I didn't disagree and two, because brilliance doesn't need to be topped. Of course, I asked both esteemed guests to pose for portraits and they indulged me. After I fed them a good dinner of Patsy's picnic fried chicken and homemade potato salad and biscuits. We opened a good bottle of cabernet Patsy and I had picked up in Sonoma and were saving for the right moment. This was a special occasion in my opinion. The second bottle I saved for when Patsy returned, and I would tell her all about my visit with Langston Hughes and Augusta Savage. After dinner, Langston recited his Weary Blues. Augusta followed with a reading of James Weldon Johnson's "Lift Every Voice and Sing," which inspired her most famous sculpture, The Harp.

They had a request for me, though I had no particular talent with which to entertain or affect them. They, however, strongly disagreed with my self-loathing tendency. Langston said I had to overcome such a thing. I did as they asked. I retold the story of my escape, breaking my rule of not talking about that life-altering night. I was in the company of greatness and goodness, and I felt a burden lighten that I had no idea I was still carrying around. Langston decided The Anglins and I were the most hunted white men in history. I couldn't disagree with him, but I did say we were also the most determined to stay hidden for as long as we had and would continue to do so for as long as we lived. Augusta told me my freedom was my armor.

"No one can get close enough to overtake you, if you don't let them." I felt she had to be right. If as a small child, her father couldn't beat art out of her, she certainly knew about the value of a battle hard won.

"May we all remain as free as the birds, Cincinnatus, and as wild as the wind in the trees," Langston said. Simple words resonate best in a complicated world.

I thanked them both for coming and for making it one of the most pleasant and meaningful days I've ever had. Augusta accepted the compliment and a nice glass of Port by the fire, as the nights had gone chilly. Langston joined us, after insisting on helping me with the dishes. Imagine, Langston Hughes and I, doing the washing up in Patsy's kitchen. Not bad for a throwaway kid from the streets of D.C. My mother would be proud of me.

Augusta Savage kissed my cheek before she left. "You are the loveliest redeemed man I've met in a good while. Keep painting, Cincinnatus." I slept with a smile on my face and dare I say, a poem in my heart.

Chapter Twenty-Nine

I was not dead. My next apparition confirmed it. It was not Billie Holiday. I wanted it to be. In my imagination she sang for me. Patsy would have loved that. She had gone back to the gallery to do some work. I was putting the finishing touches on a portrait of Sink and Circe, having sketched them on their patio in Pacific Grove. I thought about moving inside, some weather was coming, I could feel it. But I had a rhythm going, so I put on a sweater and kept at it. I was losing daylight. The clouds were winning. The wind rustled the trees scattering leaves at my feet. I ignored it. My can of paintbrushes blew over. I kept painting. I touched my shoulder and felt static electricity and quickly drew my hand back. Must be the storm. The sky had turned dark. I could hear rumbling in the distance. I took the portrait from the easel and brought it inside. I went back out to clean up and closed the door before the rain started. I left my coffee cup outside on the gate. I'd go back out it in a minute. I needed to soak the brushes before they got hard. I stood at the sink watching the sky darken.

The first big drops started to come down and were splashing into my coffee cup on the gate. I had a flashback of Oakley finding the cup that day. A sign for her to come, she'd said. Was that really over? There was a crack of lightning and a loud boom. I jumped. My coffee cup was cracked in two and lay on the gate ledge, two halves collecting rainwater. I felt a chill in the cabin. The hairs on the back of my neck were tingling. I shut off the tap, set the brushes on an old towel to dry, and walked over to start a fire. I wished Patsy were still here. "Storms are romantic," she'd say. Oakley wouldn't agree, having lost her life on a night just like this.

The fire crackled, the wood was dry as a bone. The lights flickered. I lit a few candles. Patsy always kept a supply. She wasn't coming back tonight, and Oakley would not be visiting anymore. True either, Patsy had informed me the other day. Pity. I enjoyed both their company. I needed a drink. I poured a Jamesons over ice and sat by the fire, watching the storm through the porch doors. The whiskey warmed me and I started to doze off. A piece of wood popped and bounced off the screen. I kept the screen on in case I fell asleep. It was a habit I intended to keep. This was such a beautiful place, these hills dense with trees, they had to be protected. I thought of my visits with John Muir and Joaquin Miller, both stellar men. Had they rubbed off on me? I felt myself starting to drift. Fires are mesmerizing, and they burn, like love. Was there a screen for love? No, we were meant to be open to it all, the fireworks, the burn, and the inevitable hurt. I added another log and stoked the fire. I sipped my whiskey letting it warm my insides. The storm was perfect for a ghostly visit. I put on Billie Holiday. You Go to My Head serenaded me like an old friend.

Jesus came. No, I don't mean I died. Or had one of those moments. He was in the damn cabin. Maybe he was God, I didn't know the difference. He didn't wear a name tag. But it was him, trust me. I know a holy aura when I see one. I've seen the pictures and read the books. It was him. Plus, he sort of introduced himself. Not "Hello my wayward child," or anything so pretentious. Though he could have been, he was God. Instead, he said, "So you're the guy entertaining all my residents." Yep. No lie, he said that. And you won't believe what I said to God.

"I was expecting Billie Holiday." No, I didn't say that. I said, "Holy God." At which point he smiled, a light around his head shining. It was pretty amazing. He leaned forward and extended his hand.

"That's my name. Nice to meet you, Cincinnatus."

Did I offer God a whiskey? Maybe wine.

"Water is fine." I got up and got him a glass of water. He drank it down.

"Nice place you have here," God said.

"Thanks. I've been painting. Then the rain started."

God and I were making small talk. He wasn't wearing robes and he didn't have nails in his feet and no crown of thorns. He wore jeans and a sweater. He looked like any ordinary guy you'd see in Berkeley. Beard. Birkenstocks. He had nice toenails. He saw me noticing his feet.

"All that foot washing," he smirked. We both laughed.

This had to be a dream, I thought. God doesn't smirk.

"It's real," he said.

"Are you hungry?" I offered. It was what I did, I fed ghosts. But this wasn't any ghost. This was the Holy Ghost.

"I'm good," God said. "Though I've heard you're quite the cook. I do have a sweet tooth."

Figs came to mind. They seemed biblical. Not that I had any.

"I'll take a cookie," he said, eyeing Patsy's plate of chocolate chips on the counter.

I put the plate down on the coffee table in front of him. If people only knew, they would serve Toll House cookies instead of those tasteless wafers at Communion.

"Yeah, no. It's the unleavened bread thing. You can't fight centuries of habit." He held up his hands.

"I hear you." Of course I heard him, he was God. "I was wondering what you think of all my ghost visitors. Any favorites? I know you're not supposed to have favorites."

God took another cookie and chewed thoughtfully. "I like Sylvia Plath. Sad women fascinate me. She was so talented and so tormented, and her husband was a jerk. I'd love a coffee."

I loved this guy. And I didn't even believe in him. I stood up and started a fresh pot. This was already more enlightening than I could have ever imagined. I came back to the fire while the coffee brewed and looked at God.

"I liked Sylvia too," I said, "and I agree about Ted Hughes. But I thought suicide was against the church's law?"

"Whose church? I didn't make those laws. I forgive people. Who am I to judge?"

"Um, you're God."

"So what? The woman was in inconsolable pain. Now she isn't."

"But her kids were babies. Her mother missed her. The world was robbed of her poetry."

"She feels bad about that, but it was her story. Her choice."

"I have to say she was happy when she was here. I painted her."

"I know. So you see, we don't judge. It's not up to us."

I went to pour God a cup of coffee. I was reluctant to ask if he took it black or with sugar.

"Light, no sugar, thanks," he said. "You're perplexed, Cincinnatus. Tell me." He sipped the coffee I handed him. "Nice. I like a good strong cup."

"Aren't we all going to be judged in the end? By you?"

"Again, not my laws. I didn't write the bible. Or Vatican I or II. Men like to control things."

I was shocked by his answer. I started to laugh nervously.

"Does that mean I'm not going to hell? You know my prison record and all."

"I'm well aware of your transgressions against society. Have you learned anything? Are you remorseful? Do you plan on hurting anyone or lying your way through the rest of your life?"

Now I was nervous for real. Was God insinuating I was a liar or maybe a sociopath?

"I have been learning quite a bit since I found this cabin, and Patsy. Humility. Love. People, mainly the ghosts, and some living beings, have been blowing my mind."

"Then you're good. God forgives you."

"It's that simple? Don't you mean you forgive me?"

"I forgive you. What? Should I burn a bush?"

"You're funny. Can I say that?"

"You just did. And for that I shall wreak havoc on your life. A plague upon you. Just kidding."

"Are you really here?"

"I'm everywhere, haven't you heard?"

"But are you God?"

"I am."

"So why did you refer to yourself in the third person before? Are you Jesus? Is that why? I'm confused."

"Semantics. Imagine how I feel. All these people making stuff up and claiming I said it. It's crazy. And very annoying. Imagine their surprise when there's no pearly gates or seventy-five virgins and all that jazz. Well, actually there is Jazz. I'm a big fan."

I didn't know what to think. Or do. So I stood up and put on Kind of Blue. Maybe Miles would lend some clarity to this visit. I was certainly at a loss.

"Now that's good music," God said. "They should play this at church."

"Some people's church is a music venue. I hope that's not blasphemy?"

"Wherever two or more are gathered. That one *is* mine. What's wrong? You're not buying this?"

"I like it, don't get me wrong. I am not a believer, but this I can get behind. How is it no one knows this side of you?"

"*You* do. They eventually find out."

"What do you think about the Jesus freaks?"

"Cool. Maybe I'll make the cover of Time."

"I thought religion wasn't about hubris."

"You are paying attention."

"You inspired a movement. People dig you."

"I appreciate their passion. It's more about them, in the end."

"How so?"

"It's their time. The gatherings and soul searching belong to them."

"But it's in your name."

"What isn't? Again, *their* design."

"So, what's your real message?"

"Truth."

"Can you elaborate?"

"Live your truth. Show up. Be loving. Have empathy. Dream big."

"Sounds like a poster."

"Go for it. You can sign my name to it, if you like. I won't ask for royalties."

"You care to add five more? We can call it the New Ten Commandments."

God laughed. "Respect nature, love others, sing, make art, listen."

"What would Moses say?"

"He's not the boss. Anyway, it's not like I added another tablet. Just left out a few thous and shall nots."

"I wish I had recorded this conversation."

"I'll send you a tape."

"Really?"

"No. You'll remember. I have faith in you." God smiled. He had nice teeth.

"What about the other guys? You know, like Buddha."

"We're friends. It's not a contest."

"This is *religion* we're talking about. People lose their minds over it. Don't we need guidelines and rules?"

"The Ten Commandments, you mean? Good movie, by the way. Look, people are not obedient by nature. You didn't follow the rules."

"I was a criminal."

"You aren't one now. Do you have common sense? Integrity? Compassion? Forgiveness? Love for yourself and others? A desire to create good in the world as opposed to destruction?"

"Yes. I believe I do. Is it that easy?"

"No. It isn't meant to be easy. If it were, everyone would be doing it. You served your time."

"I escaped. I didn't finish my sentence."

"I'm aware. Nice swimming. Good planning. Nobody got hurt. Move on."

"Thank you. Or I should say, thank you, God."

"Whatever you like. The labels are your hang-up. I just want everyone to love one another and stop killing others in my name. Junking up the ocean. Decimating the forests. I'm really tired of it."

"I wish I could tell them. They wouldn't believe me."

"I know how you feel."

"What can I do?"

"Keep painting. Keep listening. Stop doubting. Love a little more. The world will catch on. You'll see. It takes time."

"Maybe forever?"

"Now those girls can sing, can't they?"

"The Birmingham Angels?"

"None other. You didn't take that visit for granted."

"I'll never get over it."

"Good. Don't."

"Why didn't you save them?" I realized I had gone out on a dangerous limb. I mean you don't question God.

"People don't understand the free will thing. I don't foresee killings or disasters. They happen because human beings are flawed. Hate is not in my wheelhouse. That is mankind.

They have to be held accountable. I never taught anyone to hate. That is an ugly side to the human condition."

"Then are we our brother's keeper?"

"To a point. You have to be willing to stand up for something."

"By the way, what's with all the kneeling in church?"

"Again, not my idea. Anything else?"

"Patsy thinks that you and Mary Magdalene might have you know, been...."

"Lovers? Jumped the broom? So what? Would it be better if I was without your earthly desires?"

"It's really none of my business."

"Exactly. So don't lose sleep over it. You don't seem to have any trouble in that area that you need to pray about." God was smirking again.

"Okay. I mean, thank you. Oh Christ. Sorry, I didn't mean to take your name in vain."

He laughed. God was enjoying himself at my expense.

"No worries. I'm not an egomaniac."

"Good to know. Why do people say they have a God complex?"

"Damned if I know."

"But aren't we made in your image?"

"In your case, maybe. We do look a lot alike."

It was my turn to laugh. "It's the beard and the soulful eyes."

"Good one."

"By the way, did you really rest on the seventh day?"

"Better if God was a workaholic?"

"Just wondering."

"I like a little down time like the next person. A little baseball, a good movie."

"You get television up there?"

"How do you think I found out about your escape?"

"You're God, the all-knowing."

"That's the Wizard of Oz. Good movie, too."

"Would you answer one more thing?"

"You want to know if I moved that boulder on the third day after they killed me?"

"I thought that was Jesus?"

"We're a Trinity. Think of us as triplets."

"But isn't it God the father, Jesus his only son, and the Holy Ghost?"

"Sounds like a band. In theory, yes."

"And you died for our sins."

"Pretty nice of me, huh? And look at the thanks I get. Hypocrites. Elitists. Slackers."

"Still, you forgive them?"

"It's my job. You're welcome."

"That wasn't my question though. But did you move it? The boulder?"

"All signs point to yes."

"That's a Ouija board answer."

"Now you are going to hell. Just kidding. You want to know if you'll remain free?"

"Yes."

"It doesn't work like that. Just don't take your life for granted."

"Right. Fair enough."

"It's been a pleasure, Cincinnatus. I'll send Billie down soon. We have a jam tonight, so it'll have to wait. Good stuff."

"Cool. I'm not going anywhere. Right?"

"How should I know?" God laughed. "No. You've got time. Don't blow it."

"I won't."

"By the way, Oakley says hi." God had a distinct twinkle in his eye.

"Please tell her I said hello."

"Will do. Thanks for the coffee and cookies."

"You're welcome." I noticed the rain stopped. "Was that you?"

"Yeah, the angels are done bowling." Again, the smirk. God was some character.

"Take it slow, Cincinnatus."

"You too, God." We both smiled.

"Feel free to paint me. Just don't put me on the wall with lights and candles."

"How about next to Babe Ruth?" I might have over-stepped our familiarity just then.

"Perfect."

The fire popped loudly. I turned to look. Nothing had escaped the grate. When I looked back, God was gone. The door blew open. I went outside to look at the sky. It was clear blue and my cup on the gate was in one piece again. Inside the cup was a rolled-up note. "How's that for a miracle?"

Chapter Thirty

I hadn't asked God about the Anglins. He didn't mention he had them on the other side. Did that mean they were safe in hiding? I hoped that was the case. I put the finishing touches on God's portrait, painting the mended coffee cup in his hand. I took a break to make a sandwich. My jazz station paused for a news bulletin. Bobby Kennedy was dead. Shot to death by a lunatic in the prime of his life, coincidentally while getting the nomination for President. Another soul doing good in the world. I wondered what God thought about that. These were crazy times. I had a feeling they were about to get crazier, but I had my own life to worry about. Mainly staying out of the spotlight and loving Patsy Vaughan.

I got busy planting herbs for Pasty in the wooden boxes I'd made for her. Give Patsy a bunch of basil or a sprig of rosemary and she was a happy woman. If this relationship ever went south, it was all on me. The woman was low maintenance, and I was one lucky bastard.

I was on my knees digging away and filling the holes I made with herb seedlings. The world could have passed me by and I wouldn't have given it a thought. I was lost in my planting and about as relaxed as a guy could be. I heard humming and part of a song. I knew it. It was a song of the times and for all those other times. Strange Fruit. The Lady, it had to be. It could be no other. It was only fitting I was on my knees.

"Nice plantings. You some gardener?" That voice, that face, I was once again, undone.

"Um, no. Hardly. Just some herbs. You're Lady Day." I stood up and brushed off my hands. Was I staring? Probably.

"Hah! Lady, indeed. You're sweet. Only some call me that. You're a fan I take it? You can relax, I don't bite. Only if provoked."

I smiled. "I'm a huge fan. My girlfriend, Patsy, well she would be over the moon if she were here. Her middle name is Billie, she was named after you. Her mother was a big fan." Rambling fool, that was me.

"Well then. I suppose I should be flattered. A nice white girl having my name. You know that's not my real name, right? My given name, anyway. I assume this Patsy person is nice enough?"

"She is. You'd like her. And she's black, by the way."

"Well ain't that something? Good for you. Have anything to drink? You know my name, so what's yours?"

"Cincinnatus. Frank, in a former life."

"Which is it?" I wanted to pinch myself. Billie Holiday was on Patsy's porch, as plain as the day. She was seemingly so alive, and she was very beautiful. Unscathed. No one would believe what ravaged her later, looking at her now. Life, bad men, drugs.

"Cincinnatus Jones," I said.

"Nice. Not your given name either. I like it. So, Cincinnatus, how about we have a drink and talk some."

"Please, come inside," I managed, holding the door for Lady Day.

I poured two bourbons, and we sat by the window, quietly sipping our drinks.

"You're a solitary man, am I right? Spent some time alone away from people. People judging you, abandoning you, not protecting you from bad people, and you aren't proud of what you did to survive. Am I warm?"

I didn't know if she was talking about her life or mine. I knew she had it rough from day one. Her life had been harder than mine. But as Patsy tells it, "It's all relative. We all suffer. It's arrogant to think we shouldn't." That was Patsy, my Buddhist philosopher lover.

"You all right?" Lady Day was addressing me.

"Oh sorry. I get distracted. No offense."

"Men don't usually have that reaction to me. You've hurt my feelings."

"I'm sorry, please, don't pay any attention to me. I was just thinking, life is hard."

"Yeah, it is, and then it gets harder, and you press on. Or die. Depends on the day. We have some things in common, besides the girlfriend with my name, huh?" She drained her glass and held it out to me. I hesitated for a second.

"I'm already dead, so my liver ain't your problem or mine. That's good bourbon. You have good taste, Cincinnatus. Is that your woman on the wall? Stunning. Intense passion, am I right?" Lady Day glanced up at Patsy's portrait. "Nice body, too." I refilled her glass. We clinked glasses, I sipped extra slowly, I wanted to remember every second of this visit.

"Yes, that's her. Patsy Billie Vaughan. I think she's beautiful. And she certainly is a passionate woman. Fiercely loves. I'm lucky."

You are a kind man, I see. A lover not a fighter. Not a mean bone in your body. No bad intentions. I know the difference, trust me."

"I've heard the stories. Sorry, no disrespect meant." Who would hurt this woman?

"All true, Cincinnatus, and then some. Life is hard, you're right. People take what ain't theirs. They beat what they can't control. They hate what is not familiar or they are truly evil. You believe that? That people can be so mean, so hurtful, and so blind to their own hate, that it comes out in very bad ways?"

"I do. And I think women have it worse. This is not a fair world. Never has been. But you survived. I wish you hadn't gotten sick. You had more to sing. To say."

"Don't feel bad for me. I was a bright candle and you know what they say? The brighter ones burn out fast."

"You were more like a firework, if you don't mind me saying. Your music, your performances, they're legendary."

"Thank you, Cincinnatus, now let's get down to why I'm here."

She was here because ghosts visited me. Famous ones, murdered ones, vagabond ones, soldier ones, family ones, and one divine one. But I'd play along.

"Prison." The word sounded more ominous when she said it.

"Yes, for a good while. I escaped."

"I know that. We both did time. They shut me up and threw me in jail, claiming drugs and bawdy behavior. Lies. Well sure, I did drugs and drank too much. So what? So did others. Men. No one locked them up. I was too much. Too much gets beaten. Too much gets locked away. What's your excuse?"

"I was a thief. I kept stealing and getting locked up and escaping. No drugs. No drink. Just stupid."

'You're still a thief. You stole that woman's heart, I'll bet my life on it." Lady Day laughed, shook the ice in her glass. I was riveted to her face. I took her glass and sat there staring like a fool. A smitten fool.

"Yes, for the crime of loving Patsy, I am guilty as charged."

"You don't want to give me another drink? You need me to sing or something?"

If I said "or something…" that would be disrespectful, but she was a ghost and she probably knew what I was thinking.

"Get the drink and we'll talk about all that."

Scape Ghost

I poured Billy Holiday another whiskey. I was way out of my league. I mean, come on, Billie Holiday? I couldn't shine her shoes.

I had another whiskey and we talked about men, racism, love, money, and how no one was protecting the children enough. She was a little girl once upon a time. Things happen. They shouldn't have. "I am not whining about my life, mind you, Cincinnatus. But you've got to tell the truth. Otherwise, you're part of the dirty filthy story, you hear me?" I heard her. She was neither high nor drunk and I got the distinct feeling she could drink me under the table. And I could hold my liquor.

"I understand. Lady Day. I do. I didn't have sisters, but I have Patsy now, and she didn't have it so great either. You mind if I start dinner?"

"Stay right here, man. Listen. I ain't talking about 'so great.' I'm talking downright bad shit that went down. A whorehouse. A little girl seeing way too much. My mama working for men and not paying attention. Yes, my voice saved me. Singing was my release from that prison, long before they shackled me and locked me up. And why me, for what men do their whole life and get away with? They drug and drink and sing whatever songs they feel like singing. Not me. 'Oh, not you, Billie. You got to stay quiet. Do what we tell you.' Life is not just unfair to women; it is damn insulting to our very souls. Where is the damn humanity?" I stayed quiet, shaking my head in agreement.

"Well? You got anything to say?" Billie Holiday was not looking too pleased with me.

"I don't like the ways of men either. I hated myself for a long time. I had time to think about who I was, who I wanted to become. Not a loser in prison my whole life. I wanted more. I'm horrified at what they did to you, those men, and society. You're a queen who should be honored and revered. Your music. Your voice. Your sadness touches people. Makes them feel. I know the opposite. I was dead inside for years."

She sipped her whiskey and stared into my eyes. "That woman, Patsy Billie Vaughan, she's a lucky lady. I'm no queen, you hear? Never wanted to be. I wore a flower, not a crown. I just wanted to sing like all the men were allowed to do and be left to it. Anyway, we can't go back. The dead are dead. My mother. Your past. What's got your mind unsettled? Certain visitors? What?"

"The living are my worry. The dead know me. I don't have to hide from them."

"Here's the thing, Cincinnatus, what have you to lose if a ghost comes and hangs out with you? Nothing. But a living soul, now that's something else entirely. They know you're here. One in particular, am I right? You have to make the truth be your freedom."

"Perhaps I'm not meant to be a free man."

"That's the stupidest thing I ever heard. Don't insult me."

Billy Holiday had touched a nerve.

"You're burning a lot of wood in that brain of yours. Care to share it?"

"It's the ghosts."

"Yeah, so? They're dead."

"No, they *saw* me. Made me feel things I didn't know I was capable of feeling. It was safer not to feel. I opened myself up, felt their pain. I feel compelled to do something, live differently, maybe, I don't know, change something for the good. Is that enough?"

"Look, I believe you are here for a special reason, Cincinnatus Jones. And when you realize that you can get on with it. Now let's eat, I'm starving."

"Lady Day, I would be honored to feed you. Thank you."

You don't get to have Billie Holiday in your living room. Or sitting at the table across from you. You just don't. She let me paint her. It had to be a dream, yet I knew it was not. Just as

208

none of the other visitations were. I did not believe I was chosen specifically, but it happened to me and that was tremendous. Would it mean anything in the grand scheme of things? I don't care right now. Dinner was ready. Meatloaf and mashed and green beans all served on Patsy's good dishes by candlelight. Afterwards, Lady Day serenaded me with her velvet voice. "Don't Explain" is my favorite Billie Holiday song. She knew, of course.

Chapter Thirty-One

When Billie Holiday came to Patsy's cabin, something changed. The very thing Lady Day had been trying to get through to me. *You know now, Cincinnatus, so what are you going to do about it?*

What I knew was the road and a body of water led me here to Patsy's cabin. I never needed to be Frank Morris again. Cincinnatus Jones was a free man. But he was not a real person. If the ghosts stopped coming, could I paint ordinary people? Like the living vets I'd met? Was that why I had survived the escape? Since coming to Patsy's cabin, I was safe. Could I be content? Was it time to tell Patsy the truth?

I wanted to explore more places with Patsy. Meet all her friends and go back to Sink and Circe's place and eat garlic and mushrooms and drink good wine and listen to music. Maybe we'd head to Alabama one day and meet Addie Mae's sister. I could give her the painting of the Birmingham Angels. They could go home. Life seemed to have a simple rhythm, but I was compelled to examine it for flaws. What about Patsy? Did she need more? Did she want kids? We hadn't talked about that. I hadn't ever thought about it, to be perfectly honest. And now that I was, it made me uncomfortable. Dredged up an unpleasant feeling. Passing on my genes to another person was terrifying. What if they got the bad seeds? The ones that drove me to thievery and prison. But that was my path, not another being's, whom Patsy and I would create together, with her amazing kindness and love. That was an encouraging thought. I'd leave it up to Patsy. If she wanted to consider children, I would too. If not, we would have one another to love for the rest of our time on the earth, and who knows, maybe beyond that. I didn't really believe that it was the ghosts talking. None of this could happen without me coming clean. The truth loomed over my head like a storm cloud.

Patsy had since given up her city apartment and opened a gallery in Berkeley. I got to see her more and that made me happier than a person really had a right to be. She sold my paintings, but not the ghosts. The ghosts we kept for our own personal collection. We turned the old shed behind the house into a painting studio. Patsy and I were the only ones who went inside. On the walls were my ghosts. And Miles Davis, the only living portrait.

We were having a glass of wine in the studio. Patsy was in a reflective mood.

"You hit the mother lode, Cincinnatus. All these amazing souls came to you and you alone. You do realize how extraordinary that is?"

"You're right. It doesn't get any better, does it?"

"It could, but I'm happy as we are."

"Don't you want kids? I don't mean that in an 'aren't you supposed to have them' way."

"I know. I'm not that delicate. And no, actually I never had the inclination. I had Cole to baby. And sometimes Oakley was quite a handful. I'm good."

I treaded easy because she had been through so much. Tough as she thought she was.

"But they're gone. There's no empty space there?"

"No. Because I have you." She wrapped her arms around my neck and kissed me deeply.

I knew then. Patsy was my destiny. She was the reason I survived the swim off Alcatraz. She was the reason no one found me all these years. The very reason I came to this cabin and the ghosts came to me. She was the catalyst for my rebirth and my muse. Some people spend a lifetime searching for that moment. Or they spend years pondering how to start their journey. Then they may wonder if it is the true one for them, after all. I was gifted the answer. But Patsy was not a ghost, therefore she did not know the real me. It was up to me to tell her. I had to trust her with the truth. I would never be truly free until I began that conversation. The conversation that would make me alive rather than merely living.

Chapter Thirty-Two

May 1970, eight years after the escape

It was a pretty day. One that compels a person to venture outside and breathe in fresh air and appreciate nature in all her glory. I took a thermos of coffee and a small sketch pad and pencil; in case I was inspired on my hike in the woods. The sun was pleasant and warm, and I closed my eyes for a minute, resting on a bench by an overlook. I lost track of time. Suddenly I had an urgency to get back to the cabin. I doubled my steps and made it in record time. I heard music and smelled incense burning. Strange. It was the middle of the week, and Patsy was at work. Someone was here. I stepped onto the porch.

There were six of them. Two girls and four guys. They were college kids, except one young man couldn't have been long out of high school. There was a Navajo blanket spread on the floor in the living room and they were playing Scrabble. I didn't see such a blanket or any games in the cabin before. Patsy preferred listening to music and watching old movies. Who were these kids in the cabin?

"Hey man," one of them said. A pretty young woman with flowers in her hair. "Excuse me, I mean, I hope you don't mind, Mister. We were just taking a break between classes and the Common was closed."

The Common? "You go to school nearby?" The only college anywhere near the cabin was Berkeley. And they sure didn't walk here from there. "Are you Berkeley students?"

"Kent State," the pretty one with flowers said. She came over and gave me one.

"Flowers are better than bullets," she said. My heart went through the floor.

"You okay, Mister? You look pale. How about a Coke?" She opened a small metal cooler and drew out a cold bottle of Coke, opened it with a bottle opener attached to the cooler and handed it to me. "Allison," she extended her hand. "Allison Krause." An honor student. She dared to have an opinion about the war.

I felt faint. I chugged the Coke. One of the young men stood up.

"Thanks for letting us use your place for study hall. We were just taking a break. Our campus was closed, too. Philip Lafayette Gibbs, Sir," he shook my hand firmly. "I'm studying Law at Jackson State."

I sat down in the nearest chair. "Mississippi?" I managed, looking at the other young black man on the blanket. He nodded at me and stood up.

"I don't go there yet, I'm still in high school. I was coming home from work. Not sure what happened. But here we are. James Earl Green, Sir," he said, shaking my hand. My heart lurched. He was a baby. "Do you play Scrabble?" he asked me.

I scratched my head. Scrabble? "Don't you know who you are?"

"Just a boy, trying to live, Mister." He cast down his brown eyes.

Another pretty girl stood up, "Of course we do, Mister. I'm Sandy. Sandra Lee Scheuer, I go to Kent State." Another honor student. Crossing the Common on her way to class. Gunned down.

Students. Kids. Their lives extinguished. How was I going to do this? Was this my penance?

"I'm Cincinnatus. Cincinnatus Jones. I live here. By myself. I paint. The moon, mostly. Trees, and occasionally people. I didn't go to college. I went somewhere else."

"Prison, right? If I were a lawyer already, I could defend you." The young law student from Mississippi. A father. A husband. Murdered.

"I escaped from Alcatraz."

"Then your name is not Cincinnatus Jones, is it?" The dead law student said.

"It's Frank Morris," said another young man. "You're famous."

"You're right. About the name, anyway. But I am not that person anymore."

"No disrespect, man. I'm Jeff. Jeffrey Glenn Miller. I go to Kent State." Taking a stand against war and injustice. His whole life ahead of him. Murdered.

"None taken, Jeff. Please call me Cincinnatus. I am trying to rectify my mistakes."

"Cool," he said. "Everyone deserves a second chance."

There was a loud bang. I jumped. A car backfiring. They all looked at me.

"Jumpy, Mister Jones? Must be from being in jail. I'm Bill. William Schroeder. I go to Kent State, as well." Bill wanted to make the world a better place. Not protesting got him killed, anyway. The day a massacre was disguised as a necessary police action. I was feeling nauseous.

"Prison. I was in prison, not jail," I corrected him. "There's a difference. Like between a car backfiring and a shot fired." Oh Christ, what was I saying? What would my vet friend have to say about this visit? He hated war, I knew that much. These kids weren't in a war and they were all dead.

"We don't know anything about that, Mister," Allison said. "We're peace and love, not violence."

And look where that got you, I thought. No one cared what you believed. They shot into a crowd and killed you. Unarmed kids. Shot like ducks. What was I supposed to say? The country had gone crazy.

"Do you want us to leave? We've obviously imposed. We've upset you," Bill said.

"No, it's not you. It's what happened to you. It makes no sense. You were all going to make something of yourselves. And now you cannot. They made sure of that." I put my face in my hands. I felt a hand on my shoulder. The energy shot right to my heart. Maybe I'd have a heart attack and that would be the end of these visitations.

"Breathe deeply and slowly, Cincinnatus. There you go. You're fine. I had a wife in labor, and a baby at home, in Mississippi. I have some practice at the breathing thing," Philip smiled at me. What a kind face. I hate this world. Another child won't know his father. For what? A fucking protest?

"I'm fine," I told them. "Why don't you tell me about yourselves? I imagine you didn't know one another until after... Anyway, I mean do you have any idea what state the country is in over this? You were not all protesting, I know that. And even if you had been, the response was inappropriate, utter madness." I shook my head. They were all so beautiful. And alive.

The flower girl smiled. She was protesting. A peaceful protest. Then they were murdered.

"The war in Vietnam has killed so many. But that's war. You should be able to be on college campuses without being in danger of being shot. It was an insane response to a student protest. This is what we've come to, killing kids? I'm sick over it," I said.

"Thanks, Cincinnatus," Sandy said. "We don't understand either. We all just met up recently."

"Will you stay? I'll make you dinner. What do you like to eat?" I embraced my new visitors. Hopefully they would let me paint them. Mostly so I'd have proof of their visit and Patsy wouldn't think I'd gone off the deep end. Seems it was too late for that.

"We'd eat anything, thanks," Philip said.

"Burgers and fries, then." Thankfully, Patsy and I had stocked the freezer.

"Sounds groovy," said the flower girl. "You're very kind. Tell us about your escape. We'd dig hearing about it. So brave of you to swim that bay at night. Cool."

It was the least I could do. I didn't know why these kids came to me, but whatever the reason, I was going to let it play out. As if I had any other choice. So I told them. But somehow, they already knew.

They wanted to eat outside on the porch. They liked the trees and the way the sun set in the hills. They mentioned how lucky I was to live so close to nature and when I told them I saw a double rainbow one day, they thought that was the luckiest thing. "Good omen," they said. They were nice kids. They'd had futures. Families. Until fear and control and certainly, in the case of Jackson State, racism too, had a part in their murders. When was the country going to wake up? Why did the National Guard fire their rifles into a crowd on a college campus? Could they not have chosen another way to disperse what they were told was a violent protest, which it was not. Even if it had been rambunctious at best, how do you start shooting unarmed people? Did Nixon think he was God, ordering the National Guard to shoot students? Both campuses, Kent State and Jackson State were fired upon, like an act of war. Both campuses were attacked by what amounts to soldiers or police, shooting an enemy that is unarmed. How was this okay with anyone? How do you shoot up a dorm in Mississippi when you do not know what the hell is going on? Two innocent lives were taken. For what? Was the country safe now? Because six young students were shot down in cold blood? It was infuriating and sickening. I pushed my burger away and sat back.

"Not hungry, Cincinnatus?" Philip asked me.

"I cannot figure out why it happened and why you're here now. The world is such a fucked-up place, excuse my French. We are expected to go on business as usual."

"We don't have any answers, either" Philip looked into my eyes. "Things surely have to change. Maybe you could talk about us. Get people to see us as regular people, not different because our hair is long or some of us have darker skin, or we go to college and some of us disagree with the status quo and want to change the world. Maybe we just want to get a good education and make a contribution, see a better situation for our kids. We are all the same underneath. I don't see a problem. Why do they?"

"Well said, Philip. I would like to paint you all. Sketch you first, if you wouldn't mind. I won't forget you, trust me on that. I want to remember your faces and remind myself that goodness exists. I have to stay hidden, you understand, but I will remember this day always."

The girl with the flowers came over. "We would love that. Maybe you could share it with our families one day. They don't know why we were killed, either. You could be brave again. Like when you escaped."

I wanted to scream. She was beautiful and alive and her name was Allison. But she wasn't alive because they killed her.

"Let me get my sketchpad, " I said. "In case you have to go."

"Where would we be going? We have all the time in the world now. Plus, it's kind of nice up here," Jeff said, "Maybe we'll see a rainbow."

"Yeah, and we can sing songs," Allison suggested.

"I'd like to play a record for you," I said. I went inside and turned on the stereo. I turned up the volume. There was no

Scape Ghost

other way to listen to this song. Nina Simone's voice followed
me out to the porch.

> "Alabama's gotten me so upset
> Tennessee made me lose my rest
> And everybody knows about Mississippi Goddamn
> Alabama's gotten me so upset
> Tennessee made me lose my rest
> And everybody knows about Mississippi Goddamn
> Can't you see it
> Can't you feel it
> It's all in the air
> I can't stand the pressure much longer
> Somebody say a prayer
> Alabama's gotten me so upset
> Tennessee made me lose my rest
> And everybody knows about Mississippi Goddamn
> This is a show tune
> But the show hasn't been written for it, yet
> Hound dogs on my trail
> School children sitting in jail
> Black cat cross my path
> I think every day's gonna be my last
> Lord have mercy on this land of mine
> We all gonna get it in due time
> I don't belong here
> I don't belong there
> I've even stopped believing in prayer
> Don't tell me
> I tell you
> Me and my people just about due
> I've been there so I know
> They keep on saying "Go slow!"

221

Nanci LaGarenne

But that's just the trouble
"Do it slow"
Washing the windows
"Do it slow"
Picking the cotton
"Do it slow"
You're just plain rotten
"Do it slow"
You're too damn lazy
"Do it slow"
The thinking's crazy
"Do it slow"
Where am I going
What am I doing
I don't know
I don't know
Just try to do your very best
Stand-up be counted with all the rest
For everybody knows about Mississippi Goddamn
I made you thought I was kiddin' didn't we
Picket lines
School boycotts
They try to say it's a communist plot
All I want is equality
For my sister my brother my people and me
Yes you lied to me all these years
You told me to wash and clean my ears
And talk real fine just like a lady
And you'd stop calling me Sister Sadie
Oh but this whole country is full of lies
You're all gonna die and die like flies
I don't trust you any more

Scape Ghost

You keep on saying "Go slow!"
"Go slow!"
But that's just the trouble
"Do it slow"
Desegregation
"Do it slow"
Mass participation
"Do it slow"
Reunification
"Do it slow"
Do things gradually
"Do it slow"
But bring more tragedy
"Do it slow"
Why don't you see it
Why don't you feel it
I don't know
I don't know
You don't have to live next to me
Just give me my equality
Everybody knows about Mississippi
Everybody knows about Alabama
Everybody knows about Mississippi Goddamn
That's it!"

"Wow," said James Earl. "I never heard anything like that."

"Nina Simone," I said, "She was brave enough to sing what so many felt. People are angry, and rightly so. This music will stay with us for many years. A reminder of unrest, injustice, and hate. And the ultimate reminder, right?"

"I know, sometimes you have to take a stand," Jeff said.

"Yes. And you shouldn't have to die for it," I said, going back inside. The sounds of Crosby Stills and Nash followed me this time.

"Tin soldiers and Nixon coming,
We're finally on our own.
This summer I hear the drumming,
Four dead in Ohio.

Gotta get down to it
Soldiers are cutting us down
Should have been done long ago.
What if you knew her
And found her dead on the ground
How can you run when you know?

Gotta get down to it
Soldiers are cutting us down
Should have been done long ago.
What if you knew her
And found her dead on the ground
How can you run when you know?

Tin soldiers and Nixon coming,
We're finally on our own.
This summer I hear the drumming,
Four dead in Ohio."

Chapter Thirty-Three

I couldn't sleep. Whatever chasm in my heart the Birmingham Angels cracked open, the Kent State and Jackson State kids deepened with a pulsing anguish I could not silence. I wanted to talk to them again, hear more about their hopes and dreams. The ones that were ripped out of them by gunfire, on a college campus, not on a battlefield. I turned on the lamp and looked at the sketch. Six beautiful faces stared back at me, a double rainbow behind them. I couldn't wait to paint them. I would make them alive again, if only for a moment.

I went inside to see who wanted breakfast. The Indian blanket was folded on the couch. The extra pillows piled on the floor. The only evidence they were there. I started a pot of coffee and walked outside to the porch. The sun was shining, the trees were standing as green and majestic as ever, and birdsong serenaded me. How could everything be ordinary when only yesterday six kids with everything to live for were dead? Where was the sense in that? We had walked on the moon, yet we couldn't figure out how to act humanely when young people disagreed with the status quo. A protest was turned into a massacre, why? And we called other societies barbarians? We had such a long way to go in evolving. I walked inside to get a coffee. I couldn't fix such a Sisyphean problem, but I could paint those college students like they were alive again. I would remember them for the rest of my life. They taught me something. Tolerance. Joy. There was no color, no hate, only love and possibility emanating from their spirits. Imagine what a world that believed in that could become.

I took my coffee outside and sat down, suddenly feeling exhausted. It was then I noticed the flowers. A chain of daisies on the bench by the table where the college kids had their meal yesterday. *Flowers not bullets.* Underneath the flowers was a black and white composition notebook. I opened the cover. There was a letter addressed to me.

Dear Cincinnatus,

Thank you for a spectacular day. For a brief moment we felt alive. Remember us and never stop telling the truth. It's the only way to be free. Peace and Love always, Allison, Jeffrey, William, Sandra, Philip, James Earl

I got up to set up my easel. I had a mission. To paint six souls for posterity and tell Patsy the truth.

The painting of the college kids might be my best yet. The double rainbow shone down on them illuminating their faces, making them appear larger than life. Ironic, since they were all dead when I painted them. I felt satisfied the painting was done, but sad at the reality. I went inside and put on a Nina Simone album. Pastel Blues always managed to soothe me. I closed my eyes and that is the last thing I remember until I smelled perfume.

She was wearing sandalwood and honeysuckle and something that was in the tea Patsy liked, Earl Grey. Bergamot, that was it, a hint of orange. But why was she here? She was no ghost.

"What do I have to do to get a cup of coffee around here?"

"Nina Simone?"

"Well, I'm not Santa Claus. Who are you?"

She didn't know me because she wasn't dead. "Cincinnatus Jones. Care for an espresso?"

"Yes, I do. Nice place you got here." She followed me into the kitchen.

"Thank you, it belongs to my girlfriend."

"Treat her right. Are you the painter?" She was looking at my painting of the college kids.

"I am. I don't know why they came here."

"We don't explain art, we create it. Like music. We're compelled to express feelings and evoke those in others. What's the mystery?"

"They're dead. The kids in the painting. They were shot at Kent State and Jackson State. They came here. I talked to them. I painted them. I played your song for them, "Mississippi Goddamn.""

"Right. You dead too?" She lit a cigarette and watched me.

"No, I'm alive, like you. But I'm not as free as I look."

Nina Simone laughed so hard I thought she'd drop her espresso cup and cigarette. "Big white man like you ain't free? That's rich. You live in this world or what?"

"I escaped from prison." Why I was telling this to Nina Simone who wasn't a ghost, was beyond me.

"Are you dangerous? I don't get that from you. I'm not turning you in if that's what you're worried about. So these murdered college kids came to you? Must be for a reason. Or do you often get visited by dead people?"

"All the time, as a matter of fact. I paint ghosts. Let me show you."

We walked to the studio out back and I showed Nina Simone my collection. She was quiet, taking each painting in and looking at me sideways, until she got to the Birmingham Angels. Then she stopped.

"You gotta be kidding me. Are you saying these babies came here? After they were blown up in a church? And they looked like this? Lord, I need a drink."

We walked back to the cabin and I poured two bourbons on the rocks. I handed her one and she sat down by the fireplace. "You believe in God, Cincinnatus?"

"I don't know. I'm considering it." I sipped my bourbon.

"How else can you explain what you've seen? Unless you're a raving lunatic. I don't think so. I don't know why, but I believe you. But you can't share these paintings, or you will be labeled certifiable or found out to be a fugitive, yes?"

"Let's just say it would invite unwanted attention. Besides, I plan to give this one to Addie Mae's sister one day. And there's something else."

"They sang for you?"

"How did you know that?"

"It's only natural. They were in a choir. What did they sing?"

I handed her the sheet music. "Of course, Amazing Grace. Angels, indeed."

"I would have traded places with them. So they could be alive again."

"That's noble, Cincinnatus. It doesn't work that way. The world has gone crazy. I'm as angry as you about it. That's why I write the songs I do. I'm not masking my feelings. What's the use? Sometimes there's nothing for it but to scream." She held out her glass.

I poured Nina Simone another drink and one for myself. "Any chance you'd sing for me?"

She laughed. I may have overstepped my bounds. "You cook? I could eat. And then you may get lucky. With a song, that is. Not that I don't find you attractive."

"I happen to be a good cook. And thank you, I'm flattered. Patsy might make an exception for you, she's a big fan."

"Your woman has good taste."

I smiled like a schoolboy and got busy cooking while Nina Simone hummed a tune and drank her bourbon by the fire.

228

"This your mama's recipe?" We were sharing a meal like it was an everyday thing.

"No. A fellow inmate. My mother gave me up."

"Sad story. Get in line. You got a second chance here, man. I've seen bad men. You aren't one. You have a choice to make. What's the truth and what's a damn lie. You may not have chosen these ghosts, but they chose you. You gotta figure out why. No more hiding. It's soul-baring time. You up for that?"

"Room for dessert?"

"Are you changing the subject?"

"No, I promise. I heard every word."

"Then you're an enigma, because men don't listen in my experience. What are you serving?"

"Peach pie."

"Enigma." She shook her head. "I'll take an espresso. And then you'll get your song."

"My Baby Just Cares for Me?"

"Good choice. After we have ourselves a moment of silence for those dear girls in Alabama and the students in Ohio and Mississippi. There's a lot of work yet to do, Cincinnatus. It could take a very long time."

"Maybe forever."

"That's the goddamn truth."

Nina Simone sang for me. It was better than sex. It was fucking spiritual. She let me sketch her. I was high and it wasn't the bourbon. "Close your eyes, Cincinnatus, and imagine yourself a free man for the rest of your life. Then make that happen."

I did as I was told. When I opened my eyes, she was gone. Of course she was, she wasn't there in the first place. Nina Simone was no ghost. I'd had another dream. I got up to make myself an espresso. My sketchpad was on the counter. A beautiful drawing of Nina Simone stared back at me. I vaguely remembered doing it. But she couldn't have been here. I had imagined the whole thing. It was the shock of the dead college kids. I took my espresso over to the fireplace and stoked a fire

I didn't remember starting. Maybe I was losing my mind. I went to put my cup on the side table and noticed an empty espresso cup there. I picked it up and underneath found a sheet of notebook paper folded. I opened it. It was song lyrics.

Peaches and Whiskey
It makes no sense this senseless hate
You made your choice, there's no debate
To keep it real you cannot lie
Truth, my man, will never die.

You cannot hide behind the pain
I feel your skin and where you've lain
You're no better, you're no worse
I'm here for love, I'm not your nurse.

Feed me peaches and whiskey
Scream my name in your dreams
Feed me peaches and whiskey
It's as tough as it seems
Feed me peaches and whiskey
Give me real, let it bleed
Feed me peaches and whiskey
I'm exactly what you need.

How much bourbon had I drank? Enough to write song lyrics? This was a strange cabin from day one, so who knows? I put on Pastel Blues and got to work painting Nina Simone from my sketch. Patsy would love it. I heard a loud noise coming from outside. It sounded like howling. There were no wolves up here, as far as I knew. I went out to the porch and looked up towards the top road. Plain as day with glowing yellow eyes was a coyote. I opened the porch gate, and he took off like a shot. I heard howling again. I thought of what Nina Simone said, in my dream. "Sometimes there's nothing for it but to scream." I took a deep breath and let out a good goddamn howl of my own.

Chapter Thirty-Four

My deadline was approaching. The day I spilled my guts to Patsy. I had decided. There was no turning back. It would be the end of us or the beginning. I felt relieved. I'd been carrying this secret for eight years. Only the ghosts knew me. And Miles and Nina in my dream. It was time Patsy knew. The worst she could do was stop loving me. She wouldn't turn me in, we had too much of a connection. On some level I think she needed me as much as I needed her. And I never needed anyone until I met Patsy. Loving her was easy. Trusting anyone but myself was the hard bit.

I took a good hike to Shepherd Canyon on the old railroad trails. I needed to clear my head and get right with myself. I thought of Cab and Haggard and how we talked about "getting right with life." I wanted that so bad I could taste it. I was willing to do penance and atone for my past, not publicly of course, but to Patsy. The more I thought about it, the more Patsy was the one person who might understand. She had been to Alcatraz. She told me she felt sorry for the hopelessness of the inmates there, the desolation of that cold dark prison. Would she empathize with how badly I wanted to be free? But I'd taken my freedom, I didn't earn it. Was I earning it now with each ghost encounter? Or was I deluded into thinking I had found redemption among the dead? Were they my scapegoat? Perhaps I was not brave at all, but a coward with a fantasy life. Had I embodied Cincinnatus Jones, or did he embody me? Patsy had as much invested in me being Cincinnatus Jones as I did. She never knew

Frank Morris and she never would. He was the real ghost. As long as I was free, he could never haunt me.

I did a few sketches of an old, abandoned railroad car. It would make a good painting. Sink might like to add it to the Trainhoppers he bought. This time the painting would be a gift. Shakespeare said, "The meaning of life is to find your gift. The purpose of life is to give it away." I packed up my thermos of coffee and sketch pad and headed back for the hills. Patsy was staying in the city; she had an artist's show to attend. I had the rest of the day and night to myself, as far as I knew. I learned not to take anything for granted at that cabin in the trees. Surrender was the prelude to the difficult conversation. I had come to the place of truth. I was not afraid.

I heard the bass as I walked up the steps to the cabin. Then drums. I opened the door. I heard the voice and recognized the song, "It's Your Voodoo Working," a Charles "Mad Dog" Sheffield original. I knew who introduced him to the circuit, I followed the Blues that Oakland was famous for, back when it was known as the Harlem of the West. Slim Jenkins and his Cafe and Supper Club, the toast of Oakland's Seventh Street in the 40's and 50's. Two men were sitting at Patsy's kitchen table, drinking whiskey, one smoking a fat cigar. They looked at me and kept talking. I got myself a bourbon and took a seat at the kitchen counter. I sipped my drink and listened to the swampy zydeco sound of "Mad Dog's" Blues. If tomorrow's confession to Patsy went south, this was a perfect last night. The music stopped for a beat or two and then started up again with "I Would Be A Sinner." Charles Sheffield's resonating voice filled the room. *"If I said I wouldn't miss you, if I said I wouldn't cry, I would be a sinner, because its a sin to tell a lie..."* That tune was spot on for my mood.

"This your place?" The man with the cigar was talking to me.

"Yes, Sir. Well, it's my girlfriend's, really." I suddenly realized who he was, but his drinking partner? I had no clue.

234

"Good for you," he said. "You like 'Mad Dog?'"

"I do. You're Slim Jenkins, aren't you?"

"How do you know that? You get down The Bottom much?"

"No, can't say I ever had the chance. I heard it was something to see."

"You heard right. Nightclubs not your thing?"

"I was incapacitated, you might say."

"You mean *incarcerated*, don't you?" The other man at the table spoke up.

"Yes. I made a career out of it, unfortunately," I said.

"Coat here, knows a thing or two about careers, ain't that right, Coat?"

"Raincoat Jones, at your service," he held out his hand and I shook it. And you are?"

"Cincinnatus Jones. No relation."

Slim Jenkins laughed. "Good one. That ain't your real name, is it?"

"No Sir. I'm trying to start over."

"Can't fault a man for that. Especially one with good taste in music and whiskey."

"And women," said Raincoat Jones. "That your girl-friend in the painting?"

"Yes, Mr. Jones. Pasty Billie Vaughan is her name."

"Call me Raincoat. She's a looker. Named after Lady Day?"

"Yes, as a matter of fact she is, Raincoat. Her mama was a big fan."

"Listen, we can sit here drinking whiskey all night, but a man's gotta eat. You like ribs, Cincinnatus?"

Does a bear shit in the woods? "Yes, Sir. I wish I could have tasted the ones you served at your place."

"This might be your lucky day, boy, we got a whole mess of food to put out. Check your oven, there's ribs, chicken, and enough biscuits for a small army. Potato salad in the fridge."

I put out the spread Slim brought and we ate while listening to the best Blues I ever heard. I wondered if they'd leave the records behind when they left. Patsy would be thrilled. I was stuffed. Slim was pouring whiskeys all around. For a guy who didn't drink much before, I had become a fan of a good pour. Everything in moderation, isn't that what they say?

"There's pie, too," Slim said. "Why don't you save it for your lady friend? You expecting her back soon?"

"Tomorrow. It's kind of a big day," I said, the whiskey doing the talking.

"You proposing?" Raincoat asked. "Or you hitting the road?"

"Neither. I'm telling the truth."

Slim shook his head. "Then you better drink up. The truth may set you free, but if you get that lovely woman's nose out of joint, you're gonna wish you were dead, never mind back in prison."

"Listen to Slim," Raincoat said. "Maybe you better get some champagne and flowers. A little jewelry wouldn't hurt." The two men had a good laugh. They might have a point.

"Patsy can handle it. I think she may already suspect I am not who I said I was before. She's a forgiving soul."

Raincoat laughed. "I knew a guy who said that. Next thing I heard he was dead. His woman didn't appreciate the truth. You better think long and hard about what you're planning to say. This Patsy Billie Vaughan, does she have a gun?"

"Actually, she does. But I don't think she'll use it on me."

"Famous last words. Maybe you should eat your pie now," Slim said, draining his whiskey.

"I'd rather sketch you both, if you don't mind?"

"Better than a wanted poster," Raincoat said, striking a pose.

"Where did you get that jacket? You're not a military man, I take it?" Slim pointed to Rhodes' Army jacket on the hook by the door.

236

"A friend gave it to me. I greatly admire those who served. I made other choices. Mistakes, since we're telling the truth here. You were in World War I, weren't you? I read that somewhere."

"Yes, son. War can do things to man's head. Same as prison, I imagine. You have to move on. I suppose you know that by now. What's holding you back?"

"The truth."

"Then you're still in prison."

"I'm breaking out tomorrow."

"Now that's more like it. Let's drink to that."

We had one more whiskey and listened to Pee Wee Crayton's "Blues Before Dawn," before we all turned in for the night. When I got up in the morning, my guests were long gone and my head was not throbbing, considering the whiskey I remember drinking. The kitchen was tidied up, whiskey glasses back on the shelf, and a cherry pie on the counter. I made a pot of coffee and checked Patsy's record player. Pee Wee Crayton's album was on the turntable and a stack of Blues and Jazz on the coffee table. Can you charm a woman with cherry pie and the Blues? I'd find out soon or die trying.

Chapter Thirty-Five

I walked down to the village to get the items Raincoat and Slim suggested. A bouquet of irises, a pair of silver hoop earrings and a bottle of Pinot Noir from Napa that Patsy liked. She wasn't a champagne drinker. I probably should have stopped into the church and lit a candle, but I didn't. I was a liar not a hypocrite.

When I got back to the cabin, I put the finishing touches on a loin of pork I was marinating. I thought if I replicated the dinner Patsy made me the first night we met, the day she let me stay in her cabin, it might give me a leg up. While the loin roasted, I peeled potatoes and set them on to boil, made a fire and set the table with Patsy's favorite haint blue tablecloth. I set the irises in the center in a white metal pitcher. All we needed was music. And a Hail Mary. Maybe I was a believer after all. Bille Holiday was in order. How could I go wrong with Lady Day? The strains of "I Don't Stand A Ghost of A Chance With You" filled the cabin as Patsy walked in. Timing is everything.

Patsy took off her coat and hung it next to Rhode's Army jacket. She looked around. "Is it my birthday?"

I gave her a kiss. "No, but hopefully I'll have the chance to do this for you again."

"That sounds cryptic. Did you have a special guest today? This isn't a guilt dinner, I hope? Don't tell me Oakley came back?"

"Nothing like that." I handed her a glass of Pinot Noir. We clinked glasses. "To the truth," I said.

"Oh dear. Now I'm worried." Patsy took a sip and put down her glass. "Your wife finally come looking for you? I knew this was too good to be true."

"Patsy, I have no wife. What I have is a past I am not proud of and it's time to come clean."

"Just say it, Cincinnatus, I'm not good with suspense."

"My name is not Cincinnatus Jones."

"Of course it is."

"No. I escaped from Alcatraz. I'm Frank Morris. I mean on paper, anyway. That man has been dead for almost nine years." I let out a breath and waited. Pasty calmly sipped her wine. The fire popped. Billie Holliday was singing "Don't Explain." I put another log on the fire. If Patsy didn't say something soon, I'd know she was done with me. The woman was never at a loss for words. But what could she say to this confession of confessions?

"I knew one of you survived. Remember I said so the night we met?"

"Did you hear what I said? There is no Cincinnatus Jones. I'm sorry."

"Of course there is. You just said Frank Morris is dead. So bury him and let's get on with it."

"What are you saying? You're not shocked? Why aren't you angry? Did you know? Did one of the ghosts tell you? Are you a ghost, Patsy?"

"That's a lot of questions. I'm not shocked, or angry. I suspected for quite some time. The ghosts don't come to me, only to you. Oakley coming here years ago was a one-off thing. And no, I'm not a ghost, Cincinnatus."

"When did you know?"

"The first night. When we made love. Nobody loves with that intensity that has recently been intimate with someone. I worked on that Island. I know a little bit about deprivation of inmates. You like women, I know that. I may not have been the first after your escape, but let's just say that night, something

240

happened. To both of us. Besides sex. A connection neither one of us expected. Am I wrong?"

"I don't know what to say, Patsy."

"Thank you, would be nice. By the way, I'm not giving you up, to the police or anyone else."

"Thank you, Patsy. I don't deserve you. And you aren't wrong. Do you think it's this cabin?"

"You mean because it's haunted? Other than Oakley, I haven't ever seen a ghost up here."

"What about the White Witch of the Black Diamond Mines?"

"You read too many books, Cincinnatus. You are keeping the name?"

"It's worked for me so far. I have to say I'm relieved everything is out in the open now. And you took it so well. But then you weren't taken by surprise. Why did you not say anything all these years?"

"What would I have said? 'How was the escape, pass the butter?' People have secrets. Look at my family. Not exactly normal. And you stuck around."

"More like paranormal. And I wasn't swimming in choices, was I?"

"That isn't why you stayed. I think you became Cincinnatus Jones when you found this cabin and created this new soul. The ghosts came to *him*, not Frank Morris. He was just a catalyst."

"You may be right."

"What is it going to take for you to believe you came here for a reason?"

"Faith?"

"There's an interesting concept. In a divine power? Or yourself?"

"I don't know. But I feel like a weight has been lifted. I never thought I could ever be free while pretending to be someone else."

"You are Cincinnatus Jones, painter. Maybe that is who you were meant to be all along. 'Art is the daughter of freedom.' In your case, the son."

"I love you. And that quote by Friedrich Schiller. Let's eat. The loin is getting cold."

"Now we've come full circle. Maybe it's time to take a road trip and look for new digs."

"What about the gallery?"

"The good thing about art is, it's portable."

"Let's concentrate on tonight. And then we can plan our..."

"Escape?"

"Very funny. I was going to say trip. Does nothing faze you, Patsy Billie Vaughan?"

"My mama practiced voodoo, my father, sister, and brother are ghosts. What do you think?"

"I think there's going to be some ravishing tonight."

"But first your loin."

Chapter Thirty-Six

Later years are good for reflection. Those years in Patsy's cabin up in the trees were amazing. Maybe the ghosts did have a purpose for me. I couldn't hide who I was, because they saw something else. Someone I was meant to be. I'd found my freedom in loving Patsy and telling her the truth. I had been waiting for a thunderclap. Revelations don't work that way. That's why you have to pay attention. I did miss painting the ghosts, and I missed their presence. Pasty was right though, "It's time to paint the living." I painted portraits of Patsy's friends, who were now my friends. People she trusted and who knew me as her shy artist boyfriend from the East, whom she met in Berkeley at one of her watercolor exhibits. No one asked questions, people were either too laid back and respectful of our privacy or more interested in how I came to paint, my "process," and how I liked California. I indulged them, no harm in that. Plato said, "Storytellers rule the world."

I was a pretty good storyteller by then, spinning yarns about Trainhoppers and talking about the vets I'd met and painted. Men and women who were survivors of unspeakable war experiences. Me, a hippie looking Grisly Adams, with a bit of polish now that I was officially Patsy's man, painting Viet Nam Vets. This was very cool to these craftspeople, artists, musicians and teachers, who all loved Patsy. I was accepted on my own merit. This was a new experience for me, and I liked it. It was quite obvious the way I felt about Patsy. I couldn't hide it, I was all in.

Lady Day said that I was here for a reason. A deeper purpose. I didn't have to contemplate what that might be. I knew exactly what I wanted to do. Enough time had passed, so we took that trip down south to see Addie Mae's sister. She had recovered physically from her injuries, though forever blind in one eye as a result of the church bombing when she was just a girl. Patsy helped me explain to her how I came to paint Addie Mae and the other Birmingham Angels. I told her I had been a non-believer and through my own redemption, and after meeting The Angels, I had come to consider that there was indeed a higher power, a good force in the universe, something bigger than me.

As a devout person, Addie Mae's sister didn't doubt divine intervention had caused Addie Mae to come to me in that cabin, and "Praise the Lord she did, Mr. Cincinnatus Jones. Praise the Lord." When she unwrapped the painting, I don't think she was prepared for that intense release of emotion. We left her alone, giving her privacy to grieve once again, and take it in. When we met up later, she was most grateful and asked if she might keep it. "There was never anyone else who was meant to have it," I told her. She hugged me and cried some more. Everything, everything in my life, at that very moment came together. The search for my freedom, my soul, whatever word you want to put on it, was complete. Now I could just live. Not openly exactly, never confessing or surrendering publicly, but I had embraced my freedom and finally believed I was worthy of it. Not hubris, just no more hiding from myself. I needed no more ghosts. I was a whole man. Patsy made me a good man.

We wound up back at Sink and Circe's in the fall of 1975. The Vietnam War was finally over. Sink was not long for the world and Circe was at his side till the end. We celebrated his life with music and songs and stories and good food, as Sink would have wanted. Circe invited us to come live at the Pacific Grove house and help her tend the farm and keep her company. It was too good to turn down. Memories of sleeping on that bed rolled out from the barn, under the stars with Patsy, gave us a second wind and we relived that night over and over.

When Circe died, she left Patsy the house. "Sink would have wanted that," she told us, before she left the world for good. "This 'very fine house' needs people who know how to live here. Tenders of the fire, as it were." We were honored. It was a special house and with the beautiful view of the Pacific, it was like waking up in a dream every day.

Patsy opened a gallery in town after she decided to sell her grandfather's cabin and we moved full time to Pacific Grove. We said our goodbyes to the cabin where Patsy and I fell in love and had made love outside on the porch on warm nights, the moon as our witness. The ghosts I met there would be in my heart always. We took them with us to Pacific Grove and dedicated a room that only we went into, in their honor. We played Miles in that room. And Nina. And Billie. And read the poetry of Sylvia and Langston and Joaquin Miller. We read the words of John Muir. We gushed over the works of Augusta Savage in books that Patsy and I collected through the years. Having met her myself, they meant so much more.

On those nights, Patsy and I would cook together, a Shepherd's Pie or a rack of ribs, and some mouthwatering greens. We toasted our ghost friends on the walls with whiskey. How lucky I'd been to meet them. How grateful I was to Patsy for providing the conduit for them to come to me in her cabin in the trees. On warm nights we'd have a cookout and eat hot dogs with sauerkraut and deli mustard and watch Babe Ruth movies outside on the patio on an old television. We talked about Sink and Circe and how fortunate we were to have known them and become such good friends. We named it, A Very Fine House with a sign of haint blue paint that Patsy mixed herself. We had roots now, together. Like the redwoods, they would go on for miles, settling us, linking us to every other redwood and the earth. We would grow old, our adventures written on our souls like the rings of trees.

Patsy worked a few days at her gallery, and I painted landscapes and some portraits from photos Patsy shared with me. Oakley, Patsy and Cole as happy teens. Pasty's mama, in New Orleans on the porch of her haint blue house. An imagined one of Colton Vaughan holding back the tree branch and the sun shining on Oakley, walking back up those stairs. Patsy loved it. Another painting I dared was of my mother holding me, an imagined rendition of the locket photos. And the vets, young and alive playing sandlot ball, before their mission overseas. We both loved the one of True catching a wave with angel wings on her blue surfboard. My favorite was the Trainhoppers and me, sitting around the old Mole Railyard, our lives sorted out.

You might think a person would need more. I didn't. I had Patsy, nature, the Pacific, my painting, good friends, and chickens. Did ghosts ever come to Pacific Grove? As a matter of fact, they did. Sink popped in from time to time. And Circe could be found in the chicken coop on mornings we slept in and we'd find coffee brewing and a cup on the patio table, half empty. A portrait of them graced the living room above the mantel of A Very Fine House. Patsy's portrait hung in the master bedroom. A welcome sight on any given morning, though I had the live version next to me every night. The sex was better than ghost sex, because we shared something you don't get with other-worldly encounters. We had a future.

Patsy and I opted out of the child rearing gig. We were content as we were. We had a full life and leaving a living legacy was not on either one of our minds. Whatever we had at the end, we would leave to charity. Vets, sick kids, orphan homes, homeless shelters, and a donation to a certain church in Alabama with one stained glass window intact.

The paintings of the ghosts would be donated, upon our deaths, to the libraries at Kent State and Jackson State. They were signed C. Jones. No one would ever know who the painter had once been, and it didn't really matter. I'd be dead at that point, and you can't dig up a dead man and incarcerate him for escaping Alcatraz.

In the meantime, I kept on living. I had no regrets. My escape led me to Patsy, and Patsy led me to the ghosts and the life I was meant to live. I would make no apologies. I was man called Cincinnatus Jones until I was no more and went back to the earth and trees and soil I had come to revere. Today was for living and loving Patsy Billie Vaughan. Perhaps we would end our days on that bed under the stars, lulled by the Pacific. There was no rush. Did I ever raise a pint at the lopsided bar in Jack London Square with my old mates from Alcatraz? I'm not at liberty to say. But I am free.

Acknowledgements

I am thankful for the gift of dreams, for without them, where would a writer be?

Thank you Eric, for bringing us to Cali, and Jen for introducing us to the storied steps and forest of the Oakland hills. It was a perfect place for Cincinnatus to be born.

Thank you James, for the idea on the boat back from Alcatraz and for appreciating my ghosts.

Thank you to my first reader, Jason. Thank you to my early readers, Joie, Jen, Eric, Carrie, Cath, Eve, Donna, Carol and Lynn, and for all the encouragement. Thank you, Em and Gale, for the support and coffee book talks through the decades.

Thank you Mark Matousek for the writing time at Rowe and your advice on story and the freedom quote.

Thank you, Annali, for the road trip to Rowe and your friendship.

Thank you Dad, I could never forget your WWII stories and your penchant for nicknames.

Thank you Mom, for those precious days we had at the end. You are always with me.

Thank you Lee, for taking such good care of our mom.

Thank you Hailey, Wes and Asa, for the joy you bring into my life. I remain your champion and advocate. May you live your passion and be happy always.

Thank you Lisa, for the title. Cheers!

Thank you Kit, for the Long Road Society music, and for introducing me to the train hoppers.

Thank you Jess, for the intro to the new Oakland Bottom and your soulful harp on Cali nights.

Thank you all my awesome readers, for buying my books and liking my stories.

About the Author

Nanci LaGarenne loves to write. Scape Ghost is her fourth book. She lives in East Hampton, was born and raised in Brooklyn, and leaves her heart in California every year. She is a lover of everything Irish and has been to the Emerald Isle twice. She is ruminating on a novel set on Inis Mor having recently returned from a trip across the west. She is an avid yogi, Miles Davis fan, activist for clean water, children's safety and women's self-esteem. She loves folk music, intimate gatherings, dimly lit establishments and a real Guinness. She's never without a book and a strong cup of Irish tea. One day she will get to Montmartre and San Salvatore. She binges Scottish and Australian detective shows but is a sucker for a well-done PBS love story. You'll never find an overhead light on in her home, but you'll always find a candle burning and a string of fairy lights.